Nose Down,
Eyes Up

Nose Down,
Eyes Up

{ A NOVEL }

Merrill Markoe

VILLARD TRADE PAPERBACKS

NEW YORK

2010 Villard Books Trade Paperback Edition

Copyright © 2008 by Merrill Markoe

Published in the United States by Villard Books,
an imprint of The Random House Publishing Group,
a division of Random House, Inc., New York.

VILLARD and "V" CIRCLED Design are registered
trademarks of Random House, Inc.

Originally published in hardcover in the United States by
Villard Books, an imprint of The Random House Publishing Group,
a division of Random House, Inc., in 2008.

Library of Congress Cataloging-in-Publication Data

Markoe, Merrill.
Nose down, eyes up: a novel / Merrill Markoe.
p. cm.
ISBN 978-0-345-50021-2
1. Middle-aged men—Fiction. 2. Dogs—Fiction. 3. Human-animal
relationships—Fiction. 4. Man-woman relationships—Fiction. I. Title.
PS3563.A6652N67 2009
813'.54—dc22   2008044301

Printed in the United States of America

www.villard.com

2 4 6 8 9 7 5 3 1

Title page art by Merrill Markoe

Book design by Dana Leigh Blanchette

To A., J., G., P., and H.

Nose Down,
Eyes Up

{ 1 }

Not That Stupid

*I*f you ask me, most people are a pain in the ass. Sometimes it's all I can do to keep from telling them to go fuck themselves.

You'd get a different opinion if you asked my dog Jimmy. He thinks most people are fantastic, because he knows how to manipulate them. I've never been good at any of that.

Of every creature in the world, Jimmy seemed like the one guy who understood me. Sometimes I would just look at him and feel a whole lot better. During my divorce I started talking to Jimmy about everything, though I guess I was doing most of the talking. After five years with Eden, I probably needed to vent. I should add at this point, if I hadn't had the misfortune of running into my ex that day at the market, none of the rest of this crap would have happened. I certainly wouldn't have intentionally made a plan to see her. I may be stupid, but I'm not that stupid.

Damn!

*O*f the four dogs that lived with me through the whole thing, Jimmy was the only one I'd raised from a pup. The rest started out as foster dogs, rescued by my girlfriend, Sara, a woman neck deep in the stray dog laws of entropy, which, of course, tell us that there will always be more dogs than you will have space for, unless you make a point of trying *not* to see them. In her case, that would have been impossible.

This was a happy period in my life. I was grateful to be working on the Bremners' summerhouse in Malibu, where I'd lived rent-free for three years in exchange for doing the kind of work that I actually enjoy. It was what I called "puttering" and it consisted of things I'd do even if no one was paying me, like adding on rooms, replacing and repairing broken stuff, clearing out rot, figuring out what part of something was keeping it from working. The only hitch was that I had to find somewhere else to stay whenever the Bremners showed up. Lucky for me they had a choice of three other vacation houses, two of them on lakes.

I was getting ready to build them a new deck just off the master bedroom, so I was prepping the area—cleaning up the dog poop where I needed to reroute some sprinkler pipes. With four dogs on the premises, keeping the lawn green required a good deal of vigilance. Back then the Bremner estate was set in the center of three very landscaped acres. When I first saw the place, I thought of Thomas Jefferson's boyhood home, if Thomas Jefferson had grown up in Baja. The Bremners' five-thousand-square-foot main house was built in an architectural style that combined Colonial elements with a Spanish roof in a way that I thought of as Pueblo Tudor. Martin Bremner designed it himself. When you have money I guess you can do what you want.

Usually Jimmy sat beside me while I worked, in a position that reminded me of the Sphinx: upright on his stomach with his front feet and back feet placed fore and aft. He had an inscrutable way of staring that always made me feel like he found me fascinating. Though he was as still as a piece of statuary, every so often he would spring to his feet, run over, and lick my face like I was a delicious frozen dessert. At moments like these, when he would appear happier to see me than I have ever been to see anyone, even though he'd been sitting there for hours on end and had seen me and seen me and seen me and seen me some more, I would be reminded how much I liked his company. Jimmy was the only guy I knew who could change my mood for the better just by showing up.

You know how people say you end up looking like your

dog? That was probably true of me and Jimmy. We were both in good shape for middle-aged guys; big and beefy. Meaty, but not fatty. We both had square faces and big round brown eyes and wavy but not curly black hair. Although Jimmy had a lot more of it than I had these days.

Anyway, it was about two in the afternoon, and the radio was blasting some kind of alternative music I couldn't hear too well because I had such a lame-ass radio. Everything that came out of that sad little speaker sounded like it was a poorly recorded electronic atonal foreign language opera.

Right about then I noticed Jimmy was nowhere to be found. None of the others were around either: no Cheney, no Fruity, no Dink. So I started to worry that there'd been a massive prison break. Every few months when Jimmy detected something of interest on the other side of the street, he'd eat a hole in the fence and tunnel out. It took Jimmy to get the old ball rolling, but then the rest of the dog team followed suit. I never understood why Jimmy, a dog who'd been pampered and worshipped since he was a puppy was so hell-bent on escaping. It's not like he had the skills to make it out there on his own. But one thing Jimmy never seemed to do was think very far ahead.

After looking around and not seeing any obvious new fence hole, I thought I heard some kind of commotion over by the Bremners' four-car garage, which was a separate free-standing Tudor hacienda structure built specifically to house the West Coast branch of the Bremner car collection: The '82 Mercedes, the '59 El Dorado, the '95 Porsche Carrera, and, of course, the Prius. The usual rich-guy crap. Those damn cars had a nicer place to live out their retirement than any of the members of my family. So I headed over there to make sure my four drooling bug-infested morons weren't scratching up any of those expensively maintained paint jobs.

When I peered in an open side door, I got quite a surprise. An unusually large gathering of dogs were seated in a big group, panting and staring, apparently spellbound by something. As my eyes grew accustomed to the dimness, I realized that Jimmy was standing in front of them, holding forth like some overserved extrovert at a literary salon. Fruity, Cheney, and Dink, my other three dogs, were seated in the front row, listening intently. And behind them were more dogs I recognized from the neighborhood: Samson, the overweight rottweiler mix from down the street; Harvey, the spaniel who lived next door; Squirty, that silly Jack Russell; and a few more whose names I didn't know.

At first I stood quietly, unnoticed. Then Cheney, my shepherd-coyote mix, smelled me and turned his head, offering a cursory wag of his tail. It was one of those "Yo. How ya doin'!" lackadaisical double *thump-thumps* that meant he had seen me but wasn't interested in pursuing it.

That I could understand Jimmy as he lectured to the other dogs didn't surprise me nearly as much as it would have before I started hanging out with Sara. She was constantly going on about teaching people to turn on their inner light by talking to their animals. That's what she did for a living; Sara was an animal communicator. Yeah, yeah, I know. To be honest, I never allowed myself to really explore the idea that Sara might be nuts. Though sometimes I wondered who she'd have been if she'd been born in Ohio. My feeling was that, regardless, she was still someone I liked. Anyway, it wasn't the nuts who gave me trouble in life, because they just assumed you agreed with them. It was the sane people who tried to make you submit to their agenda. In any case, it was hard to fault Sara, because she was apparently in the right place at the right time. There seemed to be an ever growing segment of the population in Southern California actually willing to pay her to come to their house and explain why Dwayne the over-weight Siamese cat wasn't eating. Or why Tyson the pit bull tore up the carpet when they were gone. Believe it or not, she made bank leading workshops where she taught people to key into the problematic animals in question through medita-tion, and then to accept that the voices they were hearing in their head were the animals speaking to them telepathically. I said to her, "Hey, isn't that where it all went wrong for Son of Sam?" That was the kind of remark that Sara didn't find funny.

Sara and I had a pretty good relationship. She not only cooked and baked for me, I thought she was hot in that very specific way that I have only seen in crazy women. In my ex-perience, crazy girls really put out more than their better bal-anced sisters because they seemed to be under the impression that love could make them sane. That particular philosophi-cal quirk was the one thing that Sara had in common with my ex-wife, Eden.

When I first heard Jimmy talking, I thought I was catching Sara's pathology by osmosis the way I thought I was a Bud-dhist for a minute when I was married to Eden. When I live with someone, I tend to pick up their beliefs. Lucky for me I've never been hot for a crack whore.

"I've been told repeatedly that I'm a very good boy," Jimmy was saying to the others. "As far as I can tell, it's in the genes."

"Is it okay if I ask a question? I'm sorry," I heard Fruity, my golden retriever mix, ask nervously, "but is that how you got him to let you sleep next to him on the bed?"

"Nah. Anyone can do it. It takes a month from beginning to end," Jimmy counseled.

"No way that would ever work at my house," said Samson, the rottweiler mix from down the street.

"Absolutely it would," said Jimmy. "First spend a few weeks circling the bed from the floor. Then start phase two: going up to the edge of the bed and staring mournfully."

"Excuse me for interrupting," said Fruity, "but what does 'mournfully' mean?"

"Like you feel when they are eating and they offer you nothing," said Jimmy. "Memorize this phrase: 'Drop nose, raise eyes.' It's the cornerstone of my teachings." Jimmy began staring mournfully, his lower lip hanging, eyes filled with unspeakable sadness. It was a face I'd seen him make hundreds of times before. "Raise your eyes until the lip muscles tense. When you feel a slight discomfort, that means you are showing some white. Now you look the way you feel when they go for a walk without you. Do it just this way and I guarantee they never will!" Awed murmurs of delight and agreement rippled through the attentive crowd.

"Wow. You can just do that?" said Fruity, wide-eyed with admiration.

"Yes. And so can you," Jimmy said as they all attempted their own versions of the same expression, morphing into the saddest-looking group of dogs ever seen anywhere outside of the pound. "Once you master this, your next step is to place your head on the bed," Jimmy continued, "preferably as close to some part of their body as possible. Staring, always staring."

"I've tried that," said Samson. "And here's what happened: nothing. He just screamed at me 'Go to bed, Samson. NOW.' "

"How long did you keep it up?" asked Jimmy. "Were you relentless?"

"You mean, like, do it for years?" Fruity asked breathlessly. "Because wouldn't that piss everyone off? And wouldn't they lock you outside and beat you and—"

"Stop it," said Jimmy. "You're describing the place where you *used* to live. No one acts like that around here. And it won't take years. Start with an hour a night for a couple of weeks. But remember: Vibe adoration until you can almost feel it. Eventually he'll invite you up."

I was amazed and shocked, yet I also felt a fatherly pride. So much of what I'd taken for random, poorly thought-out, and endearingly dumb behavior was clearly more calibrated than I'd imagined.

"Understanding people is a hit-or-miss business," said Jimmy, "because people are unpredictable. They project their thoughts onto you. That guy you live with sees you as an extension of his personality. He can't imagine that you have a set of thoughts that don't match his."

"You mean like Sara," said Fruity, "and the way she gets it wrong every time. I'm sorry, don't hit me, but she does. She's wrong every time."

"I've noticed that too," said Cheney, "but when you try to tell her, she pays no attention." Now, to my complete surprise, all the dogs in the group began to do eerily accurate impressions of Sara trying to "read" them, raising their voices up to her distinctly nasal pitch. Cheney even got her slight northern English accent.

"He chews his feet because he was abandoned in a previous life," he said, nailing Sara so vividly that I thought for a second she might be in the room.

"The little dachshund is saying she just needs a lot of hugs because she is under stress," said Fruity, also doing a surprisingly accurate impression.

"Hey," said Dink, who was the little dachshund in question, "I am under a lot of stress."

"Look, at least she means well," said Jimmy. "Remember my general rule of thumb: When in doubt, just play along. Don't expect understanding. Just wag your tails and seem agreeable. Then when they're out of the room, do what needs to be done."

"You're saying that when they're around, we should blindly obey?" said Dink.

"Or else just fake it," said Jimmy. "But remember every situation has some options. For instance, if someone throws something, you don't have to bring it back. You can just stand there with a blank stare, holding it in your mouth."

"What? Why wouldn't you bring a thing back?" said Cheney. "Are you out of your mind?"

"It figures you would say that," said Jimmy. "I see how they have you running back and forth. Haven't you noticed that every time you bring a thing back, they throw it again? That's abusive. If they really wanted it, they'd go get it themselves."

"That's not abusive. That's the *point* of being alive," said Cheney.

Jimmy shook his head and laughed sardonically. "Whatever. Different needs for different breeds . . ."

"Can I ask a question?" said Dink. "I know you've covered this before, but . . . tell me one more time: Is it pee inside, poo inside, eat and play outside? And what about puke? Is that inside or outside?"

"Here's a mnemonic device. Everything starting with *p* is outside. *P* is for 'patio.' *P* is for 'pool,' *P* is for 'plants.' *P* is for 'poo' *and* 'pee.' And 'puke.' "

"Are you sure?" said Dink. "That doesn't sound right. If we're supposed to poo *outside*, why does Gil collect it in a bag and bring it *inside*?"

"Because Gil collects shit. No one knows why or what he does with it," said Jimmy. "From what I have observed, I think he maintains a pretty extensive collection and that's why he—"

"No. That is wrong. I don't collect it, I'm cleaning up the yard," I interrupted, unable to keep quiet any longer. Jimmy looked up, seeing me for the first time.

"Gil! Gil! Gil!! Hi, Gil! Hey! How are you! How ya been?" he said, trying to cover up the entire incident by running over to me and jumping around. "Hey, everybody! Gil's here. Isn't it great to see him?"

They all began to circle me enthusiastically, some of them hurling themselves into the air. "Oh, boy! Gil! Gil! Gil! It's so good to see you!"

"You look amazing! Let me smell you. Hey! You had chicken for lunch, didn't you? You got any more on you? Can I have some? Where you been all day!"

"That's enough, you guys," I said. "And just for the

record, after I collect the shit in that bag, I throw it out. It goes into the garbage."

"All that work to throw it out? That makes no sense," said Jimmy. "Why?"

"It stinks and attracts flies," I explained patiently.

"Yes, I'm aware of that," Jimmy said, confused. "But you still haven't told us why you throw it out."

"People find those things disgusting. You dogs as a species seem to have a greater affinity for excrement than we people do. Maybe we liked it more a hundred thousand years ago. But we've advanced since then. Now we have more important concerns like . . . I don't know. Like hair implants. And forcing democracy on people. And dancing with the goddamn fucking stars."

Everyone stared at me, expressionless.

"I guess that's all for now," said Jimmy as the other dogs all ran out into the yard. Only Dink stopped and came over to consult with me for a minute.

"Right now: Are we inside or outside?" she asked.

"You're *inside*," I said.

"Oh, good," she said, as she began to squat and pee.

"NOOO," I said, picking her up and quickly carrying her outside, where I deposited her onto the lawn. "Pee *outside*."

"Right. Right. Got it," she said as she squatted on the grass.

"How much of what I just said did you hear?" Jimmy asked, following me cautiously as the rest of the dogs ran across the yard to take a bathroom break right where I'd just finished cleaning up. "I hope I didn't offend you."

"Not at all," I said. "I found it interesting. I didn't know you gave everything so much thought."

"You're kidding. Of course I do. I'm a dog, not a hamster," said Jimmy. "Did you think I was some kind of a dumbass?"

"No, no!" I said. "Well, maybe sometimes a little. Mainly because I think of most dogs as having simpler, less convoluted notions about how things should be done. I had no idea you were so calculating or articulate."

"It's my hybrid nature. I inherited it from you," said Jimmy. "That's how I made alpha, and why it's my job to teach the rest of our pack. They're not blood, like you and I are. I'm the only one who sees things easily from both sides of the coin, so I have to share what I know to help them survive."

"Well, that's generous of you, but now I'm a little jealous," I said. "I wish you'd share more stuff with me from time to time."

"No offense, but the reason I don't is that you're not a very good listener," he said. "You fidget. You get bored easily. You're always telling me to shut up."

"That's not true," I said. "Only when you're *barking*. I'm interested in anything you have to *say*! I didn't realize you were such an authority figure."

"Yes, I am," said Jimmy, casually. "My double-edged perspective makes me a sought-after resource. Didn't you notice how everyone is always so glad to see me?"

"I kind of thought it was more a case of you being so glad to see everyone," I replied. Jimmy just stared at me, exasperated. Then he turned his head and began to chew his own back.

"Fleas?" I asked.

"No," he said. "A dry skin thing. I hope it's not scabies."

"Maybe you need a bath," I said.

"Maybe you need to mind your own business," he said, continuing to bite the area above his tail. I sat idly for a few minutes, waiting for him to finish. Eventually I got antsy and went back to building the deck. That was when I realized he was right. I did get bored easily. Damn!

The Definition of Friendship

*A*fter a couple of hours of tinkering with the sprinkler pipes, it was beer-thirty. So I ran down to that Save-Less market at the bottom of the hill to pick up a six-pack and some snacks for the dogs. Shopping in the Bremners' neighborhood was always a fatiguing experience. Everything in Malibu cost one, if not two, dollars more than the identical item on the other side of the 101. It was as if the area's merchants believed that every common household item was magically transformed into its more valuable duplicate when it came into contact with salt air, the sea breeze, and proximity to David Geffen's driveway. Therefore, I tried to limit my local purchases to small stuff. Because it was August, even the ten-items-or-less line was full of what looked like antsy, irritable holiday shoppers. The people who showed up to stay when the weather got hot were an ornery, impatient bunch, annoyed because the traffic was bad, resentful that they didn't get a heartier welcome, but too fancy to stick around for the fires, the mud slides, and the road closures common to the other three seasons. Still, every summer, there they were again—washing up on the beach like grunion. And thus it came to pass, while I was shuffling from one foot to the other holding my sad little bag of taco chips, a box of milk bones, and a six-pack of beer, that I ran into Eden, my ex-wife.

When I spotted her, my heart sank. I knew she lived somewhere in the general vicinity. I'd heard that the new place she'd bought with her next husband was at the other end of the same canyon where the Bremners lived. But those canyons were big. Those estates were spread out. I had made it my life's work to not know quite where she had landed. I also carefully avoided any place I thought she might ever be. She was one of those members of her gender who liked nothing more than spending all of someone else's cash. The market where I saw her that day seemed too downscale for anyone from her crowd.

At first I thought I was going to be able to sneak out of there unnoticed. Eden had her back turned to me and was headed left toward the cheese.

"Thank you, God," I said to the Question Mark in the Sky that I always thanked when I was dodging bullets around Eden. But of course the guy who was at the checkout had to slow everything down by buying lotto tickets. That transaction took just long enough for Eden to get in line behind me.

"Oh my God!" she said, coming toward me with outstretched arms. "I was just thinking about you today! It's so good to see you!" And the next thing I knew she was giving me the kind of hug that would lead any rational stranger to believe that we were tragically separated best friends, not two people whose last words to each other five years ago had been, "Fuck you." And "Well, fuck you too."

Politeness dictated that I at least put my hands on her forearms and kiss the air near her ears while I did my best to ignore the chill in my heart. It's hard to fake a lot of exuberant emotion about seeing someone who took your house and emptied out your pension plan.

"Oh, come on!" she said. "Aren't you even a little glad to see me?"

She looked great. But then, looking great was the thing that Eden did well. She looked better than great. She looked edible, fuckable, perfect. She was wearing her hair lighter and longer than she used to, like she had been clipping pictures of Scarlett Johansson to bring to the hair salon. She was tanner than I remembered, dressed in tight jeans and a pink tank top with some perfect midriff showing just enough toned flesh to guarantee her plenty of male attention. Eden was all about the grooming, the hair, the makeup. I didn't know that when I met her, but I certainly knew it by the time she left. The only positive thing I remembered about our five-year catastrophe was that she was astounding in bed; a sexual idiot savant, lively, theatrical, and just plain nasty. Back then I thought at least a few of those things were traits that I liked.

"Hasn't it been a long enough time now that we can be friends?" she said, clapping her hands as her face lit up with the brilliance of her idea. "Oh my God! How much fun would it be to get together!" Before I had to decide on the facial expression to use as a reaction to this, I watched her eyes dart past me to scan the rest of the market. Eden needed to know who else's attention she was able to command. A slide show of flash frames whizzed by in my head: Eden packing and leaving; Eden and her lawyer; Eden in bed, moaning; Eden losing stuff, her keys, her glasses, her checkbook; Eden's boobs jiggling. I lost the first half of my life in that fucking divorce. And the sickest thing was that the sex never died when the rest of it did. It was a near perfect example of the kind of cruel, confusing practical jokes that God seems to like best.

"Give me your number!" she said too loudly. And now the other people in the grocery line *were* turning to look at us as Eden luxuriated in their stares, compulsively checking her reflection in every nearby mirror and window. She loved an accidental audience even more than an invited one. To be fair, her exhibitionism was one of the fun parts of Eden: She liked to have sex in theaters and ballparks and restaurants, even in museums and at concerts. But if you didn't want to do it with her, why would you want to be around her, unless you found yourself craving a lot of mindless chatter?

I decided it was going to be easier to give her my number than to stand there and argue with her, so I wrote it on the back of a Costco receipt that I was pretty sure she would instantly lose. Chances were even better that she would forget the entire incident. She was one of those people who always said "Let's get together! I will call you" to everyone whenever she saw them, but then never did. Even so, I probably should have given her a fake number. But it felt wrong. *Jesus Christ,* I was thinking as I wrote down my digits, *why would anyone ever make the attempt to be friends with an ex?* Nine times out of ten it wasn't friendship that had motivated the marriage. So why would an intense period of incompatibility and fighting followed by vengeful legal actions followed by a tomblike silence be the thing that would start the whole friendship ball rolling?

"Oh, goody!" said Eden, taking the receipt. "So if I invite you over for lunch, will you come?"

"Yeah, right, sure," I said over my shoulder as I got out of there in a hurry. "See you later! Gotta run," I yelled as I jumped behind the wheel of my van.

"Fuck me!" I screamed to myself as I peeled out of the parking lot, eager to put a chunk of the highway between us.

{ 4 }

Edible or Inedible

*W*hen I walked to the front door of the house, already halfway into my second beer, I could hear that Jimmy was at it again. He had commandeered the room off the kitchen, which was where I went to kick back, watch the tube, work on the computer, or play guitar. It was also where I silk-screened the T-shirts I was trying to sell online—my sad little attempt at forming an Internet empire.

"They have all been brainwashed to think that one meal a day is sufficient," I heard Jimmy ranting, as I stood frozen in the entryway, transfixed. "How many meals do we need a day? Everyone?"

"Ten," came back the group response.

"Why?" said Jimmy.

"Biological imperative," said the group.

"Very true," said Jimmy. "But no human being will ever accept it. Acting hungry just causes them to ignore you. So you must supplement your diet in their absence. Hence my topic: edible or inedible?"

I tiptoed noiselessly to a spot where I could see them yet remain hidden.

"What does this have to do with ball?" said Cheney as he looked around hopefully.

"Nothing at all," said Jimmy. Cheney let out an exhausted sigh and collapsed onto his side on the floor. "Ball is a substitute for the urge to hunt and kill. Eating is the next step. May I continue?"

He cleared his throat. "Can it be said that everything is in some sense a snack? Or are there things that should never be eaten under any circumstances?"

"Everything can be eaten," said Dink.

I couldn't let this pass. "Incorrect," I said, startling everyone by rounding the corner and making myself visible to the group. "*Most* things can*not* be eaten. And where did you learn a word like 'hence'?"

Fruity, who was chewing her feet, looked up when I raised my voice. "I'm sorry," she said. "Don't beat me. See? I'm cowering! You like that, right?"

"No! I do not like that, and, as I have told you over and over, no one is going to beat you! Fucking rescues!" I said, perhaps too loudly, because she curled her tail beneath her and ran out of the room.

Jimmy, on the other hand, gave me only a cursory glance. "Everyone, pop quiz. A book: edible or inedible? Answer: edible. But only certain portions. The dust jacket, the front cover, and the last few pages. All totally edible."

"Do you mind if I record this?" I asked, heading over to

my computer. I turned on the GarageBand program I sometimes used to record the occasional song. The last one I wrote
was called "Leave Me the Fuck Alone." Predictably, Sara
hated it. Like every woman I'd known, once she found out
that I'd been trained to play classical piano from about age
four on, she felt compelled to encourage me to pursue that instead. They all did, never comprehending that the more they
water-boarded me with unwarranted praise and unasked-for
encouragement, the less I had any desire to play.

The piano triggered a very uncomfortable rewind for me,
from too many years spent with a mother who'd been bank-
ing on the musical genius of her sons to make her life a more
exciting place. My older brother Steve clashed with her from
day one, eventually blasting his way right past the lessons, the
recitals, and the competitions into the unsavory world of rock
and roll. He went from metal band to metal band, singing
and playing bass, until his senior year of high school, when he
dropped out. Soon after that he vanished to Europe on some
kind of unexplained tour. We didn't hear from him again until
I was turning twenty.

When Steve reappeared he was much heavier, hairier, and
the singer-songwriter behind the big hit pop song "Undercover Angel." It had been on the Billboard top five for five
weeks and in the top forty for eleven weeks during the time
he'd been gone.

Over the years I got so sick of hearing my mother confide,
speculate, boast, and fret about Steve and his great accom-
plishments that by the time I graduated college, I was fed up
with music. All I wanted to do was take stuff apart and re-
build it. That kind of work was clean. It was satisfying. It was

precise and concrete. No one else could take the credit or argue about the success of the results.

"Let's try another one," Jimmy said while I was arranging the mike. The acoustics in the den were not exactly the best, and Jimmy's voice was deep and flat and a little nasal, almost like it was playing on the wrong speed.

"Hello? Hello? Ready for me to begin? Hello? Is this thing on?" Jimmy said, testing his mike levels.

"Go ahead," I said.

"Socks," said Jimmy, picking up where he'd left off. "Edible or inedible?"

"Edible," said Samson. "At least, I eat them."

"Correct," said Jimmy. "When pulled and shredded, the toe, the ball of the foot, and the heel are an irresistible delicacy."

A murmur went through the group. "The truly sophisticated dog finds everything in the house edible to some extent, including cleaning supplies like Brillo pads and sponges, paper towels, napkins, and tissues. Ditto pot holders and dish towels, or anything fleece. Rule of thumb: Whatever you find on the floor that is mouth-size or smaller can be considered a 'starter.' So don't forget about carpet padding, gaskets, pieces of hose, or those bittersweet chewy disks they put under furniture."

"If I could write, I'd take notes," said Fruity, who was standing in the doorway and had begun creeping slowly back into the group. "I'm sorry. I didn't mean to interrupt."

"Here's a tricky one: underwear. Edible or inedible?"

"Edible," said the group in unison.

"Of course!" Jimmy chuckled. "It's very flavorful, yes. But

do *not* overindulge. One or two a year will be seen as an accident, a misguided attempt at bonding. Establishing a predictable pattern of gluttony strikes them as perverse and can lead to punishment—even the pound."

The crowd gasped. Small discussions broke out. "More questions?" said Jimmy.

"Did you already cover cat shit?" asked Squirty, the Jack Russell terrier from down the street.

"No, and thank you for reminding me," said Jimmy. "Most of us like it. Though simpleminded taboos don't allow us to admit it in public."

The group broke out into the dog equivalent of chuckles, which were weird little part-growls, part-moans.

"It's full of protein and fish oil. Great for the skin. But remember to avoid the litter, especially if it has clumping agents. I forget what chemical that is, but it'll dry you out like a piece of beef jerky. One last one. How about wood? Edible or inedible? Anyone?"

"Inedible," said Dink. "That's what I like best about eating it!"

"Wrong! *Edible!*" said Jimmy. "If something was ever part of anything alive, it's in perpetuity edible. Table legs, doors, and chairs . . . fireplace logs . . . bookshelves, even leather. Jackets, pants, shoes . . . all edible—"

"Wait a minute," I interrupted, pounding my fist on the table. "WRONG! A leather jacket or shoe in this house belongs only to *me*. And none of you are permitted to claim it for a snack."

Looking around the room for an example, I saw a pair of short black boots that I used for dress shoes. "For instance, these," I said, holding them up. "Never edible. *Never.*" Only then did I notice that there were tooth marks on the heels and a piece chewed off the back by one of the ankles.

"Jesus Christ," I said. "Which one of you did this? These cost a hundred bucks." I could feel my face getting hot as my anger started to build.

"You spent a hundred dollars on those?" said Fruity, astonished. "Oops. I didn't mean to insult you. I'm sorry. I'm so sorry."

"Well, no, they're from a thrift store," I said, a little embarrassed to be backpedaling. "But they *could* have cost that much new. The point is they're my only dress shoes. You guys are not showing the proper respect if you're eating my personal property." I brought my fist down on the table again, causing Fruity to put her tail between her legs and bolt out of the room.

"You all know better than this," I said, observing no signs of contrition or comprehension. "I have told you *all* a million times not to eat my shoes. I don't care if they are tasty. Or if you don't understand why."

"Okay, everyone," said Jimmy urgently, "Position seventeen." Hearing that, the entire group, including Jimmy, lowered themselves flat against the floor, ears back, heads down.

"Oh, lighten up," I said. "This is just a theoretical discussion. But it is important that you all listen and obey."

"I'm not saying I did it," said Jimmy, crossing the room to place his head on my knee, "but whoever did probably really missed you. Your shoes taste and smell like you. He did it to feel close to you. Or she, I mean."

"Really?" I said, surprisingly moved. As usual, I was starting to soften. "That's why you did it? To feel close to me?"

"Yes. We all love you so much," said Jimmy. Now he was

staring at me with such warmth that I felt my face get hot and my eyes begin to sting. That's when Jimmy turned to the group. "I trust you all saw his reaction," he said. "If you didn't, come talk to me after class."

"In other words, that whole 'feeling close to you' speech was just to manipulate me?" I said. "And I totally fell for it. What a pathetic old fool." I was angry and hurt.

"No. No. Not pathetic. Your reaction was typical of your species. It's one of the patterns we count on," he said.

"That's it. Class over. We're all done here for today," I said, shutting down the computer.

"Now you know why I never talk to you," said Jimmy. "You're too much of a hothead." He turned to address the group. "Remember that the human race is first and foremost unreasonable. More often than not their decisions are based on irrational rage. Therefore, the seeking of supplementary snacks, though necessary, can put you in jeopardy. Pursue such things only in the safety of your family of origin."

"This isn't our family of origin," Cheney said.

"True. It's not yours, but it's mine," said Jimmy proudly. "I was born here. I'm a native. A rare hybrid. Equipped for two worlds."

"Wrong," said Cheney. "I was here the day he brought you home."

"What's he talking about?" Jimmy chuckled arrogantly. "Home from where?"

I watched carefully. This was an avenue of discussion I'd never anticipated.

"From wherever he got you," said Cheney. Now it was Jimmy's turn to look disoriented. He began to pant, and his back legs began to tremble.

"What does he mean?" he asked me.

"I thought you knew," I said, suddenly feeling my heart begin to race. "I got you from a litter of puppies that my ex-wife was giving away. There were six. She kept two. The others went to good homes. I hope."

"When were you planning to tell me?" said Jimmy. "You should have said something before."

"Well, it never came up," I said, suddenly caught off balance and feeling embarrassed.

He sat down, looking as unnerved as is possible for an animal who only had three facial expressions: joy, fury, and nothing whatsoever. "Could everyone please leave us alone?" asked Jimmy as the other dogs exited. The only sound now was the dog door flap swinging ominously behind each of them.

"You didn't think I was your biological father, did you?" I said. "It never occurred to me that you would think that."

"A lot of obvious things never occur to you," Jimmy sniped. He turned away, and began licking his feet, refusing to look at me.

"But we're totally different species," I said. "We're not even the same kind of mammal. I come from chimps. You come from hyenas and wolves. You guys have six tits. We have two. We look nothing alike."

"I thought I was unique," Jimmy finally said after a rather long silence, "a blood relation with the gift of a double perspective. I figured I was in a transitional phase, like a caterpillar larva. That one day I'd wake up, lose a lot of this hair, and start walking on my hind legs. Maybe get a set of keys and learn to drive." When I looked aghast, he added, so quietly I almost couldn't hear him, "So, you're saying I am not related to you at all?"

"Not biologically. No." Now I found myself feeling so bad for him that I wanted to give him a hug. I lay down on the floor next to him, put my arms around his chest, and leaned my head on his back. "In my opinion we are as nice and loving a family as I've ever been part of. Yes, it's a very broad definition of a family. Not the traditional one they use when they pass laws and shit, but . . . uh . . . lots of nice families have that problem. Gay families, for example."

"What does it say on my birth certificate?" he said, looking very upset. He freed himself from my grasp and walked to the other side of the room, where he sat down and stared at me. "Well," I said to him, trying to be a little bit more diplomatic, "it says I'm responsible for you because you belong to me."

"Like property?" he said, even more upset than before. "Like a lawn mower or a vacuum cleaner? Like a slave?"

"No," I said. "Slavery involves forced labor. You guys don't do any work around here."

"Don't try to change the subject," he said defensively.

"I never thought you'd take it like this," I said, stalling. "But let me explain it to you like I heard them do on *Oprah*." I went over to him and squatted down beside him so we were staring directly into each other's eyes. "You are even *more* precious to me than a birth child. *Because I picked you*." I paused for dramatic effect. "You were *chosen*. From a group of five."

"There were five of us in my litter?" Jimmy asked me when he finally spoke again.

"Yes, but by the time I got there, there were only two of you left. And Eden had dibs on the other one . . ."

"So you *didn't* pick me," he said, barely audible. "I was a leftover."

"I guess it's not the first dictionary definition of the word 'pick'," I said.

"Why was my mother throwing away her children?" Jimmy asked somberly.

"Why?" I repeated, buying time. This was getting too convoluted for my *Oprah* strategy. "Well, it was probably more Eden's decision than it was your mother's."

"We were ripped away? Stolen from our mother? She must have been horrified. I bet she was hysterical." Jimmy looked at me with the saddest face I had ever seen. "And you wonder why I can't control my urge to eat shoes." He sighed deeply. Then he got up and walked to the side of the room, where he vomited.

The Big Emotion
Behind Snack Time

*T*he next night Sara came over to cook me dinner. She generally did this on weekends, but more and more she was showing up in the middle of the week.

Sara was a frail, ethereal, Pre-Raphaelite-looking little thing, especially when she was wearing her ironically selected Maoist army fatigues, the uniform of the palest, skinniest infantry battalion who ever fought the Battle of Malibu Beach. A devoted recycler, an animal rescuer, and a vegan, Sara was the opposite of a militia. When she cooked for me, it was a healthy experience, but a mushy one. You didn't need teeth for Sara's cooking. It was as if the entrées were part of a fine line of Gerber's baby food for fussy adults.

It seems wrong to complain about someone cooking you dinner, even if you are a meat eater at heart like I am. I have no problem with vegetables. I like a nice honest potato. What drove me crazy about Sara's cooking was the camouflage and the fraud. Don't give me a cylinder of unseasoned lima beans and call them a hot dog. There is enough disappointment in life as it is. Sara worked much too hard inventing those crazy vegetable disguises. Trying to please me was part of her nature. Sara was, after all, a very nice lady, even though no female I've ever known has wanted to be called either of those two things. Particularly in Los Angeles, where there were only two ages of people, young and pretending to be young. The women with a foot in both worlds were definitely the touchiest of all. To them, "nice" meant mediocre, bland, passive, a doormat. "Lady" meant old, colorless, and sexless. Still, in Sara's case, "nice lady" was a good description, and since my divorce from Eden, both words sounded pretty good to me.

In our five years together we'd had a lot of nice evenings and plenty of very nice sex. She'd unloaded three mainly nice foster dogs on me, though she preferred the term "placed." When Fruity, Cheney, and Dink first arrived, I thought it was for a week. I was under the impression that I was a stopover while Sara found them a more perfect "forever" home. But now, five years later, they were apparently mine by default. The list of dogs for whom Sara was finding a forever home never got any shorter.

Of the current bunch, Jimmy was the only one that I'd taken in on purpose. And truth be told, I only said yes to him to shut up the ex. We were in the most acrimonious part of our split when she discovered that Gypsy, a flat-coated retriever that I had rescued from a construction site about a month before, was with pup. "You better help me figure out what to do with them," she yelled. "They're your responsibility as much as mine." Maybe I took Jimmy under duress, but he was an easy sale. He was the most irresistible creature I'd ever seen. His blue-black hair stuck out in every direction, like a fluffy, furry pig. I fell in love. That he'd grown up thinking he was my son was an unintended consequence.

Anyway, after Sara and I polished off a sweet potato bean loaf thing that for some goddamn reason had prunes and pineapple in it, and she was clearing away the dishes, I told her about how I'd been talking to Jimmy. Sara was the one person who could hear this news and not be alarmed. It made her happy. "We're a good team," she said. "See how I inspire you? Stick with me, and you'll start playing piano again."

"If that's what you want, why don't I introduce you to my brother?" I sniped at her. "He's the musician in the family. All my girlfriends had crushes on him. Why don't I fix you two up?"

"Oh, stop it," she said, rinsing our plates, irritated. But it accomplished what I'd set out to do: put an end to the piano discussion. I never let my mother indulge. I sure as hell wasn't going to let Sara.

"When you talked to Jimmy, did you remember to meditate first?" Sara asked me. "I tell all my students it helps them key into their highest vibrations."

"Nah," I said.

"I wonder if you're getting his real meaning," she said. "If you plan to pursue this, you should attend my workshop. It can double your comprehension."

"I think I understand what he's saying," I said. "He's a lot smarter than I expected from an animal with a brain the size of a balled-up sock."

"Typical new communicator syndrome," she said, rolling her eyes. "Everyone who takes my class thinks their pet is a genius. Next thing I know they're an expert writing a book or a blog."

"Thanks for helping me feel like a cliché," I said. "I'm recording his speeches to put on my website."

She stopped and looked at me with a surprised expression.

"I thought I'd link to my T-shirt page. Look, I need some way to drive traffic, or whatever they call it."

"Oh, for God's sake," she said, annoyed. "I never thought I'd live to see the day when you had something in common with those ladies in my workshop who write in the voices of their pets. Each and every one of them thinks they came up with the idea. And not a single one really understands a word their animal is saying. Tell me you have more self-respect than to exploit those poor animals."

As she spoke, her voice became increasingly peevish. Was she feeling pushed because I was intruding into her territory? Why was she making that squinty-eyed pinched face?

"So you don't want me to do this?" I said. "I thought you'd be supportive. You know I need to make money. You told me dog stuff was a big growth industry. My T-shirts aren't selling for shit." I'd been silk-screening T-shirts and trying to sell them on MySpace for the last year, but so far my shirts hadn't made many friends. I'd sold about fifteen of THE FUCKING DODGERS and THE FUCKING LAKERS combined. HAPPY FUCKING MOTHER'S DAY totally tanked.

"That's not what's bothering me," she said, shifting into her earnest poker face, a signal that she had hit a serious topic.

"So it's the *usual* thing?" I asked.

Ah. The opening salvo in a familiar fusillade. In the beginning I liked how different Sara seemed from Eden. She wasn't silly. She didn't babble or gossip or rage. She didn't drink or do drugs or overspend. Until I found out what she did for a living, I thought she seemed grounded. But certain basic girl topics seemed to come bundled with the gender software. Intellectual or airhead, they all got around to them eventually.

"We've been together five years now," she finally said. "I need to know where we stand. What are your intentions toward me?"

"Good," I replied. "I have good intentions."

"That's not what I meant, and you know it," she said. She was right. "I'm forty-five years old. I need to know if you're in my future or not."

"I am if you want me," I said, even though I knew it didn't mean a damn thing. On the other hand, if it worked, I didn't see any conflict.

"If I want you?" she said. "You mean you don't want *me*?" Her voice got really small. "You always say you have a nice time with me. You don't love me, do you?"

"Look, Sara, of course I do. But I was honest from day one," I said with a heavy sigh. "I've just been through a nasty divorce. I don't want to get married again."

"What about living together?" she countered. This leg of the journey was tricky. "You deserve more than that," I began, trying a new angle. Sometimes when I quickly shuffled through my repertoire of acceptable girl words like "therapy," "vulnerability," "healing," "intimacy," and "universe" it was surprisingly effective.

"Right now I'm still in recovery," I added, sickening myself by going for a double play. "I don't know if I'm emotionally available."

"It's been five years since your divorce, Gil," she said. "You can't dwell in the past like that."

"Sure, I can," I said. "It's the one thing I'm really good at. I love how the past stays completely still while I wade around in it."

"Well, if you want to stay together, then we have to go to marriage counseling," said Sara.

"Marriage counseling!" I said. "I wouldn't even go when I was married!"

"You realize you're leaving me no choice but to consider my other options?" she said. That was girl talk for "I have a vagina and other guys want it." Her face collapsed into an expression of childish misery.

"You gotta do what you gotta do," I said, knowing I sounded like a dumb biker. But I hated this topic. And I really hated ultimatums. I could never change my mind after someone drew a line in the sand. It was the only time I ever had a shred of insight into what it was like to be George W. Bush.

"If you want to see other men, fine. I'll start going to strip clubs," I said, joining the pissing war, knowing how much I hated strip clubs. But I've found that if I have the energy to brazen it out, I can often turn a standoff into a win.

Sara sat quietly, staring at the tops of her velvet and bamboo flip-flops, holding herself back from any display of emotion. "Well, thank you for being honest. This makes it all crystal clear," she said, choking back tears as she gathered her belongings onto her lap.

When I didn't say a word, she got up, put on her jacket, bit her lip, and walked out.

I felt really weird after she left: exposed, off-kilter, vulnerable. Like someone had just torn my front door off its hinges. But I also had a hunch that the standoff with Sara wasn't permanent. We had been through versions of this a lot.

"Hey, you guys. Guess what time it is?" I said to the dogs.

"Beer-thirty," the dogs all recited in a monotone as I grabbed a bottle from the fridge.

"She wasn't happy," said Jimmy.

"You got that right," I said.

"Because of the mating for life thing?" he asked.

"Yep," I said. "Your species lucked out."

"Well, by instinct we know better," said Jimmy. "Love and sex are two things that we don't try to find at the same time."

"People have based whole civilizations on the notion that they are supposed to go together," I said.

"That's why a smart dog doesn't limit himself to one gender," he said.

"What is love, exactly?" Cheney asked after a few moments of silence. "I mean, I think I know, but I just want to check."

"It's the big emotion behind snack time," said Jimmy. "It's the reason why someone will take you for a walk. A good example of how it works is probably Gil and me. Or it used to be. Until that disturbing talk last night." Jimmy suddenly grew quiet, lowering himself onto the floor and into a flattened position. "Now I don't know what I understand anymore." The rest of the dogs stared in silence. Then, sensing his discomfort, they all got up and went into the yard.

"For crying out loud. Could you be a little more maudlin?" I said. "Nothing has changed. We still have the same relationship we always had."

"Everything seems different now," he said. "I was so proud of you and my noble lineage. But now I'm wondering. If you're not my dad, who are you? Just some bossy dude that we all follow around like a bunch of baby ducks. And who does that make me? I bet the others are all laughing behind my back."

"No one's laughing at you," I said. "And I'm still your . . . We're still a family. You're still my boy."

"I need to know who I really am," said Jimmy. "I need to meet my birth parents. How would I go about finding them?"

"Well," I said, "your mother lives with my ex-wife. Or she did the last time I checked. And believe me, I have not been checking. Never."

He looked at me intently. His pink tongue, spotted with black, was hanging out of his mouth in a pant that meant anxiety. It was too cool outside to be panting from heat.

We sat there like that for probably two or three minutes.

"So she's still alive?" he asked cautiously.

"Probably. Hey, who wants a cookie?" I asked, cleverly changing the subject. And in the ensuing cookie stampede, as all the dogs raced in from outside and from other parts of the house, the topic got lost and hopefully forgotten.

{ 6 }

A Conniving Little Weasel

*A*fter Sara left that night, empty bottles of beer accumulated on the surfaces around me like some kind of voracious, fast-growing mold. The more wasted I got, the more I began to curse my bad luck with women. It only worsened when I made the mistake of calling my mother.

"I never liked that one," said my mother when I told her about Sara.

"You never even met her!" I said, protecting Sara from an uninformed attack. "I'm sorry I never introduced you. You would have liked her. She was a nice woman."

"Nice!" My mother snorted. "Anyone can do 'nice.' Laura Bush was 'nice.' Milt's first wife was 'nice' too. Till she sued him. Let the whole bunch of them take that 'nice' act to someone who will buy it. They don't fool me. You can do better than that silly hippie girl, Gil." Talking to my mother was in perpetuity a double-edged sword. Her real genius was her

ability to make me want to fight against her supportive state-
ments and prove them wrong. "I wish you'd come out here
and see me," she said. "Milt is starting to think you don't like
him. And I miss hearing you play piano!" Only she didn't say
piano. She said "pi-daddo." Baby talk was always the red flag
that warned me to get off the phone.

"Oops," I said, ending the conversation like I ended them
all, with a lie. "Gotta run. Gotta take this other call."

"Your big brudda would like you to call him," she said.

"Tell him to call me," I said as I hung up, eager to purge
myself by getting back to my work.

Before I closed the computer, I Googled the words "dog"
and "blog," just to see what I'd get. And lo and behold, I
stumbled onto a site called TheirSpace, filled with hundreds
of people blogging as their animals. When a little voice inside
me whispered, "T-shirt buyers!" I plunged ahead and hastily
put up a page for Jimmy. It was just a big picture of him looking handsome and charismatic beneath the words "Advice:
What do you want to know?" My plan was to post some
audio clips from his "Edible or inedible" talk. But to my dismay nothing I'd recorded was audible except for some panting. At one point, I could hear Cheney doing his multisyllabic
yawn, and that was all. In the name of the branding of Jimmy,
I did my best to re-create in print everything I could remember he'd said in his speech.

I'm glad I did at least one productive thing that night, because when I checked my messages before bed, I realized I
had missed a call from the owner of my house, Mrs. Bremner.
I was expecting a second request to retile the kitchen. But that
was not what she had on her mind. "We'd like to come out

there for vacation this month," she chirped, as if it was great good news. It took a minute for my heart to sink.

"When are you thinking of coming?" I asked when I called back in the morning.

"Is next weekend too soon?" she said, in all sincerity, no comprehension of the tidal wave of repercussions she was causing. The longer we spoke, the more the law of unintended consequences ricocheted around my head like an echo in a drainage tunnel.

"How long are you planning to stay?" I asked, doing my best to disguise the panic in my voice.

"Well, Mr. Bremner retired this year so we have more time on our hands," she said. "We were thinking of staying out there for two months, maybe three, and then heading off to Geneva once the roof of our château is redone. I hope that's not too inconvenient!" What could I say except "Fine!" Even though by saying it I was agreeing to homelessness. This was my arrangement with them. I don't know where they thought I went when they came to town. I guess they figured that, just like a snail, I could live anywhere.

My first impulse was to rent an apartment in our area, lay low for a couple of weeks, and wait them out. But it was summer, and all the rents were quadrupled. Even if I had the five grand a week it would probably cost, I'd still wind up living next door to some jack-off family from a reality show.

So I surveyed my other options, beginning with my mother's condo in Sedona, Arizona. But there was a reason I hadn't lived near my mother since my early twenties. Our relationship was strained despite the attempt I made, like many other good enough sons, to "talk" to her once a week. While she prattled on I surfed the Internet in search of distractions. Once, as she waxed philosophical about my amazing brother, I tuned out so hard that I started to download porn. To be fair, since she'd gotten married to her third husband, Milt, her compulsion toward hand-wringing had lightened up a little. Maybe because Milt had some money he'd salted away from years of running a carpet warehouse. If you liked stories about carpet, Milt was definitely the guy you wanted at your dinner party. Anyway, I called my mother.

"Sure," she said when I mentioned I might need a place to stay. "We'd love to see you! I've been dying for you to spend some time with Milt!"

"Is this weekend too soon?" I said. "You know I have four dogs now, right?"

"Oh, we can't have dogs here." She clucked with a certain amount of alarm. "Milt is a neat freak. There must be a kennel where you can leave them!"

"Let me call you back," I said, drawing a black line through my mother's name and then scrolling down the list a bit further.

Well, there's always Kegger, I thought, fondly remembering my best friend from the construction site days. Good old Kegger: drinker, fly fisherman, dog lover. But it had been awhile. When I dialed the last number I had for him, I got a brand-new listing in Washington state.

"We're in the Cascade Mountains north of Seattle. We don't have a house yet," he said. "You still have a tent and a camp stove? Come on up, my man. It's rad."

I considered it. I had been longing for a camping trip with the dogs. Then I started remembering Kegger's squabbles with his wife after they'd both had too much tequila. There were broken dishes and a trip to the emergency room. Maybe it didn't sound so good after all.

The only unmarried friend I could think of was Wayne, a cop I sometimes hung out with at a bar in Agoura. Wayne was great for playing darts and watching the Dodgers. But couch surfing at the home of a cop seemed like asking for trouble.

The last option was big brother Steve. I was relieved when I couldn't get ahold of him. Turned out that was because he'd just moved in with Mom and Milt in Sedona. Once again his last girlfriend had "flipped out" on him. That was the phrase he used when he got caught cheating.

"Fuck me," I said when I hung up the phone. "This is my payback for being twenty-two for twenty-five years. Nothing to fall back on. Nothing to fall forward on. *And* nothing solid to stand on. Just a dead lame T-shirt business, two computers, a guitar, and four dogs."

"Beer-thirty," said Fruity and Cheney at the same time.

"Has been for the last two hours," I said.

A couple of beers later, I dialed Sara's number.

"Hi," I said to her voice mail after listening to her recite her workshop hours over a recording of pan flute music. "I'm just calling to say I'm sorry. I didn't mean to hurt you. I'd appreciate it if you would please give me a call." I hung up, and opened another beer. "Now what the fuck do I do?" I said.

"*W-a-l-k?*" Jimmy asked. The mere mention of the word, even in code, caused all four dogs to leap around like there was an electrical current in the floor. Every dog had his own take on the happy dance. Cheney twirled in a tight circle and barked. Fruity did a version with both arms outstretched, like a tenor about to hit a high note. Jimmy bounced up and down, as though propelled on hydraulic lifts like in a low-rider.

Dink, of course, came running at me like a missile. "Oh my God. I love you, I love you," she said as she pawed at my ankles.

"Nah. I'm too freaked out," I said. And when no one quieted down, I added, "That's the same as *no*." Now everyone became still.

Several of them lay down, head on front feet, nose down, eyes up, staring in despair.

"I am shocked at you guys," Jimmy said, as he alone continued to bounce. "Never give up this soon where a *w-a-l-k* is concerned. Too much is at stake."

"But we're doing 'Nose down, eyes up,' " said Cheney.

"Yes. But in this case, you have other options. Watch closely." Jimmy sauntered over to where I was sitting.

"What?" I said to him as the telephone rang. I recognized the number as being one of Sara's. After hesitating for a second out of confusion about what to say, I plunged ahead and picked up the phone.

"Hi," she said in a voice so full of hurt and defensive anger that I wondered if she had taken all the grievances and sorrows she had about me and consolidated them into a tightly written epic poem titled "Gil the Asshole." I quickly tried to figure my angles as Jimmy placed his head on my knee. He looked so sweet and supportive that I hoped he was recovering from his adoption trauma. Fondly I began to rub his ears.

"Look, Sara," I began, "I didn't mean for things to turn out like they did. You know I care about you."

"If you really cared about me, you'd care about making

this work," she said in a barely audible voice. Jimmy began slowly licking my knee.

"Well, that's not true," I said, taking a big swig of beer, instantly aware I'd screwed up. "I mean, you're not taking into account that we might have different ways of making things work. Think about what it's like to be me for a minute. I lost everything in that divorce. My house, my pension plan—"

"My credit rating, my bank account. Why would I ever want to get married again?" Sara finished my sentence and mimicked my voice. "Do you think it's my intention to rip you off like she did? Okay, so you had a bad marriage. Most people do at some point. But they get over it. And they move on with their lives and build something new. There's no way to totally protect yourself from loss. It's the universe's way of making room for you to get some new stuff."

As she spoke, Jimmy got up on his hind legs and plopped his torso into my lap. He started to lick my face like I was a Creamsicle.

"If I'm such a big mess, then you must be a masochist to want to be with me," I said argumentatively. "Don't you think you could do better?"

I reached out for Jimmy's big warm head. Running my hands through his silky fur was so comforting.

"I don't know why you bothered to call me," Sara said. "Apparently we have nothing more to say to each other." The finality in her voice made me queasy.

"Wait. Don't hang up yet," I said. We sat on the phone, in silence. The muddy sadness of the moment reminded me of the way my divorce had rushed in like a flash flood and capsized me. It had felt like a collision with a fire truck at a red light. Somehow I hadn't seen it coming.

"Okay, okay. What if I say I'll go to couples counseling?" I said, knowing I could probably put it off for months, if not years.

"Observe, now, 'the leash gambit,' " said Jimmy as he bounced off my lap and turned to address the group. "I adapted it from a Normal Rockwell calendar we used to have up in the kitchen. It's also the cover of the new L.L.Bean catalogue." Then he picked up the leash between his teeth and fixed me with another intense stare. It looked like such a piece of pure, naïve, well-intended communication that the other dogs gasped in awe.

"Oh my God! Are you serious?" Sara said to me.

"Mmm-hmmm," I said as a new approach occurred to me. "I'm getting kicked out of here while the Bremners are on vacation. This might be a good time to test out living together. A trial thing, like you suggested before?" I spoke too loudly and quickly. I think I was trying to override the voice in my head that had made me promise never to live with a woman again. Still, this seemed like my last chance at a winning strategy. I forgot that I always get this shit wrong.

"So in other words," she said, "your only motivation for working on the relationship is that you're basically homeless until October?"

"No. Goddamn it, Sara, you know that's not what I meant," I said, attempting some fast fine-tuning. "You're the one who always talks about how opportunities manifest when we live in the present. . . . So that's what we have here. The manifesting of present opportunities."

That really got her. It always helped to frame things in Sara-speak. She sat quietly thinking it over.

"Well, maybe a trial period where we take advantage of

synchronicity might turn out to be a good thing in the long run," she said. "Especially if we're also going to couples counseling!" And with that I felt the sun come out again.

I was so happy and relieved to have a temporary solution—even one that I hated—that after we said goodbye, I hooked Jimmy up to his leash. Every other dog stood frozen in complete awe at his abilities as Jimmy and I headed out the door.

"That was pretty amazing the way you engineered this while I was on the phone," I said, shaking my head as we walked down the street. "You are certainly a conniving little weasel."

"Like stepfather, like stepson," said Jimmy.

W-A-L-K

"*E*very dog wants to take a walk every minute of their lives. It's our only creative outlet. It's our church," Jimmy said as he dragged me away from the house as quickly as possible. "Every walk is a work of art in progress. An adventure of the soul. It's all the best things about living in the present linked to the best things about the past. It connects me with my ancestors, my instincts, all of my dreams for the future. When I'm on a walk, I'm on the hunt, I'm protecting my young."

"I had you fixed," I said.

"Don't be so goddamn literal," he said. "The point is that one day I get to yell 'I'm out here and you're stuck *in there*' at the dogs trapped behind that wrought-iron fence across the street. Another day I get to pee on the very rock a half block from here that others have peed on for over half a century. You know which rock I mean, I assume."

"No," I had to confess.

"I can't believe how little attention you pay to the important stuff," he said. "That reminds me . . ." And he pulled me over to a fence where he stood and barked angrily.

"What's that all about?" I asked him. I tried as hard as I could to yank him away so we could head up the hill. "Are you serious?" said Jimmy. "You didn't hear that guy call me a leash monkey? Worst thing you can call someone. On this block anyway." We stopped and he peed first on a patch of grass and leaves, and then on a rosebush, and then again on a piece of ivy.

"Why do you pee so much?" I asked.

"Well, it's certainly not because I have to pee," said Jimmy.

"Is there some set number of times you are going for?" I asked him.

"No, I improvise," he said. "I just want to exceed the totals of my rivals. For me, it's all about status. On this block I have peed more than any other dog. Except Samson. That bastard has peed *everywhere*. He is totally manic. If I didn't like him so much, I would probably kill him." He bared his teeth and growled, a very odd thing for Jimmy.

"How do you pick your spots?" I asked him as we continued to walk.

"Well, it's tricky. Around here almost every blade of grass is a guest book. Some have been signed by every dog in the neighborhood." He dropped his nose to the ground. "You have to feel your way toward the peer group that makes you look good. There still are a couple of places Samson hasn't hit yet. Ha! I just got one. That's going to piss him off. I can't wait!" He trotted along merrily, but then stopped again almost immediately. "Taking a dump works differently. You calculate that equation by counting the number of cleanup baggies being taken along, plus one. Two baggies means three dumps. Three baggies, four dumps, and so on."

Jimmy now raced forward so rapidly that I felt like my arm was being pulled from its socket. "Why are you pulling so hard? Stop it. Slow down!" I yelled.

"Just making sure I get you far enough from our house so you don't change your mind," he said, as he ground to a halt, riveted by a small patch of ivy and mud.

"Why are we stopping here?" I asked him. "What are you looking for?"

"Are you serious?" Jimmy asked, laughing incredulously. "Footprints. Holes that lead to something. Or used to but don't anymore. Nesting animals. Or better, dead ones. Insects. Oily, clear, gelatinous, or viscous goo of any kind. Hardened stuff in a lump, especially gum or jelly. Anything decaying. Any bodily excretion."

"Why would you want to find any of those things?" I asked, curling my upper lip.

"No more jokes for now," he said. He obviously didn't want to be distracted.

"Every single inch of the ground around here is equally fascinating," he said. "One day I hope to stop at them all." He began happily rooting around in the dirt with his snout like a pig until his whole face was covered with mud and wet leaves.

"Best taste in the world," he said, pushing his head into a pile of dead grass. When he emerged, he was chewing contentedly. "Unidentifiable chewy thing that's been aging in dirt. I'd offer you some, but I'm not wired for sharing."

(8)

Eden

*L*ater that night when I got back on the computer to check my mail, I was shocked but pleased to discover that Jimmy had eighty-five friends on his TheirSpace page. That was seventy-eight more friends than my T-shirts had made on MySpace in almost a year.

"Would you mind repeating what you said about taking a walk?" I asked him. "I'd like to add it to your page as a blog."

"Yes, I would mind," he said. "I'd rather we use the time to do a search for my mother."

"I told you, I probably know where she is," I muttered under my breath.

"You're sure she's still alive?" he whispered.

"You're five. She was two when she had you," I said, wondering if I was making a mistake by revealing this information.

"Can you call and find out about her for me?" he asked.

"No," I said. Jimmy looked at me intently, nose down, eyes up.

"Please don't ask me to call my ex-wife," I pleaded. "I wouldn't do that to you."

"All right, all right," I finally said, unable to resist his baleful expression. When I saw how ebullient my words seemed to make him, I had a feeling I was doomed to play by Jimmy's rules.

At the same time I was trying not to think about the fact that I had agreed to move in with Sara. I blocked it out by fretting constantly about having to call Eden. Then I did everything in my power to delay making that call. I had intentionally deleted her numbers from my cell phone right around the time of my big testosterone attack during those first blurry weeks that followed my divorce when I built a roaring fire in the fireplace, drank half a bottle of Cuervo Gold, and yelled "Good riddance, cunt!" as I threw anything she'd forgotten to pack into the flames. The following morning I was not only very hungover, but I had a fireplace full of pieces of melted hot rollers, blackened perfume bottles, metal clasps that had once been part of now-incinerated bras.

Looking back on the way it all went down, the thing that pissed me off the most about Eden was that she somehow got the last word. Stupid me for hanging around a couple years too long, trying to act like I hadn't noticed our marriage was over. How dare she not give me enough warning so I could dump her first.

Although I have to admit that I had been turning a deaf ear to her for so long that even if she had been posting warning signs on a website called "Gil Beware," I would have probably paid no attention. Maybe there were clues hidden inside some of those endless tirades I tuned out about Jennifer Lopez and Ben Affleck not being right for each other. Eden followed Internet gossip so enthusiastically that I liked to make her mad by purposefully ignoring it. My recollections of her speeches about all those Britney Spears–type people blurred together like an *Us* magazine that had been left out in the rain.

Truth was I knew that we'd had an unfixable mess on our hands, but I'd assumed for the time being we'd be polite and ignore it. It also pissed me off that she had tried my case in the kangaroo court of her unstable girlfriends without even allowing me to take the stand. How cold was it that she gave me my walking papers right after I charged a nonrefundable vacation for two to Hawaii? Then she argued that we should still go since we'd already paid for it, letting me believe it might lead to patching things up. Best of all, she waited until we checked into the hotel to tell me that she was already seeing someone else.

At first she claimed she didn't want anything from me but her freedom and her clothes. That was before she hired a lawyer. Turned out, all those things she didn't really want, she took anyway.

So I didn't want to get back in touch with Eden. Not now, not ever. No one ever needs to see an ex thriving and looking fantastic. But Jimmy had started putting on quite a show of depression and need. He would ask me if I had called her yet, and when I said no, he'd refuse to eat. He upped the ante by refusing to talk or play. He'd follow me from room to room, staring at me and moping, peppering his silence with sighs and weird little whimpering noises. That he and I had been talking to each other made it more poignant than in the old days, when I could pretend that a cookie could fix anything. I hated to see Jimmy sad. His good moods always brightened my world. Also, not to be mercenary, but we were getting lots of hits on his TheirSpace page. We had new friends and messages from other animal bloggers. Okay, yes, a quick scanning of most of them gave me a butt clench. Far too many were written in that lolcat "I Can Has Cheezburger?" cadence. "Mr. McFluffersons sends u sum puppeh wuvn" was the only one that I read out loud to Jimmy.

"What the fuck is that supposed to mean?" he replied.

"I don't know," I said. "Apparently, TheirSpace has been taken over by my mother."

Meanwhile, I kept putting off calling Eden for as long as I could. It's amazing the amount of important things you have to do when you're avoiding someone. Suddenly, I had to reseal the tiles in the bathroom and reseed the lawn. The yard always needed work because the gardeners the Bremners hired were what I called "lawn terrorists." They gardened as though they were from a land where concrete was a crop that needed tending and everything that was the least bit green had to be blown away.

It was beer twenty-nine by the time I finished pruning and fertilizing and finally picked up the phone. By now I was wishing I had just lied to Jimmy and said the number was out of service. He was a dog. How would he ever have known? But once again I felt compelled for some reason to do the right thing, even though it was making me sick to my stomach.

Most of the time I don't believe in God, though I'm fascinated by the idea of intelligent design. Because if what we see around us are the fruits of God's college sketch pad, what de-

signs did this guy have that *weren't* worth saving? If degener-
ative illness, mommies who eat their young, religious wars,
and homeless children all made it past the rough outline
stage, wasn't it possible that we, by offering unequivocal
gratitude and thanks instead of constructive criticism, were
simply helping reinforce all his worst instincts? Weren't we
what AA would call his "enablers"?

Nevertheless, I found myself praying, while Eden's phone
was ringing, that she had left the country. Please let the call go
to voice mail, I prayed. And then I said a thank-you prayer
and added an "Amen" after my prayer was granted.

"Leave a message for Eden or Chad after the beep," said a
recording. "If you want to speak to Eden right now, try her
other number."

"Eden . . . it's Gil," I finally said. "Good to see you the
other day. Just calling to say hi. Actually, I have a question. If
you get this, give me a call." I was so rattled hearing her
voice, sounding so bubbly and officious, that I hung up without leaving my number.

"I bet she's on a vacation," I said to Jimmy. Then I whispered to myself, "Please, God, let her be on a trip to the
Middle East, where she could be taken hostage. Amen." But
God was fed up with my sorry cynical ass by now. Eden
called back only a few minutes later. She apparently found
that Costco receipt. It was the first one she'd ever seen.

"Hi, Eden," I said, picking up on the fourth ring in the fer-
vent hope that she'd get impatient before that and hang up.
"Hi" was all that she needed to launch into a monologue.

"It's so weird that we ran into each other like that," she
said, the happiness in her voice indicating that she had done
a much better job of Photoshopping her memories of our re-

lationship than I had. "Everything happens for a reason. And I was just thinking about you on my way home from Pilates this morning," she bubbled. "I saw a young shirtless guy on a motorcycle, and I thought, 'Gil used to have great abs just like that.'" Eagerly I found my way to a beer. "Remember when we went to that grocery store in Morro Bay where we saw Jennifer Garner?" I sat back in my chair and took a big swallow. She had exactly one minute before I turned on my computer and started researching the erotic female form. "I'm sorry. It was Jennifer Aniston. I remember you said 'Jennifer who?' and I couldn't explain her to you since you were the only person in the entire world who still refused to watch *Friends*. That was right before we drove to that nasty motel and tore off each other's clothes. I even remember what was on the TV in that motel room! *Selleck, P.I.* I thought he was so incredibly hunky back then!"

I remembered that motel, though what I remembered even more than the hot nasty sex was almost not calling Eden for another date. Now I wished I had listened to my gut. But in those days I believed one should always give in to lust whenever possible. Kind of an homage to Henry Miller.

Eden and I met during her maiden/wench period, at the Renaissance Faire. I don't know what I was thinking using that Elizabethan toxic waste dump as a singles bar. I was there to build a bunch of stages and booths for some medieval puppet company. Eden was walking around in a milkmaid outfit, with her boobs all pushed up. She called me "kind sir" in an embarrassing vaguely Britishy-Irishy-sounding Shakesperean accent, then offered me a goblet of mead. "Sure," I said, "though I'd rather just have some fermented honey." When she stared at me blankly, not understanding my joke, I

learned that Eden's understanding of the Renaissance began
and ended with her costume. It wasn't even mead they were
selling. It was warm wine with cloves floating in it. But one
goblet of fake mead led to another. Next thing I knew she was
telling me that she really liked my eyes. Then she was pranc-
ing around my apartment, wiping her mouth on her big bell
sleeves, doing a slow striptease to a CD she'd stolen from the
puppet show guys. It was the Irish Rovers singing "John Bar-
leycorn," a song I'd never known had any erotic potential.
Eden was a sexy little thing back then. By the end of the night,
we had done it three times.

That was the first sex I ever had with a girl who didn't
shave anywhere. If memory serves, it was also the last time
she didn't. Her club-crawling punk phase started a month or
two later. For some of that she didn't have any hair at all, not
even on her head.

"So you're probably wondering why I called," I said. I
could hear in her silence that the question hadn't occurred to
her. Her voice sounded so casual and friendly, it bugged me.
We hadn't spent any time together in five years. Didn't I deserve a little more fanfare?

"Do you still have Gypsy?" I finally said.

"My dog? Of course I have Gypsy! Gypsy! Come here,
sweetie! Somebody wants to talk to you!" she called out.

"No, no, wait! Stop!" I said, knowing where this was
headed. But it was too late. Eden always did this, and I always hated it. "Eden. Pick up the phone. Eden." I shouted in
vain as she held the phone down by Gypsy's face. I could hear
vague canine breathing noises. "Hello, Gypsy," I said, feeling
like an idiot, knowing the dog paid no attention. This talking
to the dog on the phone thing never worked at all, but that

never stopped Eden from continuing to experiment. "Put Mommy back on the phone, Gypsy. Eden! For Chrissakes pick up the goddamn phone or I'm hanging up!"

All the dogs at my end of the call stared cautiously. Jimmy especially was alert and focused. He stood very still.

"Here. Say hello to your mother," I said, putting the phone by his head.

"She's on the phone right now?" he whispered. I nodded.

And then I heard Eden's shrill voice. "Gil, are you there? Pick up!"

"The window of opportunity has now closed," I said to Jimmy.

"Hi," said Eden when we resumed. "Gypsy says you two had a good talk!"

"What's your schedule like the next few days?" I asked, trying to move things along. "I was wondering if I could bring Jimmy by."

"Who's Jimmy?" she said.

"The puppy you gave me five years ago."

"Oh?" she said.

"And he . . . We . . . I thought it might be interesting to re-unite him with his mother," I said. "See if they recognize each other."

"And his sister, don't forget. Plus I have a male you never saw from another litter Gypsy had a few years ago. But, Gil, you don't have to make up reasons to come and see me," Eden said in a teasing tone. "You're welcome to come, with or without the dog!"

"Thanks," I said, pissed off that she thought this was all a ploy to spend time with her even though she had emptied my bank account.

"When do you want to come over? We're here all the time. Except Tuesday and Thursday at ten, when I have my tennis lesson. Tomorrow I have a facial peel. But I'm free after that. Except first thing Friday morning, when I'm getting some laser thing done to my jawline. Don't even ask."

"How about tomorrow afternoon around three," I said.

"Perfect!" she said, "Let's do four. That's when Mai Linn's other nanny gets here."

"Okay. Well, I have another call I have to take," I said as a preemptive tactic to keep her from bouncing untethered from one detail to the next.

"Whoa. That was so epic," said Jimmy after I hung up the phone. "I just talked to my mother."

"Talked?" I baited him. "You didn't make a sound."

"I didn't have to. We were instantly in sync. It was massive," said Jimmy. "Towering. Tremendous. Vast. I've never lived through anything like it. I probably never will again."

We sat quietly beside each other for a while, listening to the muffled snorting sounds of the other dogs chewing on parts of their anatomy.

{ 9 }

Disappointed

*T*he following morning I was awakened from a mild hangover by the conversation Jimmy was having outside my window with Samson. That rottweiler mix had a voice so deep and gravelly that it reminded me of a bass line from some classic Slayer song that they must have forgotten to write.

"I did everything you said, but it still didn't work," Samson was saying when I first rolled into consciousness.

"Give it time," said Jimmy. "If there's no progress in three months, we'll discuss a preemptive strike."

"Meaning what?" said Samson. "I don't do bodily harm."

"Don't be silly," said Jimmy. "That's not what I meant. Human beings run on empathy. They project onto you whatever *they* are feeling. So one day, while he is out of the room, jump onto the bed and get comfy. Put your head on his pillow. He will find it endearing. It will feed his grandiosity so effectively that he may actually crawl into bed beside you and try not to wake you."

"Bullshit!" said Samson. "No fucking way."

"I promise you it works," said Jimmy. "I swear by it."

The next thing I knew, I heard the thundering sounds of dog feet followed by the cacophony of a herd of animals racing in the dog door. Then Jimmy was standing on top of me, licking my face.

"You have to get up," said Jimmy. "I need to be made presentable."

"Are you kidding? What time is it?" I said, stunned that I had slept so long.

"I can't tell time," said Jimmy. "It's just a sense that I have. It's time to go call the groomer."

"It's only six A.M.," I said, looking at the clock with dismay. Nevertheless, I forced myself to sit up. "What do you mean, call the groomer?" I said as I shuffled to the kitchen, dressed in the sweat clothes in which I'd fallen asleep. I tried to make coffee. "You hate the groomer. Last time she came, we had to put a muzzle on you!"

"Well, this is different," he said. "I can't look tangled and knotty. I don't want my mother to see me for the first time with foxtails under my arms."

"It's too early to make an appointment," I said, trying to steal some coffee from the pot while it was still brewing, causing it to spill and run down the counter onto the floor. "I can leave her a message. But usually she's booked up in advance."

"Can't you tell her it's an emergency?" he whined, staring at me with the intensity of someone watching the last act of a horror movie. He was really laying the pressure on. As I sipped my coffee, I dialed the number of Gina, the woman with the mobile grooming truck.

"Her voice mail says to call back during business hours," I reported.

"Fine. Let's just sit here by the phone and stare till then," said Jimmy. "I think it might be business hours now. Why don't you try her again."

"I just called her two seconds ago," I said. "Even in dog years, that's only fourteen seconds."

"I can't take it," he said. "Let's go find her and stare at her in person."

"Not right now," I said. "Let me drink my coffee. Go outside and play or something. Go on. Go!"

"Will you play with us?" said Cheney, his mouth full of chew toys. He deposited a torn, filthy, headless stuffed bear at my feet in lieu of a ball.

"Why can't you guys go outside and play on your own?" I said. "I've never understood that."

"There's no focus if you don't play," said Cheney. "You make a big difference. For some reason, you give the ball *life*."

"He's ridiculous," said Jimmy. "All he thinks about is 'Throw it. Now throw it again.' What a ridiculous way to live."

"Ridiculous? Ever hear of a little thing called 'the thrill of the hunt'?" said Cheney, defensive almost to the point of baring his teeth. "That great feeling of release that floods your body when you know you are doing the thing you were born to do? It's like having an orgasm all the time."

"It is?" I said, suddenly interested in a new way.

"Or winning an Academy Award. Only, as soon as you win it, you win it again," said Cheney. "And all that God asks of us in return is that we bring every ball that we can back to someone. Whether they want it or not."

"That's crazy," said Jimmy. "There aren't even balls in nature. It's a sick addiction. People hate it."

"I know! I know!" said Cheney, starting to chuckle. "I have this thing I do where I go up to them and drop it into their laps, right when they're starting to work or read or something. They throw it to get rid of me. But I bring it right back. It's the ultimate high. I dictate the terms!"

"Good morning," said Dink, coming into the kitchen. "What a beautiful day. I love when we all meet outside for breakfast like this, alfresco." She began to get into a squat. "Nooooo!" I shouted, grabbing her just in time. I raced outside to deposit her on the lawn just as the phone rang.

"Oh my God. It's the groomer. Pick it up. Pick it up," said Jimmy.

"It can't be the groomer," I said, waiting for Dink to finish. "It's only six-thirty."

"Hi," said Eden when I answered. "Sorry for calling so early. But my kid wakes up at six. Look, can we reschedule? I have a meeting with my architect this afternoon. How's Sunday looking for you?"

"Fine," I said, unable to keep a smile from crossing my face, so pleased was I with not having to go see her today.

"What's she saying?" Jimmy said, staring at me apprehensively.

"Okay. Let's talk Sunday morning, then, and we'll pick a time," Eden said. "Can't wait!"

"We're not going today," I said as I clicked the phone shut. "She changed our visit to Sunday." Jimmy looked heartsick.

"She's trying to keep me from seeing my mother?" he said, filled with sorrow. "What'd my mom have to say about that?"

"I doubt your mother even knows," I said. "My ex-wife doesn't consult anyone before she makes decisions."

"But don't you think if my mother wanted to see me, she wouldn't have canceled?" he said, clearly devastated.

"I'm sure this had nothing to do with your mother," I said. "Look at the bright side. Now there'll be no problem getting an appointment with the groomer."

"She could have fought for me," said Jimmy. "She didn't even fight for me."

"Stop it. This isn't about you," I said as I watched Jimmy nervously pick up a smiling latex porcupine. He began to squeak it rapidly. The squealing noise grew louder and faster until the room was filled with the demented, feverish rhythm of an injured shrieking mouse. "She has a meeting with her architect. What are you doing? Stop squeaking that thing. It's very annoying." I was hoping to calm him, but to no avail. He kept it up with such ferocity that it sounded like he was torturing Bozo the Clown.

"It's a bad omen," said Jimmy, pausing briefly. "I finally make contact with her after all this time, and now she's gone again." With that he picked up that bright yellow porcupine in his mouth, squeaked it two more times very loudly, and then swallowed it whole.

"Did you just swallow that thing?" I said.

"What if I did?" said Jimmy, angry and defensive. "I've

stopped making it squeak. Isn't that what you wanted? I'm a loyal, obedient dog. See? The squeaking is over! Aren't you happy?"

"Well, you better hope it finds its way out on its own," I said.

{ 10 }

What Was on the
Pyloric Valve

*B*y my second cup of coffee Jimmy was moaning in agony. Midway into my third, he was mewling and pacing and making grunting sounds I had never heard him make before. Alarmed, I put him into the back of my van and headed for the emergency clinic.

"What were you thinking, swallowing that thing whole?" I scolded as I drove. "First the goddamn grooming appointment. Now this. What is it about the idea of me having a four-figure bank account that you hate so much?"

"When you first said that she canceled, it made me so hungry that I almost ate your work boots," said Jimmy through clenched teeth. "But I knew I shouldn't. You made that clear. No shoes. Nooo! Can't eat his shoes! I had to do *something* to cope."

"I didn't realize that you would find it so upsetting," I said.

"How would you like to find out your mother had another whole family and she didn't want to see you?" Jimmy gasped.

"From where I sit, that sounds like a dream come true," I said. Jimmy was not consoled. "Hey, you can't take this stuff personally. Having litters is what dogs do. That's why we get you guys fixed. All of us except Eden, who, as usual, lives in a universe with special rules that exist only for her convenience."

"That's what I want," said Jimmy. "I want a universe like that."

When we got to the emergency clinic, it was only eight A.M. I'd hoped it would be empty but there were four other people whose gazes I tried to avoid because I looked like a bum. I had barely woken up. My eyes were bleary.

A vet tech put us into the X-ray room almost immediately. I think to get me away from the regular customers. I hadn't showered or shaved. I was dressed in the clothes that I'd slept in.

"Yep, there it is," said the doctor, a short, no-nonsense guy in his early forties with big bags under his eyes. He held up the X-ray he had taken of Jimmy's abdomen. "See, right there? The ellipse on the pyloric valve? That's medical technician speak for a stuck squeaking porcupine."

All I could see where he was pointing was a vague, blurry shadow. Though I swear that X-ray was also flashing dollar signs.

After I signed some paperwork that absolved everyone except Jimmy of any blame for anything that anyone did, the doctor performed what amounted to a squeaky-toy-ectomy. I sat nervously in the waiting room for two hours, fighting the impulse to lie down on one of their plastic couches, trying to distract myself with unreadable articles in *Dog Fancy* on how to give your show dog a manicure/pedicure. Finally the emergency room doctor emerged.

"Here it is," he said, holding up a Ziploc bag with a smiling porcupine sealed inside. "Your souvenir. Jimmy's fine. If you'd like, we can keep him here overnight."

Jimmy and I had never really spent the night apart. I was concerned that given his new preoccupation with lies and abandonment it might prove too upsetting. So I hung around in the back of my van, napping and rereading old issues of *MAD* until Jimmy came out of anesthesia.

When the doctor led him out, I was very relieved. Which still didn't make it any easier to write that doctor a check for more money than I had made the whole rest of the year. Jimmy stood quietly beside me, as drugged as a reunited rock band on a reunion tour.

"Promise me you are not going to pull this kind of crap ever again," I whispered as I lifted him gently into the back of my van.

"You swallow beer" was the last thing he said before he fell back to sleep.

{ 11 }

Fresh

For the next twenty-four hours, Jimmy mostly slept. But then again he slept a lot even when he hadn't had surgery.

I spent the time packing everything I had at the Bremner house into two large suitcases and a couple of rucksacks. There were also eight sad medium-size cardboard boxes, which I pushed together onto a shelf at the back of the Bremners' garage. Eight boxes full of what looked like the unsold items from a weird yard sale: ratty towels, deflated footballs, old *MAD* magazines, cuff links my mother had given me. When did she imagine I wore those kinds of shirts? Seemed like those eight boxes had followed me everywhere. Every move I made in my life looked like this. The only thing of substance I owned was the collection of tools I kept in the back of my van: boxes of duplicate wrenches, hammers, screwdrivers, clamps, vise grips, tile cutters, wire cutters, pliers, levels, different sizes of handsaws, chisels, electrical sanders and pneumatic drills, routers and electrical testers, and a million different dovetail jigs and planers. There were untold numbers of jars, boxes, and coffee cans full of nails, screws, washers, staples, U-joints, and scraps of wire. Some of those rusted cans were old enough to still have a graphic of the World Trade Center painted on them. It was a whole van full of what-the-hell and whatever.

When I was finished, I felt like the Incredible Shrinking Man: adrift in a world where every grain of pollen and water molecule had more right to its own space on the planet than I did. The twenty-two-year-old version of me was making a racket in my head that went "Goddamn rich people. Fuck them and their multiple vacation homes and their tax loopholes and their hedge funds. Fuck their Fannie Maes and their 401(k)s." Not that I even knew what those things were. The forty-seven-year-old version of me had to sit that hothead down and remind him that Mr. and Mrs. Bremner were able to make the house payments and pay their property taxes because they had owned and run a saw blade factory for thirty-odd years. They'd made their fortune honestly and were by all accounts kind and compassionate employers. They had certainly earned the right to spend time at their own house.

The dogs, however, regarded our eviction as a joyous event, a longed-for opportunity to take a trip in the car. Even Jimmy was thrilled as I let them all squeeze into the front of my van. I put Dink in my lap so she would have to control herself. "I don't get why you're upset," she said as she circled, and then settled comfortably.

"We aren't living anywhere now," I explained.

"But we're going for a ride in the car!" said Fruity, panting from excitement. Then noticing that my expression was intense and unpleasant, she started to worry. "I'm sorry. Please don't throw me out on the freeway."

"Where exactly are we going?" said Jimmy.

"Sara's," I told them.

"I thought we liked Sara," said Cheney.

"We do, but it's a small house. It'll be tight," I said.

"Will we be staying inside or outside?" asked Dink.

"Listen carefully to me, Dink," I said. "We will be staying *inside,* but we will still be peeing *outside.* And when I say 'we,' I mean *you.* Do *not* embarrass me by peeing on Sara's Navajo rugs. Everyone has to be extra careful. Sara has three other dogs. The yard is tiny. The house is tiny."

"Three other dogs!" Cheney started to scream. "I'll kick their asses. That's my turf."

"No, it's not," I said. I slowly backed the van out of the driveway. "That's their turf. If there's any trouble, you'll have to sleep in my van."

"*Outside?*" said Dink. "Maybe I should sleep out there so I can pee whenever I want and not have to worry."

"No. My van is *inside,*" I said, pulling onto the freeway. "*Inside* the van is still inside, even though the van itself is outside. Do not even *think* about peeing inside my van."

"Seems like the list of places I can't pee keeps getting longer and longer," said Dink.

We started down the twenty-five minute stretch of canyon and freeway in between the Bremner estate, in Malibu canyon, and Sara's small two-bedroom stucco house in Thousand Oaks. "Early mid-century" is what the real-estate agents called the row of inexpensive look-alike ranch-style houses from the sixties on Sara's block.

Sara, bless her heart, was sitting outside on her front

porch waiting when we arrived. She came loping up to the
van, grinning, happy to see us. She had baked cookies for me
and biscuits for the dogs. She had cleaned out a room where
I could put all of my stuff. She had tidied up the place, waxed
the floors, vacuumed, done everything but put a sanitized seal
over the toilet bowl. Of course all of these things were more
reasons for me to feel uneasy. It wasn't just the tidiness—the
anal-retentiveness, some might call it. It was the way every
inch of the place was so full of her decorations. There were
the thrift shop antiques and American Indian hippie shit:
dream catchers, things made of feathers or antlers. But mainly
there were the miniatures. She collected tiny versions of
everything she liked in her normal-size life: tiny ceramic dogs,
cats, goats, lambs, flowers, plates and jars of tiny food, tiny
people, tiny household goods and appliances, furniture and
plants, most assembled into elaborate but tiny tableaus.

From the second I lumbered into her house hauling those
unweildy rucksacks full of my crap, I felt like Gulliver among
the Lilliputians: too large, too sweaty and hairy, too generally
contaminated to coexist in a place so full of very clean, very
delicate, and carefully arranged tiny things. Every time one of
my giant size-twelve shoes hit the floor, or I sat down too
hard on one of her antique chairs, I could see tiny populations
of miniature people and animals who had been happily attending tiny picnics and minuscule dinner parties begin to tot-
ter. It brought back the feeling that I always got when I visited
my mother, of being too big for the furniture, the halls, the
kitchen. I felt like a male silverback gorilla trying to hang a
chandelier.

And Sara's house, like my mother's, seemed to be booby-
trapped in a way that made damage inevitable. It would only

be a matter of time before the dogs and I broke something, and provided them each with a good excuse to vent repressed anger toward men. Add to that seven dogs flanking me wherever I went, trying to be the first to beat me to wherever I was heading, without ever having taken the time to determine where that might be. It all seemed as futile as trying to play a game of chess during a cattle drive.

The dogs had their own problems. As soon as we walked in, Cheney ran into issues regarding door protocol. Back at the Bremner house, the order of door exiting and entering had been carefully predetermined long ago: It was always me, then Cheney, then Jimmy, then Fruity, then Dink, then guests. Now Cheney seemed determined to grab the title of Numero Uno away from Sara's massive German shepherd, Cliff, who had held it, uncontested, for eight trouble-free years. Cliff was not amused when my platoon of half-breeds showed up acting like the Americans invading Iraq, just assuming there would be gratitude and cowed awe when they took over.

Those were just the technical difficulties. Some of them probably could have been resolved. At the root of it all was my difficulty with readjusting to living side by side with another human being. That the human was a female who wanted to share her bed, a small bathroom, and every thought that occurred to her only made it harder.

Sara immediately sensed my discomfort and tried to compensate by being generous and welcoming. There were fresh flowers, fresh coffee, fresh muffins, fresh fruit, fresh laundry. Fresh, fresh, fresh. Fresh vegetables in the refrigerator, freshly folded towels in the bathroom. She even smelled fresh. It was like there was no regular air in the house. And collapsing my life into a corner of her freshly vacuumed spare bedroom when just the day before I'd had access to my own five thousand square feet of nice stale air was pretty disheartening.

Now I had a folding card table to use as my desk, with everything I owned shoved beneath it. Even the dogs felt pushed into a corner. "That black and brown thug keeps putting his head on my back," said Fruity, edging over to me, agitated, unwilling to leave my side. "Will you do an alpha rollover on him for me?"

"I've got my own problems," I snapped defensively.

"Oh God. I'm sorry," said Fruity, crawling under the table at the same moment I was trying to wedge my suitcase down there. "You're mad at me now, aren't you? I'm so sorry. Please don't leave me. I can't live without you. I love you. Don't beat me." She tried to leap into my lap.

"Everyone relax!" I said calmly. "Fruity, stop it! I'm not going to beat you. Stop saying that, because it makes me so mad that I actually want to. Come on, MOVE." I grabbed her by her collar, scaring her further. "Look, we're only here for a month or two. Or three. God, please don't let it be three."

"Is that longer or shorter than a week?" asked Dink.

"Longer. A month is four weeks," I said. Exhausted, I lay down on my back on the floor, by my sad little corner of stuff. "Of course, I can't guarantee it won't feel like a year, if not two." Outside the door I could hear Sara clinking around in the kitchen. She was either cooking or cleaning. More than likely, it was both.

"Okay. I have one other question about being here," said Dink. "Should I pee in the outside where the trees are or the outside where the stove is?"

"The stove is *inside*," I sighed.

"Right, right. I knew that," said Dink. "I got confused for a second because I always pee wherever there are rugs."

"Yes, but that is always *wrong*," I said. "Rugs are *inside*."

"When did that start?" said Dink.

"Who gets to sleep on the bed next to you?" said Cheney.

"It's Sara's call," I said, realizing I always felt hot in this house, like I had on too many wool shirts.

"This shit is tricky," Fruity said to Dink.

"You don't know the half of it," I said to them.

Day 2

*T*his shit was definitely tricky. Every day at Sara's felt like tiptoeing through a minefield. A lot of the clearest danger zones were revealed by the second day, when cabin fever set in for me for real. As soon as I woke up, a feeling of claustrophobia crept over me like ground fog. Being rent boy was bad enough, but it was compounded by not having figured out a plan of action. I didn't know where to be. I was of no use.

"Now what do I do? Sit here and stare?" I said as I sat up in bed.

"Yes," said Jimmy, Cheney, Fruity, and Dink all at once. "It's the right thing to do most of the time."

"I wish I could agree with you," I said, longing for the safety of my morning rituals. First thing in the morning, I like to sit quietly and drink black coffee while I shake that grouchy, irascible feeling. Now I was very aware that I would have to teach my face to smile before it was ready, because

Sara was already awake and puttering around in the kitchen. I pulled on my jeans and a T-shirt, and headed in to join her.

"Don't I get a hello?" said Sara with a big grin as she looked up from a pile of newspapers spread all around her on the table. It smelled like she had been baking.

"Hello," I said.

"Is something the matter?" she asked. "Did you sleep okay? Anything I can do to help?"

"No, I'm fine," I said, longing for quiet.

"Do you want to see part of the paper?" she said. "The front page? Sports section? Entertainment? I made fresh bran muffins!" Her eyes glistened with good mood.

"Great," I muttered, trying not to be visibly surly. I reached for a coffee cup, my brain pan filled to the brim with self-loathing, like a septic tank after a big rain. "Do you mind if I make a new pot of coffee?" I said, seeing only a small amount left.

"There's still a cup left in there for you. But let me make it. That way you won't destroy all your vitamin B," she said with another big smile. "You don't read the paper?"

"Not really," I said.

"I read it every day," she said, wide-eyed and chatty. "I feel like it's my responsibility to the world to make sure I know if anything horrible is happening. In case there's something that I need to do to help."

"Mmm-hmmm," I said, wondering how much it violated the rules of guest protocol to tune her out. People who read newspapers in the morning were people that were searching for even more brand-new things to talk about. Perhaps there was a bright side to newspapers dying out.

"I find out everything I need to know from *MAD* magazine," I mumbled, wishing I had an office to go to, a project, a place that required my presence, so I could've been there right now drinking shitty coffee in silence.

I wanted a place of my own so badly that after breakfast I headed over to a construction site a few blocks away where I saw a sign that said HIRING. Turned out I was the only one applying for work that day who spoke English or expected minimum wage. I would have tried to forget the whole sad incident had ever happened, except that when I got back to Sara's, she was waiting for me at the table, smiling, wanting to hear all about how it went.

"Fine," I said, not wanting to relive any part of it. I went to the refrigerator and grabbed a beer.

"Beer at ten forty-five in the morning?" she said, incredulously. "Something bothering you?"

"No," I said.

"You're not mad at me, are you?" she said.

"I'm not mad at you," I exhaled impatiently. "Believe me, you are the last thing I am thinking about." I was instantly aware that it was the wrong thing to say. "Look, that wasn't supposed to sound so hostile. I don't feel like talking right now." I took my beer and went out to sit in my van. Every dog in the house raced with me to the door, all of them incensed at being left behind in the house. The whole group of them howled at me for a good five minutes. Or a bad one if you were the neighbors.

After an hour of self-absorbed sulking, I decided it might help center me to take a shower. This was my first encounter with Sara's tiny, tidy little bathroom full of folded pastel tea towels and little apothecary jars containing color-coordinated pastel bath salts, bath beads, and bath gels. Everything was carefully surrounded with miniature tableaus of tiny sea life: starfish, mermaids, sea horses, swimmers, octopi—all of them clean and sparkling, like they'd just been polished. And it only took one medium-length, generally restrained shower for me to ruin most of the sanctuary she'd spent hours creating. "Look, tide pools," I joked halfheartedly when she peeked in to ask if I was okay. I watched her subdue an expression of horror as she surveyed the piles of soaking wet towels, a drain clogged from my hair, a half inch of water that had splashed out onto her polished wood floor.

"Don't worry. I'll take care of it," she said buoyantly, making me feel like a nuisance for managing to create extra work for her while also doing nothing of value. I felt like a kidnapped elephant tethered to a circus tent, longing to find his way back to the jungle.

Bedtime presented other challenges. When Sara stayed with me, we both fell asleep after sex. But here, she crawled under her tucked-in sheets at around ten o'clock, surrounded by dozens of books and as many dogs as could fit in the remaining square footage. By the time I hit the hay at two or whenever, the only unoccupied surface left was under the bed. The first night that this happened I tried to be a good sport and curled up like an apostrophe around one of Sara's sleeping dogs. But the second night I got fed up and went out to drink beer in the back of my van. Come morning, Sara was mortified to find me still missing.

"Why did you have to go out to the van?" she said, before I'd had my coffee. "Why didn't you just tell the dogs to move? This is your house now too, you know!" Not that I was buying it for a second.

On the plus side, my dogs were thrilled with the way Sara

made her own dog food—a loaf of hamburger mixed with oats, brown rice, cheese, potatoes, eggs, and vitamins. "Can't I just have some of what they're having?" I suggested politely that first night at dinner when she served me seitan and Jerusalem artichokes.

"They only eat what they're eating because of primitive biological wiring. *They* don't have the luxury of making a cruelty-free educated choice based on empathy and respect for life," she explained patiently, offering me a large lump of puréed parsnips. "Studies show that people who eat red meat are agitated, aggressive, and prone to disease. Plus they pollute their auras with the fear molecules that the poor animals produce when they die a slow, painful death. . . ."

"All right! Well, bon appétit!" I said. Though what I wanted to say and didn't was "Shit! The goddamn dogs will eat anything. Plastic. Paper. Rotten stuff full of maggots. Cheney tried to eat a squirrel that was killed in a hit-and-run accident. *I'm* the only one who cares about how things taste!" Of course my griping made me hate myself more. Now that I lived here, I didn't know what I could and could not say. Or worse: who I was supposed to pretend to be.

Which brings me to sex, as everything tends to eventually. That second night Sara was so pleased to have me in residence that right after dinner she sat on my lap. "I just want you to know how glad I am that you're here," she said, throwing her arms around me and kissing me warmly. "In honor of the occasion, I want you to sit back and relax. You don't have to do anything."

She knew that was the kind of offer I'd never refuse. But in this case, with no home, no job, no prospects, I was off my own game. I know they tell you a guy is always supposed to be ready for action anytime, anywhere, but we're not. At least I'm not. I was up and down like the stock market. That poor woman was breaking her jaw trying to figure out how to please me. But I couldn't deliver. I just wasn't into it.

"What's wrong?" Sara kept saying. If I could have faked an orgasm, this definitely would have been the right time. Instead I had to deal with the embarrassment of having her sitting on the floor in front of me, staring up at me with a mouth full of dick as seven dogs watched our every move. I was horrified.

"You know, it might be all the red meat you eat. They've linked it to impotence," she said, looking as if she might start to cry. "Unless it's me. Maybe you're not attracted to me anymore?"

Now she was pissing me off. There I was, drowning in a riptide of humiliation, and *she* expected *me* to make *her* feel good.

"No, it's not you," I said, in no shape to offer comfort.

"Do you want me to wear, like, a corset or something?" she said. "Or get breast implants?"

She was really making me angry. How could she possibly have imagined that I was going to demand that she spend her hard-earned money on erotic enhancements for a goddamn rent boy?

"No, no. You're doing enough as it is," I said.

"Am I too controlling?" she asked, getting up from the floor and leaving me sitting there with my pants down around my ankles. "Is that part of the problem?"

"No. I said you're fine," I mumbled, pulling up my pants. I didn't want to have to explain how unemployment gave me vertigo.

"Now that you live here, I want you to be happy," she said, looking down at her feet. "So if there's something you want, please ask for it. Like, if you want me to wear a push-up bra, I could go buy one."

Why did women always do this? Ask me what I wanted, like waitresses bringing a menu in a sex café and it was my job to order? It's like they'd been internalizing those *Glamour* magazine lists of ways to please a man for so many generations that now they were being born with their synapses already fried. "Please don't spend any money on my behalf," I said to her.

And that was only day two.

{ 13 }

Nicer

*O*n day three, I made a vow to be nicer. If it meant getting migraines, rashes, and backaches instead of venting my rage at Sara, then fine. I deserved them. From now on I would try to be helpful if I could just figure out what that might mean on her terms.

All I could think of initially, besides converting her garage into a bedroom, was to take over garbage duty. Garbage: the last remaining domestic beachhead of masculinity—an atavistic carryover from a time when men would haul carcasses and hay from the barn. Probably a reasonable idea when it started, but even on this minor point we clashed.

We both agreed that the garbage should be taken out on a regular basis. We didn't agree on when. Sara felt that garbage should go out every evening after dinner, regardless of the fullness of the cans. My feeling was that the amount of garbage in the can should first exceed the amount of space allotted for it. "Kind of full" meant "stomp on the can for a day and buy some more time before you have to expend any more effort."

Of course, it was her house. I should have just done it her way. But I felt so useless and so disenfranchised from losing control of my fiefdom that it gave me a certain feeling of courtly generosity to offer her the use of my superior system.

So, after dinner when she said, "Are you taking the garbage out?" in that singsongy grade-school teacher's voice, I felt like she was implying that I was shirking my duties.

"Right now?" I said, to indicate that there was no urgent need.

"No," she said quietly as she got up from the table and headed toward the garbage can. "Sometime next month. Why do men think that offering to do things around the house buys them a year in which to actually do the thing. Like when you buy a wedding present?"

"I said I'd do it," I growled, rushing toward the can. "If you'd give me a fucking minute," I fumed, grabbing the garbage away from her. Here we were, seventy-two hours into my stay, already acting like my mother and father. "Don't let a woman push you around," my father used to say when he and my mother butted heads. Then he left and never returned.

"Hey, I didn't mean it," I said too late. Sara pursed her lips and fled to the bedroom. I recognized that lip pursing thing as the last stop before tears.

"I can't do this," I said.

"Dude," said Jimmy as we listened to her slam the bedroom door. "You need to mellow out." I infuriated the other dogs by taking only Jimmy with me out to the back of my van, where I opened a bottle of beer, swallowing half in one gulp. "She is making me crazy," I said.

"What do you think it's like for me to live with you?" said Jimmy. "I don't understand half of what you do in a day. I eat in a plastic dish on the floor. You eat in a glass dish on a table. You poop inside, but I poop outside. And you wonder why Dink is confused? None of it makes any sense, but I say to others the same thing I'll say to you right now, 'Just figure out what is expected and deliver it cheerfully. It's not that hard.'"

"I guess you're right," I said, open-throating my second beer before Jimmy and I reentered the house. The sounds of muffled crying were leaking from beneath Sara's bedroom door.

"Sara?" I said, standing outside. "I'm sorry. I don't know why I snapped like that." I poked my head inside the room. "Hello? Can I come in for a second, please?" I opened the door a little more and peered into the darkness. When she didn't say anything, I went to her bedside and looked down at her sweet, sad face. Her cheeks were streaked with mascara. She had shed tears over taking out the garbage? I put my arms around her and felt her relax a little. A couple of seconds later every dog in the house rushed in to join us. Half of them jumped up onto the bed and started licking her face. When it made her laugh, I was very relieved.

"I don't mean to be such an asshole," I said, lying my head on her chest. It felt comforting. I liked the way she smelled.

"I know this is hard on you," she said. Leave it to Sara to empathize with my motives for treating her badly. I climbed under the covers to lie beside her. We kissed very sweetly, and praise the Lord I was able to do it this time. When I went off like a bomb, Sara seemed perfect.

(14)

Special Moments

*I*n the afterglow of the fight, things were on a more even keel. That was the day I became too aware of another quirk of Sara's—her need to share a never-ending series of "special moments." Every time we passed each other in the hall, she'd chirp "Hi! How *are you*? Anything new?"

I think she'd always done it. But since I mainly saw her on weekends, it had never occurred to me that these weren't rhetorical questions. Now she expected real answers delivered in sentences longer and more full of description than "Fine." She wanted data on how I was feeling to increase our intimacy level.

"Hi, sweetie! How was the store?" she'd ask when I came into the house carrying a six-pack. "Christ, how the fuck do you think it was?" I would try not to say.

After all those years of living alone, I was not ready for every single thing I did to be fodder for discussion. "I never knew you did that!" she chuckled when she saw me trimming my nose hairs.

"Yeah, well, it's not a subject that comes up much," I grumbled, hoping my sour tone would put an end to the conversation.

"So, you have to trim them a lot?" she continued earnestly.

"Yes! I do! Okay? I trim them all the time," I snapped. When Fruity put her tail between her legs and ran out of the room, I made a mental note to use her as my hothead barometer.

By the end of the week, I was so fatigued from all my tamped-down rage that I had started spending my afternoons hiding out in the back of my van. I would pretend to be getting things ready for work I didn't have. I'd sit reading and rereading old *MAD* magazines. It was always beer-thirty in the back of my van. And even then I was nervous that Sara would peek her head in and say, "Can I read that with you?"

"I don't know about you guys," I said to my dogs in one of our rare moments alone when Sara had gone out shopping and taken her dogs, "but I can't take much more of this."

We were all on the floor in the extra bedroom, crowded around the card table where I stored my stuff. I'd opened my computer so I could check my mail.

"Sara's asshole shepherd keeps hooking his goddamn head over my back," Cheney agreed.

"Ignore him," said Jimmy. "Let him think he's boss. It's his house."

"But I don't have to let him hump me, do I?" said Cheney. "What is this? Rikers Island?"

This was the first time that I realized the toll this was taking on the dogs. My nerves were frayed, but these guys were in physical danger.

"Ignore him," said Jimmy. "We must respect their customs, no matter how insane. It's a different version of the way we do it with Gil." All four dogs looked at one another. Cheney yawned nervously.

"Hey, Jimmy—your TheirSpace page is picking up an audience," I said, surprised that he'd gotten almost 200 hits since the last time I looked. Somehow Jimmy now had 250 theoretical friends. Good Lord, how the definition of "friend" had changed.

"Hey," I said, "some animal expo thing wants to know if we will participate in a pet blogging event. Why don't we go and try to sell some T-shirts? If we can make you into a brand, that'd be great, right? Like SpongeBob or Martha Stewart? That jack-off Marley was a real moneymaker."

Jimmy ignored me.

"How many days till we go see my real mother?" he answered.

"Day after tomorrow," I said. "Unless Eden flakes on us again. And she might. She does stuff like that. Will you go with me to the expo?"

"Will you get me set up with the groomer?" he asked. "Will you make sure to tell her I want to be blow-dried and brushed and then sprayed with cologne?"

"You're serious?" I said. "Because don't forget that you tried to bite her the last time."

"Well, I was only two. I've changed a lot since then," he said. "Long, ratty hair balls aren't always a good look when you're over three."

"So will you go with me to the expo?" I asked him.

"Will you make an appointment with the groomer?" he answered.

"You're blackmailing me?" I said.

"I think you have it backward," he said.

I had a work trade thing going with Gina the groomer. The year before, when I resurfaced her kitchen cabinets, part of her payment was a year of free dog grooming.

So at ten the next morning, Gina the groomer arrived in her mobile dog-grooming van. She was suitably shocked to see Jimmy offering a merry greeting. "What's going on?" she said, remembering how the last time we'd had to muzzle him and lift him onto the grooming table like a sack of mashed potatoes. "Is he on some kind of medication?"

"He's going to meet his birth mother tomorrow," I said. "He wants to make a good impression."

"Whatever works!" she said, hooking his collar to a leash and leading him into her grooming truck without a struggle.

Next time I saw Jimmy, he was fluffed, blown dry, and beaming with pride. My heart ached to see him strutting, smelling all lime-scented, accessorized with a complimentary bright green bandana. He reminded me of a middle-aged guy reentering the dating scene and figuring out how he wanted to look for his picture on Match.com.

"He was fantastic today," said Gina. "Look how fluffy those feet are!"

"You can't do the same for me, can you?" I said. "Not so much the fluffy feet part, but do you cut human hair?"

"I cut my boyfriend's hair," she said. "He's almost human. I graduated from cosmetology school, but I switched when I realized that animals don't call every ten minutes for three weeks in a row, threatening to sue because their bangs are too short." She walked around me as I removed my cap.

I felt self-conscious as she examined my current hairstyle, a little "do" I had christened the Maestro Bomber because it looked like a cross between Igor Stravinsky and Ted Kaczynski. Ever since I had started losing hair on top of my head, I had been doing something I used to make fun of: not cutting it anywhere else.

"Are you happy with this?" she asked me.

"Well, 'happy' is probably an overstatement," I said. "My goal is to not look like an asshole. I'm visiting my ex-wife at her house for the first time in five years, so can you figure out a way to make me look like I'm too good for her?"

"Yow," she said, making a face filled with too much empathy. "Whaddya say we trim it? Maybe layer it at the neckline a little?"

I sat down on the stool in the back of the grooming van, surrounded by aluminum sinks, a retractable grooming table, and piles of Jimmy's shorn hair. As salons go, I preferred it to the ones Eden would frequent. They always made me feel like a bulldog in a kennel full of whippets.

At least Gina didn't ask her assistant, the undocumented cosmetologist from Central America, to lift me into that big deep sink. Although that might have been kind of hot. Gina at close range looked very inviting. She had big smoky eyes and a really great pair of tits. I didn't even notice them for the first few years because, like a lot of women with big tits, she kept them camouflaged. It was the breast implant girls who trotted those things out like they'd just won the Kentucky

Derby. Gina usually dressed in flannel shirts and khaki, like someone on safari. The twenty-two-year-old version of me saw through that ruse and was egging me on, whispering, "What would happen if you just kissed her and grabbed her boobs?" The forty-seven-year-old me had to remind him that a guy who got his hair cut in the back of a dog-grooming van was not a businesswoman's definition of a "good catch."

"Is your boyfriend still that guy Max?" I asked, trying to use friendly conversation to distract myself from further fantasy.

"Mack," she said. "Explain something to me, Gil. Are all men nuts, or is it just the ones I pick?"

"Well, we're not all nuts," I said. "Or maybe we are. It's one of the two."

"I met you at the same time I met him. If you had asked me out, none of this would have happened," she said, playfully. "You're not really nuts, are you? I seriously can't tell anymore."

"You two aren't getting along?" I said, trying to imagine Gina in bed. And then, having succeeded, trying to make myself stop. Was she coming on to me now or being sisterly? I'd always had trouble telling, but I'd definitely noticed that since I'd turned forty, I'd become more attractive to women my own age. I did okay when I was younger. I wasn't George Clooney, but there were always girls who called me "cute." Then as I got older, I noticed something interesting: The standard chick magnet types, like musicians and artists, were starting to lose their luster to the guys like me, who could at least repair your heating system or fix your sprinklers. Somehow, the horrible things that I wasn't had metastasized into badges of honor. Suddenly I was to be commended for not being a sociopath or an obvious womanizer or a felon or a pedophile or a compulsive gambler.

"There you go," she said when she'd finished trimming my scraggly locks. "Not so tidied up that she'll know you bothered."

"Perfect," I said, refusing my complimentary green bandana. A quick check in the mirror revealed that I looked the same, only cleaner. Sometimes that's all a guy like me can hope for.

I waited until Sunday to make a decision about what to wear. I couldn't ask Sara for help. She was pissed off that I was going.

"I don't get why you're trying to hurt me," she said whenever the subject came up.

"I'm not. That never even occurred to me," I said.

"How could it not?" she said. "What if I was spending all kinds of time obsessing about my ex-boyfriend?"

"I am not obsessing," I explained. "Men don't obsess. We ruminate. We examine. We review the facts. Sometimes over and over and from multiple angles. But we don't obsess." I was alarmed to learn she could tell I was obsessing. I thought about little else.

Eventually I decided on my red Ramones ROCKET TO RUSSIA T-shirt because I had long ago discovered that the best way to dress around rich people was to wear an outfit that said "Fuck you." Toss the discomfort back into their court and let them deal with it. The rest of the ensemble was a pair of black jeans, my work shirt, and a new pair of Ray-Bans that I'd found in the parking lot at the movie theater. They looked good on me. I hoped I'd make Eden miss me a little.

"I thought you didn't care what she thinks," Sara said when I asked if I looked okay. "What if I was acting like this? How would it make you feel?"

"I would take it for what it is," I said. "There's not a man or woman alive who doesn't want to look painfully good for an ex. It's some kind of Darwinian sadism passed on in the genes. Kind of a hating ritual that is the tail end of a mating ritual. Anyway, I'm doing all this for Jimmy."

"Oh, give me a break," she said. "At least admit that this is all about you."

"No! I won't! Because you're wrong!" I said. I wondered if she was right.

{ 15 }

A Visit to Bio-Mom

When we drove in the car, Jimmy hung out the window with the wind blowing through his long hair. He always reminded me of a guy standing behind a sheet in a hurricane.

Today he sat bolt upright in the passenger seat beside me.

"You want me to roll the window down?" I asked him.

"No, no thanks," he said. "I don't want to get all tangled and matted. How do you think I should greet her? Should I run up and say 'Mom'! Or wait for her to come up to me? Should I call her Gypsy? Or Mrs. Gypsy?"

"Since it's your mother, shouldn't you just trot on over and smell her butt?" I said, joking.

"Is that how you greet your mother?" he asked.

"No! Of course not," I said, shuddering at the thought. "I guess I do the human equivalent. Which is to tell her she looks great and ask if she lost some weight."

"Do you think I'll recognize her?" he asked.

"I kind of think you will," I said. "Are you nervous?"

"I'm petrified," he said.

We drove in silence until I made a left turn down a long paved road lined on both sides with cypress trees and coconut palms. Eden lived way closer to the Bremners than I'd imagined. "OhmyGod," Jimmy said. "I'm going to piss myself."

"This is it," I said. I felt a ping in my gut.

We stopped at an intercom in front of a stone and iron gate where we were visible on a security camera. Someone buzzed us in and we headed up the expensive cobblestone driveway. All around us were lawns so manicured I half expected to see golfers teeing off.

After about a quarter of a mile, we arrived at a massive two-story colonial house, about six thousand square feet if it was an inch, which it definitely was.

I parked the van in front of an attached four-car garage, then took a deep breath, expecting Eden to burst through the front door when she saw us. That would have made things so easy. I'd forgotten that making life easier for others was not one of Eden's priorities.

Hooking Jimmy to the brand-new braided leather leash he'd insisted that I buy for the occasion, I led him to the stone stoop in front of the intricately carved front door. While we stood there ringing the buzzer and hammering the door knocker for five minutes, I could smell the lime-scented cologne from Jimmy's grooming session wafting off his fluffed-up fur. The longer we stood there unacknowledged, the more I began to feel big, stupid, and foolish. It would have been so in character for Eden to have forgotten about the whole thing. She always did shit like that when we were married. Now my only option, besides leaving, was to let myself into my ex-wife's new house and stand there yelling "Hello?" I began to brace myself for humiliation as I opened the front door and tentatively stepped inside.

"Hello?" I called into a big white echoey room, my words bouncing off the white marble floor and ricocheting against the massive white walls like a confused hummingbird lost in the main ballroom at Buckingham Palace.

"I'm here to see Mrs. Eden?" I said to a lady from a Central American country who wandered in when she heard me calling for help.

"One more minute, mister." She nodded as she strode toward the back of the house. I watched her exit through some sliding glass doors and cross a patio toward a group of men dressed in sportswear, their backs to us. At the cusp of this semicircle, laughing and holding court, stood Eden, all dolled up in some type of short lime-green thing. Only Jimmy's family of dogs seemed aware that visitors had arrived. They were barking endlessly, ignoring commands to be quiet.

"Wow," said Jimmy, hearing the barking. "That's my mom. Why won't they let her in? Why are they trying to keep me from seeing my mom?"

"Eden tunes everything else out when she's got the attention of men. You have to be patient," I explained. While we waited, I looked around at Eden's opulent new digs. Her budget had gotten bigger but her tastes had not really changed. She still liked pricey early American antiques, long frilly curtains, and Laura Ashley wallpaper. And she still couldn't resist cluttering everything up with grotesquely cute statuary. Eden had a dominant Hallmark gene. When she was younger, she used to go wild at flea markets amassing collections of faux impressionist paintings and badly executed welded figurines of jazz musicians that looked like they'd been salvaged from motels that had filed Chapter 11. But now that she had access to bucks, she'd switched to life-size metal sculptures of children holding balloons and glassy-eyed couples in love. Her taste in art was one of the many reasons we'd argue. Out of bed, Eden was Thomas Kinkade. But naked, she was Picasso, Cézanne, and Marcel Duchamp. I never understood why we had such explosive sexual chemistry. Or even more puzzling, why it hung on after love had changed to contempt.

Our marriage lasted "almost five years" or "only four years," depending on who you asked. By year two I suspected she was already sleeping around.

"What's taking so long?" said Jimmy. I leaned down to rub his ears.

Right then the sliding doors rolled opened and three large black dogs stampeded toward us like a herd of water buffalo. "Gil! Hello!" Eden yelled, her arms all ready for stage one of a great big hug. I don't know who was more uncomfortable, me with Eden hanging around my neck or Jimmy with the noses of his entire family wedged between his legs. He was quickly enveloped by what looked like three other versions of him. For Jimmy it was a lovely moment. Four tails wagged furiously. For me it was a little bit too *Village of the Damned*. I was glad there weren't three identical versions of me waiting to envelop me. At least not in this part of the space-time continuum.

"Well, hi there, handsome," I heard Gypsy say to Jimmy as she sniffed his butt.

"Mom?" I heard him say in response.

"This big beautiful guy is the puppy we gave you?" said Eden. She took Jimmy's leash out of my hand and stooped over to look at him more closely. "Gypsy, you have the best-looking pups. Do you recognize your long lost son?"

"Oh, hell," said Gypsy, alarmed. "Another one of mine?"

"I don't seem at all familiar?" said Jimmy. "I'd know your smell anywhere."

"I might not remember you, but I'm sure you were a blessing. Whoever you are." I could hear Gypsy backpedaling.

"Wow!" said Eden, standing back, her hands on her hips as she sized me up. "Well, someone had a haircut!" She stood, smiling, nodding, staring at me and not saying anything. It wasn't clear if she was displaying approval or withholding further comment.

"Sorry for all the confusion but Chad is having his picture taken for *Cigar Aficionado*," she said, indicating all the guys who were now on their way into the house from the patio. "You met Chad, right?"

"No," I said, wondering when she thought I would have. All I'd really seen last time was his hairy white ass.

"Let me introduce you to your younger brother Gorgeous," I heard Gypsy say to Jimmy. "And this is your sister Party Girl."

"You're my twin brother? No wonder your butt smells so great," I heard Party Girl say to Jimmy as she play-bowed toward him. They began to wrestle. A minute later all four of them bounded off into the backyard in a big black tornado of feet and fur.

"Well, that reunion is a rousing success," I said to Eden.

"Ours is too! It's so great to see you! Let me make you a cup of tea!" she gushed, even though she should have known after being married to me for five years that what I always want is a cup of coffee.

"You've got to try this amazing tea I just bought called African Solstice. I forget what all's in it." She picked up the box and began to read, "A gratifyingly fragrant cup with a hint of vanilla. Rich in flavor, high in antioxidants."

"I hate antioxidants," I said. "You got any coffee?"

"Decaf," she said. "But trust me. You have to try this tea. It'll change your life."

"I'm not sure I'm ready for a life change today. I didn't bring the right clothes," I said, wondering why none of the women I knew ever let me have what I wanted to eat or drink. Or why she immediately assumed that I needed to change my life. Okay, maybe exchange it, but it was too much work to change it. Though Eden was already on my nerves, it was somehow tolerable because she still looked so fucking great. She was wearing one of those midriff-baring outfits all the Westside mommies wore, where the top and the pants are too short, and too tight. No more wench dresses or fishnet stockings for Eden. Now she looked like Vegas by way of Beverly Hills.

"I take Mai Linn to park now," said a twenty-ish Asian woman who entered pushing a stroller that contained a tiny infant elaborately clad in fuchsia. Now I could see that Eden's kid was an energetic, delicate little Asian girl. She was also screaming, uninterrupted, at full volume. No words, just spine-tingling, soul-piercing shrieking, like a wounded crow. I couldn't remember: Was Chad an Asian guy?

"Maa lee-an neee," said Eden to her daughter, blowing her a kiss as the child and the Asian woman departed. "Mommy love *you*," she repeated in English so punctuated with hand gestures that it looked like sign language for the deaf. "And here's my guy!" said Eden as we turned toward the kitchen and crossed paths with a Caucasian man in his late forties, a cross between a young Teddy Roosevelt and an old John Edwards: big round eyes, big white teeth, a pointy face. He was short and stocky, and his perfectly moussed and lightened hair looked like it was on loan from some other guy. Chad boldly led his posse of cigar-chomping photographers toward the enormous kitchen so he could lean over to kiss his wife on the cheek. A cloud of lime-scented men's cologne engulfed me. Chad was wearing the same cologne as Jimmy.

"Chad, you remember Gil," Eden said. Chad nodded and lifted the ends of his mouth a little, a weak attempt at a welcoming smile. I returned with a nod that said, "Yep. Here we are."

"Here we are indeed," he nodded back silently.

"Ask him what he thinks about redoing the guest cottage," I heard him say to her over his shoulder as the group moved on.

"If there's time," said Eden, "Chad would like your opinion on redoing our guesthouse. We want to fix it up so we can both use it as an office. Especially if Greta and Hayden are here." That was classic Eden: dropping names of people I'd never met, as if everyone she knew shared a common BlackBerry.

"Look at the dogs! It's almost as if they remember each other!" said Eden, getting some teacups from a cabinet. Outside in the yard Jimmy's herd thundered by again.

"I think they do," I said, filled with joy at seeing them bounding around like a pack. Jimmy looked as happy as I'd ever seen him.

"So!" said Eden, leaning back against the counter as she waited for the microwave bell to ring. "You know what, Gil? You look good!"

"Thank you," I said, assuming she was lying. Eden was being so friendly that it kind of caught me off guard. In all the vitriol surrounding the divorce, I had forgotten about the sweet side to her.

"What about me?" she prompted, apparently needing more adoration than I was offering. "Do I still look as good as I did when you met me?"

"Better," I said, squinting my eyes a little as though I were performing a diagnostic check. "You look great, Eden."

"Thanks," she said, grinning and blushing shyly as though she hadn't just insisted I say those things. "Let's go sit outside."

I followed her as she carried a tray that held the cups, a box of cookies, some stuff to put in tea, her BlackBerry, and a pack of cigarettes out to a spacious sunny patio that overlooked their back lawn. From where I was seated I could see a huge pool with a spa at one end and lush tropical gardens full of ferns and gardenias at the other.

"Great yard," I said.

"We got the same guy who did Tom and Katie's new teahouse." She nodded matter-of-factly. "Cruise." Then she stared at me expectantly. "Maybe you've heard. Chad and I have been having some problems."

"How would I have heard?" I said, irritated by the idea that she thought I followed her comings and goings. Did she think that's why I was there? Then I remembered that this was also typical Eden: revealing intensely personal information in an offhanded manner so she could reel you in and plant you where you'd rather not be.

"Gil, why do men act like such assholes?" she asked. She stared at me again.

"Well, they don't always," I said defensively. "As a gender we're kind of hardwired to effect change. If we can't, I guess sometimes we get pissed off and act like jerks. And since the only proven way to effect change when you're dealing with another asshole is to become an asshole yourself. Maybe over time we accidentally evolved into a gender full of assholes!"

I looked to see Eden's response. She was checking her BlackBerry for incoming messages. I had forgotten that Eden didn't ask questions in order to get answers. They were bridges to something else she wanted to say. "Mmm," she said, nodding when she heard that my voice had paused. I turned my attention toward Jimmy as he and his three look-alike relatives came galloping from the other direction in a giant cloud of doggy joy and dust, tongues out, paws thrusting forward. They were almost a group definition of "going nowhere fast." They looked so pleased with themselves that seeing them made me smile involuntarily.

"Gil, what happened to us?" said Eden, startling me with this new tack. "Why didn't we make it? Was I so difficult to live with?" She stuck out her lower lip, making one of her patented hurt-little-girl faces.

"Well, the way I remember it, you sued me for divorce," I said.

"I meant before that," she said. "I had no choice after I

hired that lawyer guy who did Brad Pitt and Jennifer Aniston. You know how they get. He was all, 'You have to take what you are entitled to under the law of the state of California.' I didn't know what I was doing back then." She pushed out her lower lip again. "I was only a kid!"

"You were thirty-seven," I said. "I was forty-two."

"But your thirties are your new twenties!" she said, taking a cigarette out of her pack and cupping her hands to light it. She inhaled her smoke, then blew it out her nose with great authority. Eden always looked really sexy when she smoked. She could work an exhale like it was a lap dance.

"They're still fucking old. In ancient Rome the average life span was twenty-two years!" I said, picking up my cup of tea to sniff it.

"Tell me if you like it!" she said, watching far too closely.

"Great," I said, putting down the cup of tea because it tasted like soap and twigs. I wanted coffee. What I wanted even more was a cigarette.

"See? What did I tell you? Isn't it lovely?" She inhaled the tea aroma again. "When I look back at everything now, I think in a way we were good for each other," she said in a smoky exhale. "You got me writing my poetry. I got you playing the piano. Right?"

"Nah," I said, focusing on the part of the yard where Team Jimmy was thundering past in a massive dog surge.

"Oh, Gil, why not? I miss hearing you play!" she lamented, tipping some ashes onto her saucer.

"Call my brother," I sniped. "You two always liked each other. He's better-looking too."

"Oh, for crying out loud. Aren't you getting too old to be

hung up on that crap?" She shook her head as she blew a smoke ring with great authority.

"Gypsy's in great shape," I said, trying to change the subject. It felt like the right time to shake hands and head home. But how could I shortchange Jimmy? He looked like he thought the fun was only beginning.

"She's about to turn seven. Or six. No seven. No six," said Eden. "Seven. *Plus* I think she's pregnant again."

"Are you serious?" I said. "You never got her spayed?"

"I know! I feel terrible! Six. I'm pretty sure she's six. I totally meant to before I got busy." She spoke in a very high-pitched voice, a vocal indicator that she would never give it another moment's thought. "She mostly stays in the yard, so I didn't think there'd be a problem. It didn't occur to me that she might mate with her son!"

"Eden!" I said, shaking my head. "You've got to get them neutered and spayed. You know how many healthy dogs are put down every day? Inbreeding isn't good for the health of her puppies."

"I agree!" she said, bonding with me eagerly. "I'm sorry. I know you're right!" She fluttered her eyes at me, and then stuck out her lower lip. "I am so bad! I need to be punished!" she teased. She reached out and rubbed my knee, a gesture that I found intrusive, until it turned me on.

She picked up my left hand in both of her hands. "Can we be friends, please?" she cooed. "Come on. Let's go take a look at the guesthouse."

"Fine. Then I have a real job to get to," I lied as I followed her across the yard. What, I wondered, did it mean when you were able to respond sexually to someone you wanted to throttle?

"You still live at the Bremners'?" she asked as she led me down a flagstone path and across an arched bridge over a koi pond. Was it my imagination or was she intentionally working her butt as she walked in front of me?

"Yes, but they're in town right now," I said. "I'm on hiatus."

"What a perfect time for you to do *this*!" she said. "You can live here while you work on the place! I'm sure I can get Chad to pay you too much. He always does." She opened the front gate and led me through a beautiful little yard and up another flagstone path to a smaller, more secluded version of the main house. Whoever built this place really didn't want to see their damn guests. "How perfect would that be? We can hang out! We'll have a blast!" She opened the front door and we walked into a white wooden dining room that had probably been built in the thirties.

"What do you want done?" I said, thinking it would be a shame to destroy such a nicely preserved piece of another era.

"Chad wants new everything: floors, appliances, fixtures, paint, tile. A new countertop here. A skylight and recessed lighting in here. A new bathroom with a sauna."

"Are you sure?" I started to say, before I decided not to talk myself out of a job.

"What's this?" I asked, walking down a short hall to a cozy Colonial bedroom painted a pale yellow, which was beautifully authentic-looking, except for the centrally located aluminum pole.

"That was from my foray into strip-aerobics," she said, winking. "You got here three months too late. Sorry. Now I kickbox." She pulled out some rolled blue architectural renderings from a bottom drawer of the dresser. "Here are the plans Al Takemoto drew up for us. Do you know him? He did the Anthonys' new place. Jennifer Lopez?"

"Oh!" I said. I was ready to leave.

"So you'll do it?" she asked, smiling sweetly. "There are other perks! You can have access to a new baby grand we just bought for Mai Linn's first birthday next Sunday. We're going to give her lessons—"

"Isn't *one* kind of young?" I said.

"The Chinese prodigies all start early. Didn't you start at four? I can't believe you stopped playing." She was pouting again. "Maybe you just need someone around to inspire you." She began to draw little circles on my forearm with her index finger. Afraid to meet her gaze, I stared out the window beside the bed at a little grove of poplars, aspen, and elm. We appeared to be miles from the main house. Next thing I knew, Eden stepped forward and put her arms around my waist. She leaned her head on my chest. "It's so good to see you," she said. And she stayed there like that for a very long time, cruising right past the five-second "Hi there, old friend" embrace and the ten-second "Good to see you, Mom" hug to some unnavigated terrain where she lingered at least fifteen seconds longer than was comfortable. I moved into involuntary arousal.

"So you'll do it?" she said, staring at me so intently for a second that I thought she was Cheney waiting for me to throw her a ball.

"Do what?" I said, looking down at her. I was hard now, and she seemed to know it. Her eyes were blazing back at me.

"Oh, you! You know what I mean!" she giggled, moving in a little closer and hugging me a little tighter until she bumped her pelvis up against me. Just a tiny little move, but it made my whole body shiver. One short, hard thump. Impossible to miss. One little thump. That was all.

"Let me think about it," I said, moving away from her. But, man, oh man, that little thump began to haunt me.

(16)

Seeing Clients

*A*s I drove away from there, I was hosting a raging debate in my head: What would be worse? Living in too little space with Sara and seven dogs? Or reveling in quiet luxury too near Hurricane Eden? Then I'd think about that thump and wonder, was it an accident? It had that mysterious, intoxicating, mind-warping electrical power that only unexpected and forbidden sex can have. The kind of sensory overload that can distract you so completely that you find yourself driving through a red light. I kept reliving the details of that moment: how she'd drawn circles on my arm. How she'd hugged me a little too long. Then I'd be back at that thump, seeing it first in a long shot, then in a close-up.

Remaining at Sara's didn't feel like an option anymore. Every time I turned around, there she was, smiling, wanting to talk or go for a walk or go to a movie or cook me a meal. And, yes, I realize those are all nice things for which I should have been grateful, not grouchy, edgy, jumpy, angry, or any of the other members of the Bizarro World version of the Seven Dwarfs. But there was no getting around it. That was what I felt.

Then there was Jimmy's newly whetted appetite for his family. It had been difficult getting him back into the van so we could leave.

"At last I am whole," he said while I merged the van into a lane full of slow-moving cars on the 101 freeway going west. "They complete me."

"I didn't realize you felt so incomplete," I said. "I never notice a feeling of completion when I see my mom."

"Well, your mom doesn't wrestle with you after breakfast, now does she?" he asked.

"I don't even want to imagine that," I said, and shuddered.

"My mom is a lot of fun," he said, looking rapturously happy. "I can't wait to see her again."

I reached over and patted his big block head. We drove the rest of the way back to Sara's in silence. In the grand L.A. fashion, even on Sunday evening the freeway wasn't moving. That gave me too much free time to keep revisiting that thump. There it was as the camera zoomed in from a medium shot to an extreme close-up, filling the screen in my head like it was a hundred feet tall. Thump. Just the right amount of pressure to make the erotic parts of our marriage that I'd spent the last five years blocking out come tumbling back in vivid color. Random scenes of athletic electrifying raunch, sometimes with accompanying sound bites of bitter fighting. There were also flash frames of the incident that ended everything, where I had the misfortune of seeing Chad's hairy ass staring up at me from my own bed. Then it occurred to me: Chad must have been the one who paid for that lawyer that Eden hired to rake me over the coals. Who else would have financed that great litigator from the halls of Harvard who was willing to pit the legal system against a barely solvent handyman from the Valley? Chad, the guy I was supposed to go work for, was the man who had emptied my bank account.

I was dying to run this whole weird scenario by Sara in a bid for sympathy, until I reminded myself that a girlfriend is a girl first, a friend distant second, and definitely not a guy friend. As if to prove my point, when I walked in the door to her house she seemed to want to pretend that the whole day had never happened. "Guess what!" was the first thing she said, in a cheerier tone than seemed appropriate. "I have the answer to your job problems!"

"Excuse me?" I said.

"I got the idea because I need you to give me a ride to my client's house at seven. My car battery died. That got me thinking: Now that you're interested in the field of animal communication, you should come along tonight and watch me. We can see how we'd do if I took you on as a partner. If it works out, I can give you a job."

Sara's beaming face rendered me speechless. Oh, dear Lord, how I wanted a cigarette. I could almost feel those delicious little fibers on my lips. "I don't know," I said. "Maybe sometime. But tonight you can just borrow my van."

"Don't be freaked out. I think you'd be a natural once you got the hang of it," she continued. "There are practically no men in the ani-com field! It's entirely women. A lot of men think it's silly. You would prove that it's not. You could dominate the field! How great would that be? Please come tonight!"

"I don't think it's a good time for me to leave Jimmy alone," I said, scrambling, hoping she'd let me use it as an excuse. "He had a heavy day today."

"Then bring him along!" she said.

All the other dogs looked miserable as they watched the three of us leave the house without them. United as one, all six of them sat peering out of the window behind the sofa, howling a heartrending chorus of "How come *he* gets to go?" as we boarded the van.

"How'd it go today?" Sara asked, finally acknowledging the elephant in the room as we drove across town.

"Annoying," I said, doing my best to play it down while at the same time trying as hard as I could not to think about that thump. But the memory had become so fierce I was worried Sara would see it on my face. "It's a beautiful estate. Her husband is loaded," I added, making sure to emphasize only the details Sara wouldn't find threatening.

"And Jimmy and his mom?" she asked.

"They had immediate chemistry," I said.

"That's not what he's telling me," she said abruptly. "He said he doesn't want to go through that again. He says it upset him and he resents you for making him do it."

I looked at Jimmy. He stared out the window. Neither of us bothered to argue. Instead, I got lost again in that mystical thump. Now I felt guilty, sweaty, delirious, overstimulated as I sank into a swirling eddy of sex. Thump.

"I've seen this client twice before," Sara explained when

we headed down Wilshire toward Culver City. "Deandra has Chihuahuas. One is suddenly angry and hostile. The other one now refuses to eat."

"So we go in and tell her what her dogs have to say about this?" I said. "How would she know if we were lying?"

Sara looked at me, appalled. "Gil, she's a repeat client. My work comes from referrals. Lying is not an option."

"You sure I shouldn't just wait in the car?" I said again, doing my best to push away that boomeranging thump again. Immediately it came back, this time in dazzling color and with a soundtrack that blended heavy breathing and a female moan. Floating behind it was Eden's face, eyes glistening. Thump.

"I want you to consult," Sara insisted. "I'll take the lead. Don't worry." We pulled into the carport of a fourplex on a manicured suburban street. I put Jimmy on a leash and we followed Sara into the house.

"Hi, Deandra!" said Sara as we entered a small, tidy apartment full of lacy cloth coverings and photos of Chihuahuas mounted in expensive art deco frames. Instantly two bony Chihuahuas were yapping at our ankles.

"Hi, Cecile. Hi, Fellippe!" Sara greeted the dogs. "This is my partner, Gil. And his dog Jimmy." The Chihuahuas circled Jimmy and bared their teeth. Jimmy stood quietly, looking at me, forlorn.

"I hate Chihuahuas," he said.

"Cecile, Fellippe . . . ENOUGH!" said Deandra. "My children are terrible hosts. But that's why you're here, isn't it? Cecile isn't himself. You can see the effect that it's having on Fellippe."

"Cecile," said Sara jovially, getting down on bended knees to visit with him. "What is going on, buddy?" He immediately rushed to her and started to kiss her.

"Should I leave you alone, like I did last time?" asked Deandra apprehensively. She watched me carefully, not sure if I should be trusted.

"That might be best," said Sara. Deandra nodded slowly, offering the dogs tentative little goodbye waves as she backed out of the room. "Stay," I said to Jimmy as I crawled over to join Sara on the rug. Both Chihuahuas stared me cautiously. One of them, I think it was Cecile, got up on his hind legs and pawed at my knees.

"Hey, how ya doin'? Nice to see ya. Pick me up," he said to me. "Come on, dude. Now. Don't leave me down here."

"Okay," I said, reaching under his front arms to lift him.

"No no no!" Sara scolded me. "What are you doing? He just told you he hates to be picked up. That's one of his issues. He has a complex about his small size."

"I heard him say just the opposite," I said. She looked at me, stunned. Her eyes were widening into a stare that said "What is wrong with you?"

"You've got to listen more carefully," she said, speaking slowly as she might to a misbehaving grade-school child.

She picked up the other Chihuahua and held him in her arms. "Why have you stopped eating?" she asked quietly.

"That new holistic stuff she feeds me tastes like shit," said Fellippe.

"Wrong," said Cecile. "I have eaten shit. It's tangy. That crap she buys tastes like soap."

"Interesting," said Sara. "He is telling me that he has been too upset to eat because he is so concerned about Deandra's emotional problems. The man Deandra is in love with won't commit to her. They see her alone at night, sobbing and think it's their responsibility to try and fill the void for her."

"Are you sure that's what he said?" I asked.

"Of course," she said. "I do this for a living."

"Dude told me she's buying holistic food that tastes like soap," I said.

Sara looked at me with great condescension and sighed deeply. "Gil, animal problems are much more complex than you seem able to grasp. If you want to do this for real, you need to dig deeper. But don't be discouraged. It took me quite a while to learn too."

"What makes you so sure that I'm wrong?" I asked her. I regretted it immediately.

"Do you think I could be earning a living in a field like animal communication if I wasn't great at it?" she said, matter-of-factly.

"Well, it helps that your clients are all fucking nuts," I said, now unable to keep the twenty-two-year-old juvenile delinquent contrarian from taking the wheel. He was intoxicated by that thump and holding my id hostage while he tried to drive us both over a cliff.

Sara bit her lip. Her face went white.

"Not now," she said, very quietly.

"Here. Drive yourself home. We'll walk," I said, handing her the keys to my van.

"Fine," she said, so angry that she couldn't look at me as Jimmy and I headed out the door.

"She wasn't listening. As usual," Jimmy said as we turned

down the street toward the 7-Eleven. "She hears what she wants to hear."

"Might be all women," I said.

"My mother listens," said Jimmy.

"Yeah, well, my mother doesn't," I said. "And she's been a woman longer than your mother by a factor of ten. You'd think I'd know how to keep my big mouth shut by now."

Groveling

*A*ll six dogs were lying on their stomachs staring at the front door when we walked into Sara's. Apparently time had stopped while we were gone. Our return was met with so much pent-up excitement that after an initial burst of ecstasy, small fights began to break out. Cliff went after Cheney. Chopin, Sara's Lab mix, went after Fruity. I pulled them all apart, which so humiliated Fruity that she went after Dink. "What the fuck!" said Dink. "I'm on your side!"

"Cheney! Fruity! Dink! Jimmy! COME!" I shouted, leading them all down the hall and into the guest room. I closed the door and handed out pieces of Slim Jim that I'd bought at the 7-Eleven.

"Situation sucks," I said to a chorus of assorted mouth noises. "Too much hostility. What do we do?"

We all sat down on the floor together and chewed.

"Oh my God. I love you, I love you, I love you," said Dink as she jumped into my lap and started licking my neck. "Does that fix anything?"

"Groveling would have worked," said Jimmy. "Always works on you."

"Really?" I said.

"Yep," he said. "When Sara gets back, sit at her feet and place your paw on her thigh." He demonstrated. "See?" he said when I smiled. "It's very persuasive. Of course, with my *real* family this kind of dishonesty isn't necessary. That emptiness I used to feel when you left the room is finally gone. No more need to eat shoes. My family has cured me."

"I had no idea a family worked like that," said Cheney.

"It doesn't," I said, opening up a beer. "In my experience, it's a harrowing combination of mind-numbing tedium and nerve-racking hysteria. Tell you the truth, it's only you guys that make me feel better." I looked down at myself lying in the midst of them all. Cheney was stretched out alongside my left leg, Fruity had her head on my ankles. Dink was sprawled across my lap. Jimmy was flanking my right side, resting his big head on my thigh. It was so warm, comfortable, and genuinely touching that I closed my eyes for a minute, and drifted blissfully in my dog nest. The five of us all must have fallen asleep, because when I woke up a short while later, Sara was peering through the doorway.

"Oh, that's where you are," she said, her voice still angry and hurt as she turned to leave.

"Sara," I said, "Come. Sit down for a minute." I pointed to the empty chair by my card table desk. As soon as she sat down, I crawled over and sat on the floor by her feet. Then I reached up and put my hand on her thigh. But I think it was "Nose down, eyes up," that made her break her silence and start to laugh. Next thing I knew, she was bringing all five of us cookies.

{ 18 }

Something I Want to
Talk to You About

*W*hen Eden called at eight A.M. the next morning, I didn't answer the phone.

"The guesthouse," she said in her message. "Are we on? I talked to Chad, and I told him your rate was fifty bucks an hour. If that's not enough, let me know." Then she brought out the big guns. "Please, please, please, please, please, please," she purred.

It was a very bad idea. The cons were obvious. The pros were: (1) I needed a job, and fifty bucks an hour plus free room and board meant I could stockpile some money. (2) Thump.

Yet I didn't call Eden right back because Sara and I were getting along. I wanted to figure out how to enlist her support. So I devised a plan to get her into a good mood before I delivered the news.

That evening after dinner, I took out the garbage (even

though it was only half-full). Then I pulled out her always amusing collection of erotic toys (taking care to hide the round vinyl one full of tooth marks that Cheney had mistaken for a ball). I thought I'd deliver all of the things that she really liked in bed. I'd drive her wild with a lot of foreplay, flood her with endorphins. I even broke out that goddamn patchouli-scented massage oil that she likes, though I'm not crazy about that smell. (What I hated more was the way it made us both look like we'd been basted and then breaded in little specks of bed residue such as stray pubic hairs, lint, and assorted things that fall off the dogs.)

Everything started out great. Once I knew she was in the zone, I began making sure I nailed all those weird off-the-beaten-path spots that had taken me most of our relationship to locate. The guy who invents a GPS to use for this sort of thing will one day be a special hero to all men.

Anyway, it was going so well that she even let me throw the dogs off the bed: a form of self-preservation she didn't always allow. I don't know what it is about the proximity to human coupling that gave Sara's dogs gas, but I do know that nothing enhances cunnilingus less than the sulfurous odors of dog flatulence.

This was one of those times when I was an artist, if I do say so myself. She was really screaming, and that made me happy. I liked watching her get off. It ended with Sara and me lying in bed wrapped in each other's arms, feeling that crazy degree of sleepy and relaxed that comes on right afterward. She cuddled up next to me, nuzzled my neck, and with eyes still full of an appealing amount of lust said, "I had a feeling this was all going to work out."

"Yeah, it's been nice," I said, waiting for the right moment.

"I'm feeling so close to you," she said. "Like we're both on a whole new level. Like now there's nothing that we can't say to each other."

"Exactly," I said, seeing my opening. "Interesting you bring that up. There's something I want us to talk about."

She looked at me all dewy-eyed and compliant, open to suggestions, eager to make plans.

"I found a guesthouse," I said, watching her face light up. "A nice one with a big yard."

"Oh my God!" she said, sitting up. Her eyes were full of hope. "That sounds amazing!"

"Good. I'm so glad you think so," I said, "because all of us crammed into this little house doesn't feel fair to you." I was thinking, *This is about making* you *happy!* "This other place is three bedrooms, two bathrooms. Colonial," I offered proudly.

"It sounds almost too perfect," she said, breaking into a grin. "When can I see it?"

"Well," I said, "I don't know. The people who own it want me to do a remodel on it for them. It's the old 'two birds with one stone.'"

"Oh," she said, furrowing her brow a little. "So it's a job. Does that mean they want us out after you fix it up?"

That was when I saw the giant chasm in my genius strategy. How could I not have predicted she'd think I'd found a new home for us all?

"The remodel might take four or five months. Maybe more," I said. "They want a whole new layout and brand-new plumbing. There's a loft where they said I—*we*—could camp out . . ."

"Oh. You weren't talking about *us*, were you?" she said, her face falling out of its smile. "You're just talking about *you*."

"No, no," I began. "I just took the job a minute ago. I didn't think it out that far ahead. I was going to work out the details after I settled in . . ."

"You're completely full of shit, aren't you?" she said, her eyes starting to blaze.

"What?" I said, using my all-purpose line for getting caught red-handed. "Hey, I am not," I said, knowing I totally was.

"I thought the premise of you moving in here with me was that we were using this time as a living-together trial," said Sara, her facial expressions begining to retreat behind an immobile mask of deadened features. It was as though she were willing herself invisible.

"We are," I said, starting to scramble. "But I don't know if it's a good idea for us to be crowded and uncomfortable while we are making such an important decision. This guesthouse is nearby, so it's practically in your backyard."

"How did you find the place?" she asked, starting to look at me with suspicion.

"Craigslist," I lied. "But you know how life is so full of weird coincidences? Turns out that I knew some of the people who took out the ad!"

"Oh?" she said, staring hard. "A coincidence?"

"I might as well just say it," I said. "One of the owners is my ex-wife."

Sara's expression went from dead to enraged in a flash.

Her face got red. "Shit," she said as she sprang from bed, naked. "Shit, shit, shit," she continued. I could almost see her soul retracting to a point on some internal horizon. "Did you find this ad before or after you went over there yesterday? So that's your interesting Craigslist coincidence: You're moving in with your ex-wife?" Now she was too quiet, like the calm in the center of a hurricane.

"No!" I said, "I am not moving in with my ex-wife. The guesthouse is way out in her backyard. At the other end of their huge estate. You can barely even see her house from the guesthouse."

"I don't believe this," she said. "All that sex and affection just now was to butter me up so you could dump this shit on me? You fucking asshole!"

"You are way out of line!" I started repeating over and over, trying to barricade myself behind a tone of outrage now that she had nailed me. "How can you accuse me of that?" I said, buying myself more time.

"Gee, I don't know, Craigslist," said Sara, pulling a sweater on over her head and getting dressed so rapidly she couldn't get her foot into the hole of her pants leg. "I must be delirious."

"You're reading this wrong again. Yesterday *was* all about Jimmy. This guesthouse thing was Eden's husband's idea," I said, adding some heat to my voice. "He's the one who ran the ad. She didn't even know about it. He wants to build himself an office. . . . Look, I'm broke, Sara. They're offering me fifty bucks an hour. I can build up a savings account to help us pay for a real place down the line." There it was. The ultimate idiot-boy tactic: When caught in a losing strategy, overcommit.

"I can't believe you made love to me like that to manipulate me," she said in disgust. "That's so sad, Gil. Why did you have to bring sex into it? Why couldn't you just talk to me straight?" She headed out of the bedroom with most of the dogs following her.

"Now see what you made me do," I said to Jimmy. "This is where groveling gets you."

"Everything I suggested worked great," he said. "You did too much improv."

"Believe me, Sara, I do *not* want anything to do with Eden," I shouted, jumping out of bed and pulling on my pants so I could follow her into the other room. "That's not why I just made love to you."

"Living here together could have worked if you'd given it a chance," she said when I finally caught up to her. "If you feel like a rent boy, it's because you act and think like one. I don't know how you expect me to deal with you moving in with your ex-wife."

"I am not moving in with her!" I yelled, trying to win a flimsy point by relying on volume. "I'm the one with the problem. How do you expect ME to deal with it?" She sat down at the table in the kitchen and refused to look at me.

"How about if we just start the evening over again?" I said. "I'll come back in the door. You just said we could talk about anything. If anything was ever anything, well, that would be this."

"When I said 'anything,' I meant things that we could work through together," she said. "Things that would make us closer. Things that would bond us. Like getting a time-share. Or planting a garden. Not impossible hurtful things.

Like having an open relationship. Or getting reinvolved with your ex."

"But I don't want Eden," I pleaded. She stared down at the floor. "I had five years with her. That was four and a half years too many."

As my voice got louder, Fruity put her tail between her legs and ran out of the room. The other dogs flattened themselves on the floor.

"I can't take this anymore," said Sara. "We've been playing this game for years. Obviously you're planning to leave. You should do it right now."

"Right this minute?" I said, resenting that I had lost control. I was sleepy. I needed an after-sex nap.

"Yes," she said. "Go be with your ex-wife. Have a nice time."

"I never said I wanted to be with my ex-wife," I argued. I wanted to go back to bed. "All I did was take a job. Now you're punishing me for it?"

"You can leave the dogs here for tonight. But you can't stay," she said calmly. Her voice contained an unfamiliar but terrifying iciness.

"Fine," I said, realizing the only card left to play was to ask her to marry me. Not that she would have gone for it right then. But the offer would have impressed her. "Just remember, when this all blows up, you were the one who started it," I said. Then I turned on my heel and headed for the guest bedroom.

"Well, that went well," said Jimmy, unable to disguise his delight as he sat down to watch me pack. He'd been campaigning to go back to see his family ever since we'd left. I looked around at my small pile of personal belongings, most of which had never been unpacked, and I exhaled deeply. Then I picked up the cell and called Eden. Jimmy stared at me eagerly, panting, wagging his tail. "Would it be possible for me to move into the guesthouse tonight?" I said to her voice mail. For the first time ever, I was glad she called back right away.

"Yes!" she gushed. "Come over! Come over! Get your ass over here now!" Her voice was full of the kind of ebullience she had when things went her way. "I was going to a mommies' night out, but I should be right back. Those mommies all get cranky by about ten. I'll leave the key under the mat."

"I guess this is it," I said to Jimmy. "Brace yourself. We're going in."

Jimmy was overcome with unbridled joy. He picked up a latex lamb chop in his mouth and ran rapidly in a circle.

"Listen," I said to Sara when I returned to the kitchen, interrupting her in the midst of aggressively, furiously, purposefully cooking a dog loaf. She didn't bother turning to look at me. "I'm only leaving because you want me to," I said, speaking softly in an attempt to recast my behavior as considerate.

"Good," she said, her back still turned. Seven dogs looked up at me, ready for anything, expecting the best.

"Are you taking the dogs with you?" she asked, still not looking at me.

"Just Jimmy," I said. "I think the others would rather stay here tonight."

"No, we wouldn't. Are you insane?" said Fruity and Cheney.

"He's kidding. I know for a fact he's taking me," said Dink.

"Hey, we'd be up for a ride in the car," said two of Sara's dogs, Cliff and Chopin.

"I'll be back for the rest of you tomorrow or the next day," I said to them. "Just give me a chance to get settled."

"Fine," Sara muttered, pretending to be so engrossed in cooking that she couldn't look up. "Fuck you," she whispered quietly, under her breath.

"Sara, this was your idea. I've tried to do things your way. I even agreed to marriage counseling. By the way, you're the one who dropped the ball there," I said. I was so eager to win a point that I was bringing up things I'd hoped were long dead. "This fight is silly. I took a job. Period." I said. "Think it over. Once things settle, it will look different." She said nothing. "Do you want me to call you when I get there? What would you like me to do?"

"I would like you to go." She spoke in measured tones, eerily firm in her resolve, clearly fed up with my bullshit. "Go. Just get out of here."

This was a side of her I'd never seen before. And now that she was fed up for real, turned out I wanted her back.

{ 19 }

Déjà Vu All Over Again

$\mathcal{E}$den came walking out of her house the moment she heard the car door slam. She smelled like alcohol and Rive Gauche, but in that short black dress and four-inch heels she looked like a decade of aerobics classes and a shopping trip to Neiman Marcus. "I decided to cancel my plans so I could help you move in," she said. She gave me a full body hug.

"That explains why you're wearing your work clothes," I sniped.

"Come have a glass of champagne. I just opened a bottle." She grinned at me, trying to lead me by the hand.

"Eden, go see your friends," I said, taking my hand back. "I just have a couple of bags."

"I didn't want you to have to spend your first moments in a new place all alone," she said. "Moving is one of the top three upsetting things, after death and divorce."

"Congratulations. Now you represent two out of three of those things for me," I said as I followed her down the path to the guesthouse. I was mesmerized by her twitching butt. The air felt clean and lush, and full of the scent of night-blooming jasmine and a freshly mowed lawn.

Jimmy was trotting behind me, as eager as I had ever seen him.

"Voilà," she said, turning on the lights and opening the front door. Thump. The house smelled like furniture polish and cleaning solvents. All the rugs had those semicircular vacuuming marks that could only come from getting the once-over by a housekeeper. Eden wouldn't have been able to make a place look that thoroughly cleaned, even if she had been able to develop an interest in bothering.

She went over to the refrigerator and removed an open bottle. "I was actually going to try to make you some mead," she said, pouring me a glass of champagne. "As an homage to our first date. But I went on the Internet to look for recipes, and, geez, you need yeast. Who has yeast? At Ren-Faire alls we did was put red wine and a clove in the microwave!" She poured herself another glass after handing one to me. "You'd probably rather have a beer, but Chad bought a couple cases of this champagne, so . . . cheers!"

"That Chad!" I said. "Does he still have a hairy ass?"

"I make him get it waxed," she said, giggling as she flopped down onto the couch in front of the stone fireplace, exposing a lot of her left leg. I hadn't seen those legs in a long time. When we split up, nothing about Eden seemed remotely appealing. Except her legs, and her ass, and her tits. And now they had a new companion: the memory of that thump. I sat down in an upholstered leather chair across from her and tried not to look up her dress.

Jimmy positioned himself right in front of me and began scratching at my knee with his paw.

"Oh," I said. "Jimmy would like to visit his family."

"Just let him into the yard. They'll hear him and come running out," she said.

I opened the front door, and Jimmy took off. A couple of seconds later there was barking, then the sounds of a dog stampede.

"Eden, you're all dressed up," I said as I watched the herd gallop through the dog door into the main house. "Go see your friends. I'm fine by myself." I was trying to sound considerate, but the truth was that I wished she would leave. It seemed like forever since I'd had any place to myself. Silence and solitude were like a couple of long-lost friends I missed desperately.

"Ah, screw 'em," she said. "I've been looking forward to this."

"Where's your husband, young Teddy Roosevelt?" I asked.

"Is that what you call him?" she laughed, pouring herself some more champagne. "It's his poker night." She rolled her eyes. "He only plays poker because everyone plays poker. He's at least three years late to that party."

"Three?" I said, trying for a little hard-edged authenticity. "Try thirty. I've been playing poker since the seventies."

"I know. He is such a cliché." Eden rolled her eyes.

"Did you talk that way about me behind my back when we were married?" I asked her.

"No, never!" she said, plopping back onto the couch and running both of her hands through her long hair. She began piling it up on top of her head and then letting it fall again, seductively reaching up to expose her underarms in a way that gave me a jolt because I remembered that move as an unintentional signal she wanted to have sex. "Well, maybe a teensy bit toward the end when you were being such a prick." She got up and walked around behind my chair and poured a fourth glass of champagne.

"I want to hear what's going on with *you*!" she said. "Tell me everything!" This time she repositioned herself on a chair that she pulled up next to me so she could put both of her feet in my lap. Some kind of instinct for self-preservation kicked in and I picked up the remote, thinking I'd turn on my old co-conspirator, ESPN. Eden hated televised sports. My mind cycled through a rapid slide show of moments involving Eden storming out of rooms, furious at being upstaged.

"Ha!" she said, piling her hair up again, then letting some strands fall forward to frame her face. "I hid the remote batteries. Now you have to talk to me! Don't be rude to your landlady. How's your mother?"

"Fine," I began. "She got remarried to a guy in Sedona—"

"My mother got remarried too!" Eden interrupted. "They moved to San Diego right after our divorce. He owns a thirty-five-foot yacht? Dwight the fire captain." I tried to follow what she was saying, but when Eden hopscotched and zigzagged through a personal anecdote, it was like trying to understand a Korean newscast without knowing Korean. There was something about a townhouse outside of La Jolla, an orthopedic surgeon, and a woman whose daughter-in-law went to knitting classes with Lindsay Lohan's mother. At that point we both heard a car pull into the driveway and a door slam shut.

"Oh, shit. Chad," she said, sitting up and straightening her clothing.

"E?" we could hear him screech like a hawk pursuing a mate. "Ee? Eeeee?"

"Dammit. He's going to wake up the fucking kid," she said, jumping up. "I better go sshh him. Be right back."

"Eden, go be with your family! We can talk tomorrow!" I said. I meant it. I was thrilled she was leaving me alone. I didn't need champagne or even beer for once. All I needed to drink was the voluptuous peace and solitude. "Please, God, don't let me fuck this up," I chanted as I started to realize how much I loved it here. Too soon, I could hear the clack of high heels on the flagstone path that led to my front door, signifying the return of Eden with her waxy-assed hubby.

"Welcome!" bellowed Chad, bounding in first and offering a big toothy presidential smile and a handshake. "Thank God you're taking this project over, Gil. We've had the worst luck with contractors. What an unholy bunch." I half expected him to add "Bully."

"My pleasure," I said, returning the handshake in as forthright a fashion as I could, surprised to find his hand moist and soft like a peeled orange. Eden was right behind him. Behind her was Jimmy and his three identical relatives. They galloped in as though this was the destination they had been looking for their entire lives.

"E, do you think we should let the dogs run loose through here like this?" said Chad. The swarm of them raced toward him to say hello in that way a boisterous group of dogs sometimes seems to single out the one person in a group who'd rather be left alone. "We just had the place cleaned. . . . Hello, Gypsy. Hello, Party Girl. E, can you please put these guys outside? Gorgeous, get down. I said DOWN."

"That's my dog Jimmy bothering you," I said. "Jimmy, get down."

I grabbed Jimmy by the collar to restrain him, but as soon as I did, Gorgeous took his place. "Eden, can you please . . . ?" Chad pleaded.

"Come on, you guys," said Eden, holding the door open. And just as quickly as they had all rushed in, now they all rushed out.

"Do we have a lint roller anywhere?" said Chad, brushing his pants to free himself from the pounds of freshly shed hair that rose around him in big clouds, like dust at a track meet. "We have one back at the house," Eden said, sitting down on the sofa. Chad sat down beside her, his arm around his wife's shoulders in a gesture of nervous ownership, while she continued picking hair off his thighs. "So, when do you think we can get this whole show on the road?" he asked. "Is tomorrow too soon?" Eden sat still, rolling her eyes. *Poor confident bastard,* I thought as I watched them together. I was already worried about Chad. Slick and rich as he was, with his spiky hair lightened at the tips, he seemed too naïve and benign to be a match for Eden. He was clearly the more enamored member of the couple. That was the kind of advantage you didn't give Eden. She knew how to use it.

"No, tomorrow's fine," I said.

"Give me a ring on my cell in the morning when you get up," he said. "We can go through the plans." He rose from the sofa and headed for the door. "Well, I'm wiped out," he said. "Honey, you coming to bed? I bet Gil is tired."

"You got that right," I said, yawning and hoping that Eden had noticed.

"In a minute," said Eden. "I just want to make sure Gil knows where everything is." Chad nodded, waved, and bounded out of the room. Eden stood still, listening as his footsteps grew faint.

"Towels in that closet there. Bread, milk, eggs in the fridge. Do you still like Grape-Nuts? I remembered Hot Pockets. Jimmy will sleep in our living room," she said. "He can share a bed with our three. That'll be so cute!"

"Great," I said. "He's been looking forward to this."

"Okay. Well, sleep tight. I'll see you in the morning," said Eden. Then she stepped toward me and put her arms around my waist. Next thing I knew she was planting a kiss on me that was soft and wet and deep and long. It sent me swirling into a steamy montage: our first date, our last date, the time we did it in the bleachers at Dodger Stadium, the time we did it in a booth at Domino's Pizza. The time we did it in the bathroom of a tour bus, almost got locked in, and had to pound on the door from inside. Peppered throughout were moments from ugly fights: the slamming of a car door when she decided to try to display her rage by getting out on the 405, the day she actually threw a book at my head like some peeved, rolling-pin-waving hausfrau from a sixties comic strip. Followed by even more outrageous sex that was so good, so athletic and nasty, that even after we hated each other, I had to block myself from revisiting those memories for fear of getting trapped in a kind of sensory quicksand. Which sent me back to that thump. But wait. There it was again. Eden had done it again. A real one. Thump number two. And this time there was a tiny little grinding move added in to make sure that it registered.

Having accomplished what she'd apparently been planning the whole night, Eden stared me right in the eyes, sent a beam of electrical current my way, and smiled.

"Nobody kisses like you," she said, shy for a moment. Then she sashayed to the door, where she paused for dramatic effect before her exit.

"Jesus fucking Christ," I said to no one after she left.

Then I took a swig of champagne straight from the bottle.

(20)

Reparations

When I checked my messages, I learned that Sara had called ten times: First to apologize for making unwarranted assumptions, then to apologize for being unreasonable and to say she was sorry for sounding so abrupt, then for leaving such a long message, then for forgetting to tell me that she loved me and missed me. There were also apologies for sounding stupid and girlish and for leaving so many messages. There was even one for apologizing too much. I wanted to scream "STOP!" so badly that I started to listen to only the first word of each message just to get the emotional tone. I was afraid to call back too quickly for fear she would read my mind and know that her paranoia about Eden had been well founded.

Instead, I debated my menu of excuses. The time-honored favorite was, of course, calling her when I knew she wouldn't be near a phone. But Sara's freelance work schedule made that difficult to predict. When did she go to yoga again? Or the dog park? In the middle of stressful contemplation, I fell asleep.

There are those who say I make light of things and don't show enough appreciation for the good. By "those," I guess I mean my mother. But it was certainly not the case when I woke up that first morning in Eden's guesthouse. I liked the quiet sunlit rooms with no one in them so much it made me wonder why I'd ever had roommates. Lots of people don't like anything as much as I sometimes liked the absence of others.

Last night's fight with Sara put a damper on things, but I'd made the right decision. This was so much better.

Chad showed up at about nine A.M., before I had a chance to call him. He brought me a huge cup of latte from Starbucks and a blueberry scone. Better still, he brought Jimmy.

"I didn't know if you'd already had your caffeine quota for the day," he said.

"There is no such thing in my world," I said, going over to my wayward dog-son and giving him a hug. Was it my imagination, or was Jimmy acting aloof?

"The architect who drew up the remodeling plans should be here in an hour if you have any questions," Chad said. "He and my wife have gone to pick out tile." He paused and looked thoughtful. Then he unrolled a very extensive set of blueprints on a table before us. I became fonder of them by the second as I realized that their complexity would provide me with a great many months of work. "Alan Takemoto," Chad said. "Do you know him? Eden said he did a lot of work for Beyoncé. Maybe it was Queen Latifah."

"I thought she said Jennifer Lopez," I said.

"Really?" he said, furrowing his brow. "I thought Jennifer Lopez was the landscaping." He opened up his briefcase. Arranged inside it were a dazzling array of paint swatches; wallpaper; wood swatches; glass, brass, and carpet samples. This guesthouse was going to be my annuity.

"Why don't we begin with the upstairs bedroom?" Chad suggested. "My son, Hayden, is supposed to come visit in a few weeks so I thought we'd start there. Here's a credit card and a blank check to get you started. I'll be in and out all day. Call if you need anything."

"Know what? This might actually work out," I said to Jimmy when Chad left.

"It better," said Jimmy. "I'm so happy to be here with my family, I feel like I've just eaten! My mother showed me how to use her dog door last night. I mean, obviously I already knew how, but I loved that she bothered to teach me. And she let me drink from her water bowl. She's an amazing mother. We're all like soul mates. Totally in sync. My brother even tried to hump me."

"That's a little weird," I said.

"Of course you would think so," said Jimmy. "You take a dim view of everything. It's a power issue. We have a few things to straighten out, but we will because we're family. We think alike. We all like to kick backward into the dust right after we poo. I used to think I was the only one who did that."

"Great thing to base your identity on," I said, rolling my eyes.

"As a matter of fact, it is," he said abruptly. "You want to know what didn't make sense? Me living with you." Jimmy's voice was now testy, defiant. "You're not even my same species. I know so much more about myself after spending *one* day with my family than I learned in all five years living with you. Which, by the way, are thirty-five years to a dog. A long time to learn basically nothing."

"Really?" I said, feeling very defensive. "What did you learn from them?"

"Well," he said, "in our world there's no 'bad.' There's no 'stay.' There's no 'no.' You made all that stuff up!"

Before I could argue the point, there was a rapping on my open door.

"Hey! Okay to come visit?" said Eden, grinning like a teenager as she entered the room, uninvited. She was dressed in a short tennis skirt, a tank top, and tennis shoes. Her tits looked fantastic. "Who were you talking to? Someone else here?"

"Just Jimmy," I said.

"Just Jimmy," said Jimmy with disgust. "I love that. No one important. *Just* Jimmy. I am so over this." He stared at me for a moment, then galloped out the door. I watched him as he gleefully ran up the hill toward the patio and other dogs.

"Don't look so worried. He'll be fine," said Eden. She was not alone. "This is my life coach, Halley," said Eden, nodding her head toward a shorter, slightly younger woman with bright magenta hair and a teensy silver ball pierced into the side of her nose. Ms. Life Coach was dressed in jeans and a black tank top, the better to show off the tribal tattoo on her upper right arm. I recognized that tribe: Divorced White Middle-Aged Women from the Westside Who Seek to Obscure the Ravages of Age by Acquiring a Dense Patina of Pop Culture

Camouflage. "It's because of Halley that I'm starting my own business," Eden gushed. "You can thank her for the guest-house remodeling job! Did I tell you I'm starting a line of frozen organic Chinese baby food?"

"No!" I said, withholding further comment by nodding. I began unpacking my tools.

"Chad told you to start with the kitchen?" asked Eden.

"No, Chad said to start upstairs, on the bedroom," I said.

"No way. He didn't say that!" she said. "He knows I'm going to need to test stuff in the kitchen. You have to start down here."

"You want to check with him . . . ?" I asked.

"No. I have the right of way! You need to start down here," she said, looking to Halley for affirmation and getting a tight-lipped nod.

"How about giving Chad a quick call . . . ?" I said, not sure what "the right of way" was or how it affected my job. Eden looked at Halley quizzically.

"You definitely have the right of way!" Halley pumped her.

"Halley's been helping me focus on getting what I truly want," said Eden.

"When did you ever not get what you wanted?" I said incredulously.

"Ex-husbands!" said Eden, winking at Halley.

"Men in general," said Halley. "But in this case, I have to point out that Gil is simply stating his truth. So he has the right of way!" She looked at me with a raised eyebrow and a nod that indicated she was accepting my thanks.

"Gil, I'll handle Chad," Eden said. "Just start down here."

She leaned toward her life coach and whispered something as they walked off together.

"Don't you dare!" I heard the life coach return. "The universe does not provide the right of way for you to act like an idiot."

Thwap

*P*ulling down the wall between the first-floor bedroom and the living room was cathartic on-the-job fun. I enjoy the clear-headed feeling of completion that comes from a concrete physical action. I was wedging in the pry bar, looking forward to yanking out a big-ass chunk of plasterboard, when Chad appeared at the front door.

"I thought we agreed to start upstairs," he said.

"Yes. We did," I said. "But Eden showed up and told me to do downstairs first." He looked at me openmouthed, frozen like a cartoon character who'd seen a ghost. It was almost as though he were on pause awaiting a foreign subtitle. Life with Eden often brought this kind of a moment.

"Damn. I love when she shows up and changes everything," he said.

"Maybe you and your dearly beloved should talk amongst yourselves," I said. I was pissed because this controversy had stalled my momentum. Oh, how I wanted a cigarette. "Let me know what you two lovebirds decide," I said, sitting down on the couch, with the crowbar in my lap.

"Give me a sec," he said, clicking open his cell phone, and heading out the door. As he crossed the big green stretch of hill between our houses, he reminded me of a condemned man walking toward a firing squad.

"Hon, I'm here with Gil," I heard him say before the call was reduced to the Morse code of Eden's voice; the staccato beeps and chirping sounds one heard from a distance. As I watched him out there mmm-hmmming her on the lawn of his magnificent estate, it was hard not to see him as a little kid who was trying every sweet, polite, correct thing he knew how to do to console his angry mother. "But . . . But . . . But . . . " I heard him repeating like a cross between a sitcom husband and an outboard motor. "Right . . . Right . . . Got it. Okay. Yes. Love you." He stood completely still, unaware that his fallen face was being observed. In that transparent moment I felt compassion for him again. I watched him take a deep breath, compose himself, and lick his lips before he headed back across the lawn toward me, young Teddy Roosevelt striding purposefully once more, his facial expression arranged to show that a momentary misunderstanding had just been negotiated in his favor. "We're going to go ahead and start with the first floor," he said. "Sound good?"

Poor bastard, I thought to myself for the second time in two days.

I was only too happy to get back to work. My hands, face, and hair were already chalky from plaster, but it felt good to be busy. I was pleased with all the progress I'd made. The only downside was that I missed the presence of Jimmy hanging out with me, keeping me company, making me feel interesting. I was starting to regret facilitating his family reunion.

In the next couple of hours I took down most of the wall that separated the bedroom from the small adjacent bathroom as well as the wall that separated the bedroom from the living room. I was wailing, a one-man wrecking crew. And then suddenly there was Eden in the doorway, finished with tennis, and two kinds of hot . . . overheated and oversexed. There were beads of sweat glistening on her chest that sent me colliding into a moment after we first got married. It was 103 degrees at our home in Glendale and we were both so slick with perspiration that when we made love, we created a layer of suction between us that made squeaky fart noises whenever we moved. Even the fart noises had an erotic glow. After I merged those memories into the file with thumps one and two, it was impossible to refocus on work.

"Wow, you've been busy," she said, surveying the growing pile of plasterboard fragments. She came up behind me and wrapped her arms around my chest, leaning her head gently against my back. "I've always loved the way you smell," she said. "I'm so glad you're here!"

"Eden, for crying out loud," I shouted, as she rubbed her body against my back and nuzzled my neck. I swung around to face her, grabbing her shoulders, attempting to hold her at arm's length. That only made her laugh. She ducked underneath the bridge of my arms and then slithered up to kiss me.

"You are such a good kisser," she said. "Sorry, but I needed to double-check. Am I? Still a good kisser? You used to say I was."

"Yes," I said, ping-ponging between resentment and randy opportunism. "But what difference does it make?"

"Oh, come on! Can't we just have some fun?" Eden said. "Who in the world can it hurt?"

"Well, your husband," I said.

"And why would he care?" she said. "You're no threat, for Chrissakes. You're my ex. We already did the whole Kama Sutra. We successfully performed every raunchy thing at least twice, and we still got sick of each other. I'm not exactly going to run off with you!"

"You're crazy," I said as she began to bury her face in my neck. "Chad told me he'd be in and out all day. He might show up here any second."

"I know! That's what makes it so much fun." She giggled, rubbing her tits against me, kissing my chin and my cheeks, brushing her lips across my lips. Leave it to Eden to turn me on and make me debate my worth as a human being at the same time. The more I wanted sex from her, the more I felt like I was sullying the last nice clean spot I had on my tarnished soul. Until right now, at least I had never messed around with somebody else's wife. The forty-seven-year-old guy in charge of my decisions wanted to tell her to please go away. But the twenty-two-year-old who was now a fan of Eden's kept offering me glamorous parallels to use, like Tommy Lee and Henry Miller. "Eat, drink, and be merry," he kept whispering. "Life is for the living." As though a string of platitudes would provide me with strength.

"So you and Chad are over?" I asked, no longer trying to pull away.

"Well, he's a nice man. A good provider. Very generous. But the poor guy has no imagination. I mean, we have a sex life. Sort of. But . . . Well, I guess it's good for *him*." When she kissed me again, I felt as if I had boarded a ship full of ne'er-do-wells. I was watching myself wave goodbye to those dear old friends, my instincts, as we pushed off from the dock.

Good Lord, I really want this woman, I was thinking. I should have been able to control myself. After all, I had Sara. Sara could be exciting. Well, "exciting" wasn't the right word. Besides, it was wrong to make a comparison. Sex with Sara was about bonding, warmth, and familiarity. Eden brought to sex the psychotic's thirst for dramatic resolution.

"Oh, come on, Gil," she teased. "All we're doing is making out, for Chrissakes. At our age, that doesn't even qualify as sex."

I considered her homage to Bill Clinton for a few seconds.

"Look at it this way," she said. "When we were married, Chad wasn't worrying about you."

"So this is how it went down behind my back when we were married?" I said, needing a cigarette. Something unfiltered. A fresh pack of Camels and a shot of Courvoisier.

"No!" she said, indignant. "Oh, come on. Like you didn't do anything behind my back?"

"I don't know why I didn't. I was a blockhead. I really should have," I said. "And I would have if I'd known that you were. There were opportunities."

"What opportunities?" she said, very interested. She ran her finger along my belt, playing with the buckle. Each time she upped the ante, I wanted her more. "Tyler?"

"Maybe," I said, acting coy because it was turning her on. Now when she moved in to kiss me, she was on fire.

"Who else?" she said. "Kelly? Jen?" She leaned in, put her lips to my ear and began to talk dirty, asking me nasty questions about my intentions. That was another thing about

Eden. She could really talk dirty. That was a rare find in a woman, though still not a fair trade-off for losing my house.

"Slow down," I said, taking her by the wrists. We locked eyes and smiled. Licking her lips, she pushed her hips forward and started rubbing her panties against my thigh.

"Not now. I'll tell you when," I said, watching it turn her on when I took control. Like that time when I blindfolded her in that no-tell-motel in the Valley one New Year's eve. What was the name of that damn place? Or did I have it mixed up with that hot springs in Santa Fe where they had that weird seventies porn on tap?

My cell phone rang. "I have to take this call," I said, seeing it was Sara.

"Okay," said Eden, eyes blazing. "Is that shower still working?" She pointed to the bathroom, now visible because of the missing wall.

"Should be. I haven't started in there yet." I nodded. Locking eyes with me again, Eden started slowly unbuttoning her shirt. Then she climbed through the two massive holes in the walls to get to the shower, clearly pleased that she had a rapt audience.

So what? I said to myself, shaking my head in disbelief as I watched her strip down to her panties and bra and then enter the shower. I'd seen Eden naked millions of times. *No big deal*, I thought as I turned my back on The Eden Show to focus my attention on Sara.

"Hi!" said Sara. "Did you get my messages last night?"

"No. I went to bed early," I lied, unable to stop myself from thinking: *Thump! Thump! Thump!* Now I could hear Eden turning on the water in the shower.

"I'm so embarrassed," Sara was saying. When I checked to see what was going on, Eden was unhooking her bra, slowly and methodically, as though it had hundreds of tiny little hooks. She was clearly visible behind the glass shower doors. "I completely flipped out last night." Sara continued, "I am really sorry." Now Eden was rolling down her panties a little at a time. She looked amazing. She'd been working out. She even had tan lines. Did she remember that I liked tan lines? "I need to get back into therapy," Sara was saying. "We were just getting to issues of trust when I decided to quit last time." Eden grinned and began soaping up her naked tits.

"Well, don't be so hard on yourself," I said to Sara, hoping that I was making some kind of sense in this context, because I was having trouble tracking what either of us said. My twenty-two-year-old dickhead alter ego was now haranguing me. "Look! Dude! She's soaping her tits. One of the rarest sites in all of nature! Memorize it! Print it! It may never happen again!"

"I was crazy thinking we would be happy in my teensy house," Sara said.

"Hey, no problem," I replied a little too quickly, hoping that it sounded like a reasonable response. I was trying harder now to turn my attention away from Eden so I could more fully appreciate this second equally amazing thing: Somehow I was coming out ahead in a situation with Sara in which I had been the asshole. Somehow I was winning! In a way I felt bad for Sara. She could have won this one easy. It was so like her to find a way to take the blame for something that wasn't her fault. Sara was too nice. She made it impossible not to take advantage of her.

"I have to learn to appreciate a good man when I meet

one," Sara was saying, when *thwap*, Eden's wet panties hit me on the back of my neck. I turned quickly, and there she was, the shower door wide open. She stood there naked, wet, giggling as she taunted me with a bunch of silly centerfold poses.

"You were right about the way I dropped the ball on the marriage counseling," said Sara. "Maybe I was afraid of what I would hear. The weirdest part of it all is I have always prayed to the universe to send me a guy sane enough to get along with his exes. A guy who doesn't feel the need to burn every bridge. I even wrote it down in my 2004 New Year's ritual. Those exact words! And here I am punishing you for being the very guy that I wanted!"

"Don't be so hard on yourself," I said, concerned I'd just said that a minute ago. My brain was so overstimulated from watching Eden go through her soap and rinse cycles that my synapses couldn't keep track of my speech. "A lot of people would think it was weird for their boyfriend to move into his ex-wife's guesthouse," I said, feeling the need to help Sara defend herself against me.

"But it's right that you and Eden would be friends now that you've settled your differences," she went on. "You were family. And family is forever."

"Well, thank you for seeing it that way," I said as Eden stepped out of the shower, wrapped her lower half in a towel and walked back into the room, topless and wet. She came up behind me and clamped her arms around my chest.

"It's a sign of maturity and wisdom that you two can have a sane business relationship!" Sara was saying as Eden was rubbing her naked boobs on my back. "You needed a job, and the universe provided one. Everything was fine until your stupid neurotic girlfriend with her childhood abandonment issues stuck her nose into your affairs and tried to ruin your chance for success."

"Wow!" I said to Sara, not sure what I was "wow"ing. Eden had unbuttoned the front of my shirt and slid her hands inside. "Hey, Sara, listen . . . can I call you back? I can't talk right now. There's a shitload of bricks. A shipment, I mean. Of bricks. And a load of cement and shit that I have to sign for. What I mean is I gotta go."

"I want to come by and bring you dinner," she said sweetly. "The dogs really miss you. And I do too."

"Can I call you back?" I said, eager to get off the phone before I made an accidental moaning noise.

"Was that your girlfriend?" Eden asked after I clicked the phone shut. "You never talk about her. I don't even know her name."

"Sara. Her name is Sara," I said as Eden kneeled down in front of me and began to pull on the zipper of my jeans with her teeth. Eden had apparently learned a few new tricks in her dull boring marriage. She was still the only woman I'd ever met for whom oral sex was foreplay. Now there was a worthy example of intelligent design.

I deserve some kind of compensation for losing so much to this goddamn woman, I thought as I stopped resisting and moved Chad's credit card and check to a drawer where I couldn't see them. *I'm sorry, God,* I was thinking as I began to enter the dangerous rapids of infidelity. *It appears I'm going to fuck my ex-wife now. I know it's crazy, but since your oldest religions don't believe in divorce, doesn't that make Chad the interloper and me the avenging angel?*

{ 22 }

Exploited

*E*den and I went at it for an hour longer than necessary. Probably to prove that we hadn't lost a goddamn thing to age.

"Well, I gotta go," she said only a minute or two after we were done.

"No afterglow basking for you," I said, a little hurt.

"That was kind of abrupt," she said as she was buttoning up her tennis skirt. "I'm sorry. How about this? *Oh, baby! That was amazing! No one does it like you. I feel so safe and happy lying here in your arms.* Do you feel a little bit better now? Because I gotta run up to the house and pay the nannies before they start a picket line."

After she left, I fell asleep and didn't wake until the phone rang. "Shit!" I yelled as I realized I'd forgotten to call Sara back. "I must have dozed off. I'm sorry. But I'm not done yet. With my work, I mean."

"Aren't you going to take a break for dinner?" she said sweetly.

"Can we do it tomorrow instead?" I said, searching for an excuse. "It's a mess around here. I'm so goddamn tired."

"My poor baby," she said, and she said it with so much empathy that she made me feel like a sociopath. "Are you sure you don't want me to come over with a bottle of wine? I could help you relax?" Now Sara made an awkward little attempt at phone sex. God love her, she meant well, but she still didn't understand. She needed to tell me what she wanted to do to me, not ask me if it was okay.

The good news was that once I succeeded in postponing our reunion, I was free to lie back and watch the Lakers game on Chad's brand-new forty-eight-inch flat screen HDTV. It was practically beer-thirty when I opened a cool frosty bottle, and then a second one. Blissfully I floated in my newfound quiet and space.

During a long commercial break I remembered I needed to call my mother so I thought I'd get that over as quickly as possible. I generally preferred calling her during a televised game because it gave me something to concentrate on while she was babbling. "Hi, Mom. Just thought I should probably tell you that I've moved," I began.

"To where?" she said. She sounded far too excited.

"Well, same general area," I said. "I'm at Eden's new place remodeling their guesthouse."

"Oh, honey, that's wonderful," she said. "So how's your music?"

"Fine," I said.

"Are you gonna do any shows?" she asked.

"No. I haven't done any shows in twenty-five years," I said.

"Well, keep on plugging! That's all that God asks of us. That we plug away. Did I hear you say Eden? Could that be right?" she said. "Don't tell me you two are dating? After what she did to you?"

"No," I said. "She's happily married now. To someone else. What're you up to?"

"Oh, all kinds of exciting stuff," she said. The best thing about my mother was how easily distracted she was. "Milt is taking a seminar in pruning. He'll tell you all about it. He pulled our money out of the market and invested in gold so now we'll be all set before the Fed does whatever it is that they do. You know I don't understand that stuff. Gil, I'm worried about you. Not a day goes by that I don't think about that scholarship to Juilliard you turned down. Is it too late to reapply?"

"Yeah, I think there's a quarter-century statute of limitations on those college scholarships, Mom," I said. "Oh, well. Those are the breaks. I gotta run. If you need me, call me on my cell."

Every call to my mother ended in a state of emotional backwash. It took me another beer to regain my center of gravity. While I recovered, I checked in at TheirSpace, where I was delighted to see that Jimmy now had three hundred friends. If we could sell a ten-dollar T-shirt to each of them, it would be a nice piece of change. That alone seemed like a damn good reason to keep freshening the site. The easiest way seemed to be to update the blog.

For that I needed Jimmy. I stood out in the front yard and

called to him. When he didn't appear, I headed over to the patio where he and his family were lying on their sides in a row like a platter of giant hairy sardines. I felt a twinge in my gut when I approached the group and Jimmy barely noticed.

"Jimmy, it's me," I said, hooking a leash to his collar. "I need to talk to you."

"Hey, what's going on?" his mother said, lifting her head as she surfaced from a deep sleep.

"Yeah. What's going on?" said Jimmy's brother Gorgeous, looking very concerned. "To hell with him. You should take me," he said, pushing in between us.

"Dude, lighten up. We'll be right back," Jimmy said to his brother as he begrudgingly followed me. For the first time since I'd known him, he wasn't excited to see me.

"I miss you," I said to him. "Don't you miss me at all?"

"Well, I guess I miss you a little" he said, once I got him away from the group. "Like I miss someone I just saw a few hours ago. Because I did. I saw you earlier today."

"That's cold," I said.

"The new me is very honest," he said. "It's my heritage. My whole breed is forthright and spontaneous."

"Honesty is fine," I said, "but one day remind me to explain tact. Meanwhile, we have some work to do. I need a blog from you." I led him to the door of the guesthouse. And when he was reluctant to enter, I tried to ply him with cookies. He took them eagerly but remained rather distant.

"I'm so not into this anymore," he said. "Go ahead and write whatever you want. I don't care. No one in my family can read."

"Oh, come on," I said. "We're in this business together."

"You're thinking of the old me," he said. "I had some

strange ideas when I used you for a role model. I used to feel bad that I couldn't read or cook or use tools. Now I know what I am and from whence I came."

"Whence?" I said. "How do you know the word 'whence'?"

"I'm not dumb," he said. "I'm just a different kind of smart than you. I'm perceptive. I know how to manipulate you far better than you do me. Your species is so brutal and lacking in subtlety. You can never figure my kind out at all."

"Come on!" I argued. "That's not true. I think I understand you pretty well."

"No you don't. Give you an example," he said. He put out his tongue and started to breathe hard. "When I do this, I'm panting. You always say, 'Look, he's smiling.' No. I'm either hot. Or sometimes I'm in pain. But the truth is, we all have it in frequent rotation because it makes *you* smile. And when *you* are smiling, that's when you start giving out treats. But we're not fucking *smiling,* so just stop saying that, okay?"

"A perfect blog topic," I said, coaxing him to my side as I sat down at the computer.

"Go exploit one of the others. I'm not into it," he said. With that he lay down in front of the door, head on his paws, and just stared.

"You feel exploited?" I said, shocked and hurt.

"May I go back to my family now?" he asked. "I have pack order issues I need to work out with my brother."

"Come on!" I said. "You're not being exploited. Don't you want to be heard? We're invited to speak at a pet bloggers forum this weekend! People love you! We can sell them T-shirts with your picture. This is for both of our futures. It'll be fun!"

"As usual, it's all about you," said Jimmy. "Our priorities are different. My future is running around mindlessly with my family. Or napping." He stared at me with an especially intense version of "Nose down, eyes up."

"Oh, hell," I finally said to him, sighing as I opened the door. "Go do what you want. Hang out with your damn family." I stood there, hoping he'd succumb to all the guilt I was heaping upon him. Instead he ran out.

He was right. He was much better at manipulating me than I was at manipulating him.

{ 23 }

The Lucky Snake

I dealt with the pain of being rejected by my very own boy by pretending it never happened. I got up early in the morning and threw myself into my work. As I was dragging another enormous mass of garbage and dust out to the dumpster the phone rang.

"We're coming over," said Sara. "We miss you."

"Nice to hear somebody does," I said. "Jimmy's off with his family again. He sleeps with them. He eats with them. I'm persona non grata."

"I'll have a talk with him," said Sara in a calm, measured tone meant to inspire confidence. "Tell me again how to find your place. We're bringing lunch."

Now I was looking forward to seeing them all. The timing was perfect until Eden appeared at the door. She walked right in without knocking.

"Eden, I know this is your house, but you can't just walk in here," I said. "I have a private life too."

"I knocked," she said defensively. "Do you want me to make an appointment?"

"Yes, I do," I scolded as she came up behind me and clamped herself to my back like she wanted a piggyback ride. "What private life do you have? I think I'm jealous."

"Sara's coming over and bringing me lunch," I said.

"Oh?" said Eden petulantly. "How would she feel if she knew I was doing this?" She started to push her hand inside the waistband of my pants.

"Eden, not now," I said.

"Come on! You used to get off on a little danger. Remember when we did it on that roller coaster at Magic Mountain? Remember the Wiltern during Pearl Jam?"

"I hate Pearl Jam," I said. "I didn't go to that show. Remember? That wasn't me."

"It was too! Wasn't it?" she argued briefly before letting it drop. "Well, anyway, we'll hear the dogs start to bark if someone is coming."

"This is quite a little marriage you have going on here," I said when she started to unbutton my shirt again.

"Look at it this way," she said, grinning, "you're helping to keep it alive."

"Enough!" I said. I lifted her by the waist and carried her to the sofa, where I threw her down onto her back and pinned her by her arms. "Do you want me to remodel your guesthouse or not?"

"It's nice to have someone to play with again." She giggled. A canine commotion began to erupt in the distance.

"Dogs are barking," I said. "I'm going to let you up now. Someone is coming. Please behave."

I unpinned her, and she sprung forward and grabbed me around the legs. She was trying to pull me down onto the couch when I heard Sara's voice outside the front gate. "Hello? Hello? Gil? You around?"

"Coming," I called to her. "Eden! Sit up. Be nice!" I whispered sternly. I headed out to unlock the front gate.

"Hi," said Sara, looking as happy to see me as a child meeting Santa. She looked lovely. She was less fresh-faced than usual because she was wearing some makeup. She had gotten dolled up for this. I was touched.

Her arms were filled with Tupperware containers and grocery bags. Fruity, Cheney, and Dink all squeezed through the gate and charged in ahead of us. "Oh my God," said Dink as she rushed at me like a gust of wind. "I love you, I love you, I love you." Fruity and Cheney barreled in the front door. They started circling the room, ramming their big rubber noses into every crevice and corner.

"Back in a sec," I said to Sara, as I made a quick run for the bathroom to spritz myself with deodorant and cologne, lest Sara nail me for smelling like Eden. Sara was like a drug-sniffing dog. If there was something being intentionally hidden, she would be on it in a heartbeat.

"Sara, there's someone I'd like you to meet," I said, trying to infuse my voice with benign good nature as I returned to the room. "This is Eden," I said, relieved when Sara rushed toward Eden, extending her hand.

"Great to meet you," she said. "I've heard so much about you."

"I'll bet!" said Eden. "You look familiar. Did I meet you through Halley?"

"Halley?" said Sara. "You mean Tarnauer? I spoke at one of her seminars!"

"She's my life coach," said Eden.

"Oh my God! Halley was one of the first people I met when I moved here from Denver! Talk about coincidences! First that Craigslist thing, and now this!"

"You and Halley met on Craigslist?" said Eden.

"No, I'm sorry. I'm getting everything jumbled. I meant the weird way you and Gil connected about the guesthouse through Craigslist." Eden stared at me with steely eyes. When Sara looked toward me, grinning, Eden mouthed the word "liar."

"Now that I'm moving in here with Gil everything has come full circle," Sara said. "He must have told you."

"Gil never tells me anything," said Eden, rolling her eyes at me.

"You really have to keep on him, don't you?" said Sara, looking at me cautiously.

"We'll exchange notes someday," said Eden.

"I can't wait," I said. "Try to give me a couple hours' notice so I can slit my wrists."

"Halley is one of the names I have on my list of couples counselors!" Sara said brightly.

"Couples counselors?" said Eden.

"Well, you know," said Sara, "a lot of people think it's a good step to take before you make the commitment to live together."

"Seize the moment," said Eden. "If you two get married, there's zero chance he'll go for it." I shrugged and looked down at my shoes. "I have a mommy-baby yoga class at one." said Eden. "Good meeting you, Sara. Gil, can we talk for one second?"

I followed Eden out to the driveway.

"Your girlfriend is Little Sara Army Pants?" Eden said in an astonished whisper. "She's been around forever. I am really shocked."

"She's a very nice woman," I said.

"Gil, no offense, but she's ridiculous. She's a local crazy. She thinks she talks to animals. She's a *nut*."

"Well, I like her," I said.

"You could do a lot better," Eden clucked. "She's too Greenpeacey and global-warmy for you. But I guess if you're with her she must be really gooood at something." She wiggled her eyebrows lasciviously.

"I met *you* at the Renaissance Faire," I said. "That's not exactly Harvard Business School."

"Yes, but we were kids. At least I outgrew that shit. Oh, well. None of my business! Go enjoy your organic seedcakes or whatever," said Eden. "I'd give you a big wet smooch, but . . . I'll just stop by later."

"Knock first," I said, heading back into the house.

"She seems nice," said Sara when I rejoined her in the kitchen.

"Really? She does?" I said. "That's a new one. Let's eat."

"She's so beautiful. I don't get why you're with me." said Sara, putting the containers of food in the microwave. "Don't you think she's still kind of into you?"

"Sara, please don't start this again," I said.

"Sorry," she said, "but it's hard not to pick up that vibe. Maybe because things have been weird with us and you were married to her . . . Maybe I better hurry and make that couples counselor appointment."

"Please don't go getting paranoid on me again," I said, trying to maintain a tone of neutral jocularity to underscore my innocence, as Sara stared at me. That minute and forty-two seconds still left on the microwave felt like an eternity. I could chart my own deteriorating mental infrastructure by the way I felt about the microwave. When I got one five years ago the idea of making a baked potato in three minutes was magical, astonishing. Now having to wait three minutes for anything was too much to bear. Especially since I felt myself being scrutinized by Sara's X-ray vision.

How did people who cheated deal with the stress? What did you need to do to make sure you weren't turning transparent? Why didn't Bill Clinton use his free time now to write an advice column?

"Sorry," Sara said as the microwave dinged. "I'm sorry I doubted you." She leaned over and gave me a big, deep kiss. It started out more well intended than hot, but as she persisted, it began to get pleasantly heated. We fell back onto the couch in an embrace that was at least partially fueled by all the days of crazy monkey business with Eden, egged on by a dialogue I had been having with that twenty-two-year-old moron my id had taken on as a full-time collaborator. "Dude," he was saying, "A two-vag sampler right in a row. You didn't score this well when you were my age the first time." Next thing I knew, I was deep into one of my all-time steamiest encounters with Sara. It was eye-opening, and even a little staggering. Right until she got wedged between the sofa cushions. When she reached down to balance herself, she pulled out a pair of Eden's panties.

"What are these?" she said, holding them up and staring.

"What are what?" I said, careful to maintain a tone of bewildered bemusement.

"I'm getting out of here," she said, standing up. "I can't believe I apologized to you."

"Sara, that's not what you think," I said.

"Just for fun, go ahead," she said. "How is it not what I think?"

"Eden lives here. This is her house," I said, trying to add a layer of indignation to my tone of bruised piety, while at the same time taking pains to seem both intrigued and a little concerned about being falsely accused. "I only got here the other night. Her stuff is everywhere. She uses this bathroom after she takes tennis lessons."

"She undresses here on the couch?" she returned.

"Sara, I don't know what she does or does not do," I said. Now I was throwing in a touch of understandable rage. "I am not her guardian. Maybe she was here on the couch having marital relations with her husband!"

"So you're saying that these panties may have been here for days, weeks, or even months? I accidentally unearthed them from their ancient burial place? Just another amazing Craigslist coincidence?" As she talked, my brain was racing ahead. Could she put a date on them somehow? She would never examine them too closely. If she sent them to a forensics lab, probably they wouldn't be back for weeks. I was safe for now.

"Swear to God," I said, "I have no idea when they got stuffed in there."

Sara stared at me. Then she sat down again.

"For Chrissakes, Sara," I said, "Eden's the *ex-wife* who

totally screwed me. Would *you* want to have sex with someone like that?"

"You're giving me your word?" she said.

"Absolutely," I said, feeling like a snake. A very lucky
snake.

We finished eating our soggy vegetarian whatever it was in
silence. It wasn't too bad. All that flavorless soy cheese substitute gave it a rubbery appeal. And by affecting tremendous
calm, I somehow managed to make Sara feel comfortable not
only about Eden but about the guesthouse and everything
else. That filled me with both cocky pride and rank self-
hatred. It's unsettling to know how easy it is to lie.

24

1,440 Rounds a Day

$\mathcal{S}$ara left a few hours later to go see a client. The minute she departed the premises, I got in the van and drove down to that rip-off market to buy a pack of cigs. Then at beer-thirty, I sat down and had a beer and a smoke for the first time in almost six years. It felt like a reunion with my best friend from high school. The only thing that would have made it more superlative would have been the companionship of Jimmy. At least the others were there with me now.

"Cheney," I called to him. He was lying on the other side of the room taking a nap.

"Yeah? What?" he said, lifting his head, opening his eyes. "You want to play ball?"

"I'll make you a deal," I said, glad to see him. "I'll throw the ball if you help me write Jimmy's blog. You can be the guest columnist."

"Sure," said Cheney. "As long as you're promising ball."

"What should we write about?" I asked him.

"Ball," said Cheney.

"What about ball?" I said.

"Exactly," he said. "What about it?"

"Okay. Go ahead, start," I said. "What about ball?"

"Are you saying you want to play right now?" he said. "Because if you are, I have to go find a ball. I usually have one on me."

"No!" I said. "I want you to speak to the topic."

"What topic is that?" said Cheney.

"The topic of playing ball. Tell me your views about it. I will write them down," I said.

"Right," said Cheney. "Well, it's always a good time for ball. Always. That's about it."

"More," I said. "How about rules? Explain your technique."

"Okay!" said Cheney. "Usually I bring the ball to someone in my mouth. Then I either release it, or else I stand there with my jaws clenched and make them pry it loose. It's surprising the number of people who don't want to reach into my mouth to get it. It makes me feel very powerful. The main thing is I try to keep focused. I never let up until it is airborne. Then I run like hell. But it's those seconds right before, when I try to predict where it will land in order to get there and be waiting for it, that are really critical. I check the wind velocity, factor in the sex of the thrower, and their age. Try to determine whether it will be underhand or overhand. Got to get there first. First is very important."

"Good," I said, making notes as rapidly as I could. "Good boy, Cheney. A few more questions: What if you bring a ball to someone and they won't throw it?"

"Relentless staring. That's the number one strategy. Sometimes they will throw it just to get rid of you. It's a win-win situation."

"What kind of ball is best?" I asked him.

"What kind isn't? I like 'em all," said Cheney. "Small, pointy, furry, squeaky, flat. With a face or without. In a perfect world, I play continuously. I figure it takes between a half a minute and a minute and a half to complete a ball cycle. I don't know math, but how many of those could I fit into a day?" he asked me.

"There are 1,440 minutes in a day," I said, doing a little multiplication on my calculator. "So you're thinking 1,440 rounds of ball a day? Every day?"

"Well, ideally," he said. "More if you can make the day longer. Or use smaller balls. It's frustrating to want something so much and not get anyone to cooperate."

"Why don't you guys start your own teams?" I said. "Why wait for me to play?"

"Why don't you guys go for your own walks?" he asked me. "Why do you wait for us?"

"We do go for our own walks," I said, lighting up another cigarette and inhaling deeply. "We don't always wait for you."

"You don't?" he said. "Whoa. Who else knows about this?"

"Well, hopefully I've got enough to fake my way through another blog. Thank you, Cheney."

"I know how you can thank me," he said, staring relentlessly.

25

Saturday

$\mathcal{M}$y plan for the evening was to silk-screen some T-shirts with Jimmy's face on them to sell at that pet bloggers event on Sunday. I was thinking of a picture of Jimmy over the words "Walking is my church." Was that too precious? Or not precious enough? Should it be "Walkin iz mah church," like they'd say in lolcat?

Anyway, that was my plan until Eden turned up at seven, unannounced, uninvited, raring to go.

"What is going on with you?" I said. "Are you ovulating or something?"

"I guess I was more bored planning this damn kid party than I knew. I told you I'm having a party for Mai Linn to-morrow? Of course you're invited. She's going to be *one*."

"Please apologize to her for me when she can talk, but I'm speaking in Pomona at some pet bloggers expo," I said.

"You're speaking?" she said, astonished. "Are you taking Little Sara Army Pants?"

"Don't call her that," I said, even though it was kind of a perfect nickname. "No, just me."

"I'm so pissed that she got you to go to counseling. I couldn't get you to go when we were actually married," she said.

"I don't remember you wanting to go to counseling," I said.

"Maybe I want to go now," she said. "I maybe need to get closure."

"Fine. If I can go to marriage counseling with a woman I'm not going to marry, then I guess I can also go with the one I divorced. Set up the appointment," I said as Eden started rolling up my T-shirt and kissing the hair on my stomach.

"If I'm not going to see you tomorrow, can I please have my way with you right now?" she purred. "Let's put the dogs outside?" she asked me as she undid my belt. "They're staring at us. It's a little freaky. Haven't they seen you having sex before?"

"You add a layer of special effects they're not used to," I said as we kissed. "But I'm expecting a visit from Sara. Now is not good."

"Well, how about a quickie, then," she said, hoisting up her dress. In a nanosecond she had her legs wrapped around my waist, and my pants were around my ankles. She was moaning and sweating and hanging on to me when the dogs started barking again. I heard tires on the gravel driveway. I heard a car door slam.

"What's Chad doing home so early?" Eden said. We pulled apart.

"Hi," Sara said cheerily over the intercom. "I'm at the back gate. Let me in! I've got fresh pears!"

"Shit! It's Sara *and* Chad," I said, zipping up, making a run for the bathroom sink and the cologne. "You should get out of here."

"Fresh pears?" said Eden. She looked all smeary like a Toulouse-Lautrec painting as she pulled her dress down and pulled her hair back into a barrette at the nape of her neck. "Is she worried they'll go bad? You better tell her she can't just show up here unannounced. That is so rude." There was a knock on the gate.

"Coming!" I yelled to Sara.

"I'm back!" Sara sang, smiling broadly as she stood on her toes to give me a kiss. Fruity, Cheney, and Dink all ran to greet her. "Oh my God, I love you, I love you, I love you, I love you," said Dink as Sara picked her up.

"Hello, sweetie. What's that?" she asked, as Dink kissed her face. "Dink says she needs to be fed twice a day."

"That's not what I said," said Dink. "But it's true! I do!"

"What?" said Sara, looking at me. "Why do you look upset?"

"I'm not upset," I said, paranoid that I looked like a man who had been having sex. "It's great to see you!"

"Hi, Sara," said Eden with a little too much friendly aggressive force. She had repositioned herself in the kitchen, where she was pretending to examine the hinges on the cabinet doors.

"Oh, hi, Eden," said Sara, seeing her for the first time and returning the smile everywhere but in her eyes. Sara was on the scent of a couple of things she didn't like: too much stilted friendliness, too many pheromones.

"Well, I'll leave you kids alone," said Eden, picking up her purse. "Nice seeing you, Sara," she said, scuttling out the door.

"Why don't I go find Jimmy? I know he'd like to see you," I said, grabbing the opportunity to disappear for a minute, compose myself, and let some air into the room. Sara stood silently, staring at me. "Anything wrong?" I asked.

"There was something going on just now with you two, wasn't there?" she said.

"Going on?" I said indignantly. "Come on! No way."

"Just the usual humpy stuff that everyone does when they could be playing ball," said Cheney, dropping a deflated soccer ball at Sara's feet. Thank God Sara never understood a word he said.

"Why don't you come help me find Jimmy," I said to Cheney, thinking it wise to get him out of there in case Sara's comprehension improved.

"Why do I get the feeling Eden doesn't want me here?" said Sara. "I was looking right into her eyes and seeing hostility."

"I know for a fact that you're wrong," I said, darting out the door, hoping things would neutralize in my absence.

"This way," said Cheney, leading me toward the patio where Jimmy's family was relaxing. Jimmy was lying on his side between his mother and his sister. His brother Gorgeous was standing over him, stiff-legged, sniffing him aggressively. "That used to be my spot," said Gorgeous.

"Get a new spot," said Jimmy.

"You know, when I was alpha, there was never a single complaint," said Gorgeous.

"Who's complaining now?" said Jimmy.

"I am," said Gorgeous, wrinkling his upper lip.

"Jimmy?" I said. He rolled his eyes toward me and lazily wagged his tail. "Friends of yours are here to visit."

"Oh," he said. "Tell them hi. I'm kind of busy. I've got a lot of alpha shit to do today."

"Come tell them yourself," I said. I reached down to attach a leash to his collar, but when I tried to lead him, he growled at me.

"Are you serious?" I said. "What's that about?"

"It means knock it off," he said. "I learned it from my mother."

I stepped back in shock.

"Big tough guy," taunted Gorgeous.

"You don't want to see Fruity and Dink?" I said. "Or Cheney?"

"Hey, man," said Cheney.

"Hey," said Jimmy. "He can smell me from here. He'll tell the others about it."

"Okay, fine," I said. I reached into my pocket and pulled out a handful of dog biscuits. "More cookies for me and for Cheney and anyone else who wants to spend time with me."

"Me! Me! Me! I'd like to spend time with you," said Jimmy's brother, sister, and mother all at once. The three of them leapt to their feet and clustered around me like I was an ice cream truck on a hot day.

"You're not playing fair," Jimmy scoffed. "You know my family has very poor treat resistance." Reluctantly he followed the group of us as we headed back down the hill to the guesthouse.

"I gotta tell you, I don't like this," I said to Jimmy, slow-ing down so I could walk beside him. "The only way for me to spend time with you is to bribe your whole damn family?"

"We're an inseparable unit. Treats for one, treats for all. That's how we roll," said Jimmy stoically.

"Look, I know you don't see me as family anymore," I said. "Fine. I understand. Sort of. But you also used to be my best friend. Can't we still hang out together? I love having you in my life."

I didn't know quite how to explain to him how much I missed having him around. The way we used to be together relaxed me. It was the easiest kind of companionship. It was also the only family tie I'd ever known that wasn't burdened by obligations I felt I couldn't fulfill. Part of me was a little sorry I'd never had kids. But the truth was I had never wanted to pass on my genetic shortcomings. Knowing that the future would contain no Gil replicants didn't bother me in the least. Yet I couldn't imagine living the rest of my life without Jimmy. Our time together was one of my favorite things about being alive.

"I hate to sound like a Hallmark card, but, I just like being with you," I said. "Can't we still get together and talk and stuff?"

"About what?" he said. The sun was setting. The sky was a beautiful pale shade of lemon as we made our way back down the hill to the guesthouse. But as we got close, I could see Sara out front looking angry.

"Well, her, for starters," I said. "Look at that face she's making."

"Whew," Jimmy said. "But know what? Not my problem."

"Whose cigarettes are these?" Sara said, holding up the pack I'd been smoking.

"Mine," I said.

"You're smoking?" she said. "When did this start?"

"Today," I said. "I just had one."

"There are four missing," she said, heading into the house and walking briskly toward the bathroom. "I'm throwing them out."

"Don't you dare," I said, catching up to her and trying to grab them away. "Seriously, Sara. I'm a forty-seven-year-old man. It's my constitutional right to contract the diseases of my choice. Give me my goddamn cigarettes."

"Wow. They *are* yours," she said. "I was sure they were hers."

"This whole house is hers," I said, "but if you flush those fucking cigarettes, I'm going out to buy a carton. I promise I won't come back till I've smoked them all."

"My spirit guides say that their alarm bells are ringing," Sara said, putting the cigarettes down on a table.

"Look," I said, "I need a fucking smoke. Apologize to your spirit guides for me. Explain to them that I'm in a tough spot in my life right now. And while you're at it, tell them even if I believed in them I'd still have trouble buying that they have alarm bells."

"I don't think Eden's the only one who doesn't want me here," said Sara. "You're overtly hostile. Even the dogs are picking up on it."

I looked at the dogs, and sure enough, Jimmy's brother Gorgeous was being aggressive. Cheney was standing quietly, looking miserable as the big black dog dominated him. Fruity curled her tail beneath her and ran out of the room. Luckily for Dink, she was too little for anyone to pay much notice. She was slowly moving across the room, licking the floor.

I interceded by opening the door, knowing it would distract them. Gypsy and Party Girl ran outside. Gorgeous immediately followed.

"Nice seeing you. I gotta go," said Jimmy, racing after them.

"I guess I'll go too," said Sara.

"I'm sorry about all this," I said to her. "My timing is off today. I'm behind in my work. I've got a lot on my mind. How about if tomorrow we pick up where we left off?"

Sara shrugged as she gathered up her belongings.

"I'll call you," I said, trying to gauge her response. Silently she opened the door. On her way to her car, she ran smack into Chad.

"Oops. Did I come at a bad time?" said Chad. He was holding an open bottle of Scotch. The young Teddy Roosevelt having a night on the town.

"No, I was just leaving," said Sara, not looking back at me. Knowing Sara, that was a very loaded gesture.

"So things are going good?" said Chad, completely oblivious.

"Never better," I said.

"Have a drink with me?" said Chad, holding up the cut glass bottle to show me what he was offering. I didn't know Scotch, but I could see from the choice of font and the colors on the label that it was an expensive brand.

"Sure," I said, lighting a cigarette.

"Rocks?" he said, removing tumblers from a liquor cabinet.

"Why not?" I said. He grinned and made ice chips shoot

out of the refrigerator door. Some of them even went into the glasses like they were meant to. "I'm glad we're finally getting this project under way," Chad said, sitting down on the couch and taking a giant swig of his very full drink. "I need something to focus on. Oh. I forgot. Cheers!" He held up his glass.

"Cheers," I said, clinking my glass against his.

"To the success of our new project," said Chad, during another big swallow. His eyes were becoming glassy, his words were starting to slur. "You're my kind of guy, Gil," he said. "You're honest. A hard worker. I like a hard worker. I'm a hard worker. My father was a hard worker. To hard workers!"

He held up his glass for me to clink again, so I did.

"I gotta hand it to Eden. She knows how to pick good guys!" he said. "I know we had our differences in the past, Gil, but I'm glad that we can be friends now." He finished his drink and poured himself another. "You probably didn't like me at first because of what happened way back when. But I swear dude, I didn't know you guys were still married. . . . She said me you were broken up."

"Oh, really?" I said, trying not to have visions of his hairy ass dancing in my head.

Out the front window I could see Jimmy's family running around in a pack, taking bathroom breaks and admiring what they'd done.

"Look at those crazy guys," said Chad. "Can you see them? Look what a nice family they are, all together like that." He went to the door and yelled to them. They all came galloping toward him. "Hey, you guys. Hello, Gorgeous. Hello, Gypsy. No, you're Jimmy. No, you're Gorgeous. Hello,

Party Girl. I mean Jimmy. See how they love me, Gil? They are nuts about me. I must not be such a bad guy after all."

Stumbling a little, Chad got down on his knees. Eagerly, the dogs climbed onto him like a swarm of locusts. "I love these guys. Look at them! They're like four twins. I guess you can't have four twins, can you?" He laughed through a mouth full of ice cubes.

"I guess not," I said. Chad fell on his side and was blanketed by an avalanche of friendly dogs.

"Okay, now open the door and let us out of here," said Jimmy. "When this guy is smashed, he sometimes gets dominant. I've got as much of that going on with my brother as I can handle." I did as he asked, and all four dogs ran out of the house.

"Am I interrupting anything?" said Chad as he struggled to get to his feet. "You don't mind if I talk to you, do you?"

"No," I said. I was a little worried.

"I think maybe Eden is screwing around on me," he blurted out, sitting down on the couch with so much force he almost knocked over a lamp. "There. I said it. I don't have all the evidence yet. But I recognize the pattern. The body language."

"Why are you telling me?" I said.

"Well, I kind of feel like I know you," he said. "Come on, dude, we've both been through the same goddamn wringer. I've been hearing about you for years. She talks about you all the time."

"Personal stuff?" I asked, feeling my breathing quicken.

He nodded and bit his lip. "She has a big mouth. Remember?"

"I seem to remember that vaguely," I said.

"I know all about how your sex life died. Everything," he said.

"Christ, really? She said that?" I took a deep breath.

"I'm sorry. I don't mean to turn you against her," he slurred. "It's just that I feel like you're the only one who knows what I'm going through." He looked at me with a pained expression, then poured himself another half glass of Scotch. Was he setting me up, I wondered? In a movie, this would be the scene where he pulled out a loaded revolver and accused me of something.

"Who do you think she's doing?" I asked, making sure my voice sounded neutral, like a man on an impartial fact-finding mission.

"I'm not sure," he said. "I think she's fucking our architect. Have you met that putz? Designer to Jennifer Lopez? Eden loves that shit. They're always going off to look at faucets and famous people. They stop for lunch someplace where he introduces her to someone related to Goldie Hawn. Or Donald Trump's daughter Whoseewhats. He knows everyone's daughter and mother. I never liked that guy."

"Well, I'm sorry to hear that," I said, buying some time.

"You know what?" he said, looking around. "Fuck this whole remodeling horseshit, dammit. Why should I use my money to build an office for Eden? Why the fuck does she need an office? When did she ever do any work? Suddenly she needs an official place of business? Fuck that. And fuck her, right, Gil?" He sipped some more Scotch and crunched some more ice. "I'm looking out for me. And me wants a functioning guesthouse. Because me knows it's better for resale value. This is *my* house. Why should I do what *she* wants? I should have my goddamn head examined."

"Did you confront her yet?" I asked.

"No. Not yet. You're the first person I've told. Ssshhhhh," he said, spraying the room with tiny droplets of water as he lifted his index finger to his lips. "Top secret. There's one other person who knows." My heart stopped again.

"The detective," he said. I felt something in my circulatory system change levels. "I hired a guy to stay here next week and snoop around and shit. Take some photos, find out who she's seeing."

"Wow," I said. "You mean follow her around? Won't she notice?"

"Well, here's where I need you to help me, Gil," he said. "She thinks he's my son, Hayden. From my first marriage, coming to stay for two weeks. She's never met Hayden because he's been living in Tokyo. I tried to show her pictures. She never even looked at them, Gil. She doesn't give a damn about my son, Hayden." Now he started to get morose and weepy drunk. "So now it's this PI who's coming to stay here instead. He's the same age as my son. He gets here next week. I mean tomorrow. Did I already say that?" he said. "We've got Linn Mai's party. I mean Mai Linn. Eden'll be so busy she won't notice what the guy's up to."

"You want me out of here?" I asked him, sipping some Scotch.

"No, no. Stay. You take it easy," he said. "Finish up what you started. Put those walls back up. Do whatever you feel like."

"The ones I just took down?" I said. "Put them back up? In the same spot?"

"Sure! Why not? Fuck that architect and his curvilinear space and his important goddamn angles, am I right, Gil? I don't even like textured surfaces, do you? Fuck him and fuck Frank Gehry and Frank Lloyd Wright and all the Franks in the goddamn Bauhaus. And thanks for talking to me. I feel better just getting it out. You know, I gotta tell you, I really admire the way you and Eden have put aside your differences. You figured out how to have a mature adult relationship with her, Gil. I hope for the sake of our kid that somewhere down the road I can be that mature. But for right now, fuck that shit. Am I right, Gil?"

I polished off quite a bit more Scotch that night after Chad stumbled off. Now I was filled with a pounding, white-hot anxiety. This should have been a real victory moment for me. The hoped-for day of retribution in which Chad would finally pay for all the pain he had caused me. But it was joyless and ugly. And leave it to me to have ruined it for myself by not owning the moral high ground. Somehow I had wound up casting myself in the role of the evil home wrecker.

I spent the rest of the evening weighing my options. Only I could put myself in a situation where every way I played it, I was still the asshole. Meanwhile I silk-screened Jimmy T-shirts to sell at the pet expo; a picture of his intense face over the words "When all else fails: Nose down, eyes up."

The big question, as I saw it, was this: Who was I going to betray? Chad was paying me well, so I felt a loyalty to him. I had empathy for his situation. It was sadly familiar. Seemed like he was a decent guy in over his head.

Eden, on the other hand, was still blowing me, and dammit, she was good at it. That had to count for something.

Was it all a sign that I should let Sara move into the guest-house? It didn't seem like putting her in the middle of all this would help anything.

It also seemed only right to somehow warn Eden before she got us both into trouble. I was her co-conspirator.

{ 26 }

Cheezburger Sunday

*E*den woke me at eight A.M., when she showed up at my door, unannounced, accompanied by two fireplug-shaped piano movers from Central America. As soon as I opened the door, they began angling a piano into the room with that amazing grace and economy of movement that piano movers all acquire. They'd removed its legs in order to slide the instrument on its diagonal on quilted movers' rugs. Eden stood beside them, dressed in a short kimono, black leggings, and high-heeled flip-flops, grinning mischievously.

"I'm storing this here for the time being," she said. "I need the space in the living room for a Chinese dragon they're delivering at nine. It was part of a Rose Bowl float I got them to let me rent. It'll make the party! Wait'll you see it."

"You can't put that piano in here," I said. "The room is full of plaster dust and garbage."

"Yes, I can," she said. "It's my house. I need the space for the party. Isn't it beautiful? It's the same model Nicole Kidman bought for Keith Urban. Put it here!" she said to the movers, gesturing to a spot between the kitchen and the living room. "There aren't any walls coming down on this side of the room, right?"

The two unsmiling piano guys reassembled the piano as Eden strolled around the room examining my stuff, picking up my papers, opening and closing my drawers and looking inside them.

"I don't know," I said. "Ask your husband. Or Jennifer Lopez. Or whoever makes these decisions. This place is a mess. And you and I need to talk."

"That's why God invented drop cloths." She grinned as she sidled up to me and whispered, "Honey, have you got a couple of twenties to tip these guys? I forgot to bring my wallet with me. I'm good for it. I promise." She reached back and patted me on the butt. I glowered at her, concerned that the movers could see. But because my ego wouldn't let me look broke in front of the grim-faced El Salvadorans, I opened my wallet and handed Eden forty bucks.

"Why don't I meet you guys back up at the house. I need you to help me move stuff around for my party," she said matter-of-factly as she turned to the movers and handed them the cash.

"Sorry, ma'am. We work for the piano company," the shorter one said to her. "We're on the clock."

"My husband will make it worth your while," Eden insisted flirtatiously. Goddamn pretty women get away with shit that gets the rest of us punched. "Just tell him what you want and he'll meet your price. Look for the guy in the tennis outfit with the Beatle haircut." The two guys eyed each other and then walked out the door and crossed the yard. "Good. I thought they'd never leave. Now come here and play me something before I have to run off," she ordered.

"No," I said, resenting her tone.

"Oh, come on!" she said. "Don't be a pill. I just need to make sure the piano didn't get damaged in the move or anything. Quick. Do it now before they leave." She pulled me to my feet by my arms and started to push me toward the piano bench. "Go on. Sit," she said, pushing down on my shoulders, expecting me to buckle at the knees like a rag doll.

"Do you mind if I have my coffee first?" I said, locking eyes with her. I was still half-asleep.

"Here! I'll wake you up," she said, winking at me as she started to run her hands down my chest. "Come on! Play something for me. I'll return the favor. Please, please, please, please, please, please?"

Exhaling with exaggerated contempt, I sat down at the piano. It was a beautiful instrument, much better than any one-year-old needed for lessons. It was polished, perfectly clean and lacquered, irritating and alluring at the same time, much like Eden herself. I hadn't been behind a keyboard since our divorce. Fixing her with a resentful stare, I played precisely twelve bars of Rachmaninoff's Concerto Number 2 in C minor. When I was a kid, that was the piece I always fished out for people to shut them up. I liked to play just long enough to astonish them, then stop abruptly and leave them slack-jawed.

"No! Don't stop!" said Eden. "Keep going." Eden had regained her confidence with me enough to be giving me orders. This was not a good trend.

I got up to make some coffee. "Oh, come on! You owe me!" she said, petulant. "Here I am giving you all the sex you can eat and a free place to live. You used to say I inspired you." She stuck out her lower lip. "Remember?"

"I was on the make," I said. "Or I was drunk. Or both."

"What did you want to talk about?" she asked.

"I gotta have my caffeine first," I said, savoring a chance to deny her.

"How about if I come back in a couple of hours," she said. "My guests don't arrive till two." She stood there staring, sucking on her index finger suggestively.

"I'm speaking in Pomona at noon," I said. "But we need to talk. And soon."

"Then after the party. Tonight," she said, pleased, standing in front of me on her tiptoes so she could kiss me on the mouth. And she held that kiss until she was sure the charge she was sending had been delivered. "We'll talk. You'll play piano. And whatever else comes to mind!" She blew me another kiss and strutted out the door.

I was thrilled that I had someplace to go for the rest of the day. I had decided that Jimmy was going with me, whether he wanted to or not. He was still my dog, dammit. I had the right to insist on his company occasionally. Though I was unprepared for how bad it felt when I had to force him into the car.

"You love riding in the car," I reminded him.

"Why can't my family come?" he said.

"Have you ever heard of the word 'co-dependent'?" I said

as I sat behind the wheel. "All of nature's creatures leave the nest when they're grown. What about developing your individual identity?"

"I'm a pack animal. Remember?" Jimmy huffed, refusing to look at me.

"But didn't the other dogs and I seem like your pack?" I asked, backing the van down the driveway.

"Not really. Did they seem like one to you?" he returned.

"No, I guess not," I said. "But I thought you might see it that way."

"Why? Because I'm a dumb animal?" he said. "And you wonder why I'm so alienated."

We drove the hour to the Pomona fairgrounds in silence.

After we found a place to park in the enormous lot, we made a lengthy trek past booths selling animal products and services, each one seeking a corner on the overextended dog and cat novelty market. Someone was selling dog socks. Someone else was selling bottled vitamin water for cats. Just beyond a dog agility competition I saw some folding chairs set up around a small riser that was being used as a stage. A gigantic photo blowup of the "I Can Has Cheezburger?" cat was mounted at the rear as a backdrop. Beside it was a big hand-painted sign that said WELCOME PET BLOGGERS. And standing by a podium holding a hand mike was a large-boned fiftyish woman in a floppy tan felt hat. "Can I help you?" she said, checking her clipboard when she saw us staring.

"We're speakers," I said. "We're 'A Message from Jimmy.' "

"Oh! 'A Message from Jimmy!' Excellent!" she said, her voice all lilting and upbeat, like a QVC saleswoman. "I'm Heather, the woman who contacted you, aka 'Rough Ruff-

Ruff from Rufus.' Maybe you've seen our page!" I nodded like I knew what she meant. "We're all such big fans of your blog. I'm so glad you could make it. This is going to be a fun event."

"You think so?" I said, as Jimmy retreated to a spot behind my knees. "What do you need us to do?"

"Just hang out," she said. "We're going to start in fifteen minutes. You're our only male reader! Isn't that a hoot? You'll be reading fifth."

"Yes, a hoot," I said, in a voice so small I was stunned it had come out of me. My entire being seemed to be retracting like a tortoise into its shell.

"Do you mind if I introduce you to someone who is dying to meet you?" she said. "She'll be here in a second. You may know her blog. 'Beatrice the Kitteh Bee'?" She giggled at her own lingo.

"Great," I said. "Can I ask you a question? What about selling stuff?"

"Well, you're supposed to have made those arrangements last March," she scolded. "There's a waiting list, and a table fee. There's a nonrefundable rental fee."

"But I only heard from you a week ago," I said.

"Oh. Hmmm. Okay. Talk to Janeane over there. Tell her I said to ask if there's any space left." She winked.

A woman who looked like Eden's middle-aged massage therapist was fussing in the aisle between two rows of manned tables. All around her were vendors selling everything from cat perfume to parakeet tiaras. Some were mom-and-pop start-ups. Many were corporate franchises.

"Well, you lucked out," Janeane sighed, clearly depleted from a long morning full of requests. " 'DogGone

Jewelry' never showed. I love these people who flake and never bother to call! Their empty table is right there. Might as well grab it."

"Thanks," I said, leading Jimmy to our designated spot. I piled my three dozen Jimmy shirts in stacks on the tabletop. Beside a small sign I'd printed out the night before, I thumbtacked a couple of shirts to the edge of the table like banners.

"Well," I said to Jimmy, "congratulations, CEO. We are open for business." I sat down on a folding chair behind the table and tried to get Jimmy to sit down beside me. "Can we go now?" he asked. "I hate it here," he said, retreating under the table.

"No," I said emphatically. "This is the first day of the rest of our lives."

"This is embarrassing," Jimmy said as we sat there being completely ignored.

"It is pretty nasty," I had to admit.

"Stop it," I said.

"Let's go," he said, now beginning to make high-pitched whines and whimpering noises.

"Gil, this is Jenny, the girl I was telling you about," said Heather, bounding over with a short, stocky woman in tow. Jenny had a shag haircut, wore green eye shadow, and was dressed in an I WUV MY KITTEH! T-shirt. She was holding a cat carrier. "This is ma bebbeh, Beatrice!" she said. "And we're both so glad to meet you! Where's Jimmy?"

"Hiding under the table," I said.

"Damn you," I heard Jimmy mutter. "Damn you to hell."

"Nice to meet you," I said to Jenny.

"Can we please go now?" Jimmy whined, poking my ankles repeatedly with his nose. "Go. Go, go, go, go, go," I heard him whimper.

"Well, we're about ready to begin," said Heather. "Jenny is going on first. She's one of our superstars. I'm going to go introduce her in just a minute. The rest of our speakers will be in the seats I've roped off for you all in the front row. There's a chair there with your name on it."

"Okay," I said.

"Oh, noes! I guess we has to go gets ready," said Jenny. "I'd tewtully love to continue our conversation laters. Dey has deelishus kookiss and other delectabuhls ovar thar." She pointed to a food stand a hundred yards away.

"Sure. Fine," I said, surveying the area.

"Wish me lucks!" she said, heading toward the stage.

"Now can we goes?" said Jimmy. He looked at me with a combination of sadness and fear. It was a look I'd last seen when we'd had to get the squeaky toy removed.

"If our bloggers can please take a seat in this area here," I heard Heather say into the microphone after the mandatory audio feedback shriek. "Is everybody ready to speak lolcat?" The small group of ardent fans all applauded.

"Dees shud bees tewtully redonk, ehn?" said Heather. "We's goink to hear six peeps who is ritings da bwogs for daze dawgs and daze kittehs."

"What did she say?" said Jimmy.

"She said you're right. We gotta get out of here," I said as I hastily packed the T-shirts back into their cardboard boxes. Then I scribbled a note on the back of the sign I'd made: " 'A Message from Jimmy' had to leave. Family emergency."

"De foistist bwogger is a prosh fawty-pound kitteh from

Woodland Hills who loves to snorgle! He also likes hees peelows and hees speshul feeshes. It's the tewtully redonk Beetrix the Bebbeh Kitteh Bee."

Jenny, dressed in a yellow and black striped vest and a baseball cap on which she had sewn a pair of cat ears, now took the stage. When she put the cat carrier on a table beside the podium, the fourteen people who were seated in front offered a hearty round of applause.

I tiptoed over to the roped-off section of seats where my fellow bloggers were waiting. "Please give this to Heather," I said, handing my note to a middle-aged woman wearing a gray I LOVE MY DOXIE sweatshirt with sequined trim.

"We is proshness mcsquirmesons and I am dee snorgling queen" is the last thing I heard Jenny say before Jimmy and I took off running.

"I'm sorry about putting you through this," I said to him.

"Now do you understand why I would rather be with my family?" said Jimmy, as we drove out of the parking lot, both of us still panting.

27

Red String

*W*hen we pulled into the driveway at Casa Eden, I was stopped by a beautiful young girl in a white tuxedo jacket from a valet parking service. I was so worn out by the lolcat women that I thought she said "I can has your car?" and I barreled past without stopping to flirt. I didn't get very far. The driveway was totally blocked with what looked like hundreds of new high-end SUVs or luxury sedans: Lexus, Prius, BMW, Mercedes. I thought to detour around them but wound up blocked by a fence. This was the best-attended party for a one-year-old I had ever seen. Not a bouncy tent or a petting zoo in sight.

As it happened, Eden saw us sneaking around to the side of her property. "Gil," she screamed, running over, "come celebrate Mai Linn's birthday!" Grabbing me by the forearm, she began to pull me toward the front door. Jimmy began to whine disagreeably. When I let him loose, he barreled off to find his family.

"Come see my beautiful party," Eden said, pulling me into her living room, which had been totally transformed into a feverish vision of China. On one side was a thirty-foot inflatable Chinese dragon, hinged jaws wide open, a big red silk tongue hanging down. On the other side was a massive catered Chinese buffet table decorated with a red silk tablecloth. Chinese-silk-pajama-clad waiters and waitresses were serving Chinese food and drinks. The décor was very red: red curtains with Chinese lettering on them; red paper lanterns; red fans; large red baskets filled with eggs dyed red; a big red and black lacquered Chinese gong on a stand; a multitiered birthday cake in the shape of a pagoda. Over the din of a hundred happy mommies and animated toddlers the soundtrack to *Mulan* was playing full blast. Perhaps the most remarkable weirdness was the ceiling, where, among dozens of bright red Chinese paper lanterns, were hanging millions of different lengths of red thread.

"It's a red thread party," Eden said. "I got the idea from an old Chinese saying: 'There's an invisible red thread that connects those who are destined to meet. The thread stretches and tangles but will never break.' Here." She handed me a cold bottle of Tsingtao beer. "Chinese beer. It'll change your life."

"So in China when you turn one, they give you a red thread party?" I asked, taking the beer but resisting the idea of another of Eden's beverage-induced life changes.

"No. I made it up. But one is a very big birthday for the Chinese. They invite all their relatives and friends. Since we didn't have many of either, I put up a MySpace page for Mai Linn. I put the word out that we wanted to connect with other adopted Chinese babies and mommies. Ten months later, Mai Linn has two hundred and sixty friends! And look how many of them came!"

"That's a lot of friends for a one-year-old to manage," I was about to say when I realized Jimmy had three hundred and ten.

"Did you see the red eggs?" she said. "Red is the color of good luck in China. The egg is a symbol too. I forget for what. Go get some food. It's classic Chinese."

"Full of lead and fake protein made out of coal?" I joked. "Here's what I don't get, Eden. You brought your baby here when she was only two months old. Why so much emphasis on the culture of the anonymous birth mother who abandoned her?"

Eden was already scanning the room for better opportunities.

"Back in a sec," she said, making a beeline for someone on the other side of the room. Pretty much everyone there had a Chinese baby except me.

Deciding I might as well grab a plate of food before I made my retreat, I was helping myself to some cashew chicken when I realized Chad was standing beside me.

"Hi," he said. He looked particularly grim-faced.

"Great party," I said.

"Ridiculous," he said. "The baby is *one*. That's only twelve months away from none."

"Well," I said, playing devil's advocate and being unaccountably upbeat, "as the lolcat ladies say: 'You can has egg rolls.'" He looked at me blankly. "Enjoy yourself, dude. You paid for this," I said. "You deserve to have fun."

"In that case, let's grab some fried wontons and go to a titty bar," said Chad, grabbing a beer. He stood very close to me, but his eyes were always on Eden. "Look at her with that Jennifer Lopez guy. Mr. Muted Colors, the architect," whispered Chad, nodding toward the edge of the room where Eden was offering a beer to a handsome Asian guy in gold-rimmed glasses. He was wearing a gray cashmere sweater tied around his shoulders and beige linen pants. "Read her body language," said Chad. We both watched her standing a little too close to him, piling her hair on top of her head, letting strands fall down around her face.

"You got a second? There's someone I want you to meet." Chad waved to a tall, lanky, curly-haired guy in his twenties dressed in a long-sleeved hockey shirt and Dockers. "My son, Hayden," Chad said, as the guy approached us from the other side of the room.

"Oh, really?" I said. "I see a little resemblance. Around the mouth. Maybe the eyes?"

"No!" Chad whispered. "This is the you-know . . . that I told you about. I put a rush on him. Sorry to be landing you in the middle of this, but I gotta get things moving. I've had a stomachache twenty-four hours a day for the last three months."

"Nice to meet you," I said, shaking his hand. He raised his eyebrows, bit his lip, and nodded.

"I'm going to show him the guesthouse," Chad said. "We'll meet you down there whenever you're done here."

"Right," I said, my stomach starting to knot. I finished up the rest of my Tsingtao in one gulp and was about to set off in search of another when the whole room froze as Eden bonged the big gong.

"Everybody, we're going to cut the cake!" Eden shouted. She moved to the center of the table to stand behind the gigantic multiple-layer pagoda cake. As she picked up a sharp piece of gleaming cutlery, the background music changed to twelve-tone Chinese symphonic music. It took me only a minute to recognize the overture from *The Red Detachment of Women,* a revolutionary Chinese opera that used to be part of my record collection. I'd wondered what had become of it. Like my youth, my optimism, and my pension plan, my record collection had vanished into thin air after the divorce. Now here was a piece of it, providing a change of tone and ambience so stark and foreboding that a half dozen little Chinese toddlers began to cry. "I want to thank all our wonderful MySpace friends for following your red thread to Mai Linn's birthday party," Eden said. "We were all destined to meet. So be sure to take home the little phone book I printed up with everyone's phone numbers so we can stay in touch! Now please help me sing a little 'Zhu ni sheng ri kua le' to Mai Linn." One of the costumed waiters hit the big red and black gong, and everyone in the room began to sing: "Zhu ni sheng ri kua le. Zhu ni sheng ri kua le. ZHU NI SHENG RI KUA MAI LINN. Zhu ni sheng ri kua le."

"Yay!" Eden cheered, clapping as she jumped up and down in front of Mai Linn in her high chair, her face smeared with red icing. "Everyone get some cake!" she shouted above the din. "And please take home as many red eggs as you want! I don't know what to do with them!" A room full of happy mommies and babies began to swarm toward Eden like a giant nest of termites attending to their queen.

I grabbed the chance to get some more food since there was only one woman in line at the buffet table. It took me a minute to recognize Halley, Eden's life coach, dressed in a clingy hot-pink kimono.

"Quite a party, isn't it?" she laughed as she took a plate of lo mein. "How are you? Everything good?"

"Great," I said, ordering a plate of sesame noodles.

"Look, between you and me, I realize Eden's been kind of a handful these days," said Halley. "I don't know if she told you, but she's going through some intensive 'me' time."

"Eden lives in a circular vortex of intensive 'me' time," I said, scanning the room for the quickest route out.

"This is special," Halley said. "She probably mentioned how we are reraising her from infancy?" When I stared at her blankly, she continued. "She just got in touch with her molestation after I hypnotized her last week. She is seeing the world through the eyes of a wounded child right now."

"What?" I said, so shocked I almost choked on my noodles. "I know Eden's family. Who molested her?"

"We're still not sure," said Halley, nibbling daintily on a fried wonton. "It might have been a family member or a friend of the family. Even a neighbor or teacher. She has stopped speaking to all of them while we are MapQuesting her anger." She dipped her wonton into hot mustard before she continued. "We all need to be patient with her. She's making wonderful progress. Every day she is closer to her walled-off self."

"Go, Eden!" I said, spotting a cooler full of Chinese beer, then grabbing a couple for the road. "Well, I gotta run," I said, absolutely intending to leave when the twenty-two-year-old slacker who squats on my soul like a drunken frat house version of Jiminy Cricket noticed the slit that ran up the side of Halley's dress. I could see a lot of thigh. She had great-looking legs.

"What about you, Gil?" said Halley, touching my forearm. "Eden tells me you play piano. Why did you stop?"

"Ah, it's all bullshit," I said, realizing that despite a pronounced lack of desire to talk to this woman, her tight kimono was holding me captive. The silky fabric was clinging to her in all the right places, and even better, all the wrong ones. "My mother used to make too big a deal out of it when I was a kid," I said, running on at the mouth while I MapQuested Halley's body. Turned out she had some very nice tits attached to her torso.

"You don't still make your decisions based on the approval of Mommy?" she said.

How had I missed seeing those tits the other time I met her?

"My brother's the star of the family. But my mother wanted two musical sons. In my case she failed," I mumbled on autopilot. I had no energy for this subject, but that goddamn twenty-two-year-old bonehead wanted to stand there and stare at her tits.

"Well, Mommy isn't around now, is she?" Halley said, with too much understanding.

"Not unless you count the yapping in my head," I said. This conversation was over. I was tumbling into a funk. "Gotta get to work. Sorry. Gotta run," I said, handing my dish to a waiter and ordering the twenty-two-year-old simpleton back into my subconscious for a time-out.

When I decided to grab a few more egg rolls and fried shrimp to eat for dinner, I bumped right into Eden. She was so preoccupied with bringing a plate of food and another drink to that Japanese architect, she never looked up or said hello.

28

The Son Shines Brightly

Fruity, Cheney, and Dink were beside themselves with joy to see me coming toward them with a full plate of food. Their happiness level increased exponentially with each egg roll that I offered. Once upon a time they had all played second fiddle to Jimmy. Not anymore.

Checking my messages, I was not pleased to learn that I had two from Jenny, the lolcat woman. "Hopingks evwe tink is tewtully . . ." was as far as I got before I deleted them both.

"Hi there," said Hayden, appearing unannounced at the top of the stairs in the guesthouse and scaring the piss out of me. I had forgotten Chad said he'd be staying down here.

"Dude," I said, "you scared me."

"Many apologies!" he replied cheerfully.

"Hey, no biggie," I said, not meaning a word of it. The phone rang.

"Sorry. I gotta take this," I said, seeing Sara's number. "Be with you in a sec."

"Fine," he said, descending the stairs and heading to the kitchen. "Mind if I make a pot of coffee?"

"There's a can in the fridge," I said, answering the phone. "Help yourself."

"Hi," said Sara. "I was just calling to apologize for being such a pickle yesterday. Seems like all I do is piss you off and then apologize."

"Not a problem," I said.

"I'm sorry things have been weird with us," she said. "Mind if I come over and talk about it?"

"Now?" I said.

"No, in a month. When neither of us can even remember what happened," she said. "Yes now. What's wrong with now?"

"Well, Chad's son, Hayden, is here. I have to show him around," I said.

"Chad has a son?" she said. "This is more BS, isn't it?"

"He's right here," I said. "You want to talk to him?"

"No," she said. "*You know what, Gil?* I give up. Why don't *you* call *me* when you have time to talk."

"I'll call you back in an hour," I promised, seeing an even bigger problem headed my way. Eden was coming down the path toward the front door.

"Hi!" she said, entering without knocking.

"Talk to you later," I said to Sara, hanging up quickly.

"How are you?" Eden said, coming toward me. "God, I

am so overstimulated. I drank a ton of Maotai. . . . It's that Chinese hootch? Did you try it?"

"Stay right where you are," I said softly but firmly, holding out my arms to prevent her approach.

"What? Why?" she said, continuing to come closer. "I came to tell you about my hot new fantasy. Check it out. I want to crawl under the piano while you play and—"

"No," I whispered, my heart beating rapidly. *"Not now."*

"Geez," she said. "It's coming back to me what it was like to be married to you."

"Stop," I said softly. "You find what you needed, Hayden?" I flashed my eyes at Eden to alert her to his presence in the next room.

"Yep, I think so," he called back.

"Oh!" said Eden. "Hi, Hayden! I just came down to tell you guys there's plenty of food left if you get hungry!"

"Maybe later," said Hayden, walking in with his coffee. "I'm good for now."

"Great!" she said, backing out the door. "Well, let me know if you need me to do anything . . ."

"Thanks, Eden," said the detective genially.

I sat down on the sofa with my beer and clicked on ESPN.

"You a Dodgers fan?" I said to Hayden.

"Not really," he said, sitting down with me on the sofa. "Mets."

"What's it like being a detective?" I asked him.

"Fun. Boring. Depends," he said.

"Where does this gig fall on the spectrum?" I asked.

"Not sure yet. Somewhere in the middle probably," he

said. "How long have you and Eden been renewing your marital vows?"

"What?" I said. "Me and Eden? No way. You need to do
your research, dude. We had a bad divorce. I don't need that
stress again."

"Mmm-hmmm," he said, watching me as I watched the
game. "Well, you seem like a nice guy. I thought I'd give you
a heads-up."

"What do you mean?" I said.

"I was here with a long-distance listening device last
week. I've got audio of you two going at it. Or that's what it
sounds like. I haven't done a voice print yet. Or checked
the video footage. I set up robot cameras all around here.
They're everywhere. I've nailed that architect too." He took
a sip of his coffee. "If I were you, here's what I'd do: I'd
write me a check for five grand, and take off. Make myself
scarce."

"Five grand!" I said. "Are you serious? I don't have that
kind of money."

"Gil," he said, "I've seen your bank account. I have your
monthly statement on my computer. You have $5,562 as of
this morning. I'll take cash or a check. I'm letting you keep
$562 for moving expenses."

"Why are you doing this to me?" I said. "Can't you get the
money from Chad? Isn't he paying you pretty well?"

"Couple reasons, Gil. And I'll tell you what they are. One:
I'm helping you learn a valuable lesson. I like that. Makes me
feel good about myself. If it hurt you less, you might not
really learn. Two: I like you. You seem like a nice enough
guy," he said. "This way, I know you'll never forget me.
Kinda heartwarming, really. And three: To be perfectly hon-

est, the power trip of it all makes me feel a little bit tingly inside. It's a real rush. I just dig it. It's why I love this job. I don't get that many perks, so I grab the ones I can. Excuse me. I gotta get a little more Coffee-Mate," he said, and then he got up and walked out of the room.

29

Apples and Snakes

*A*ccording to Hayden, or whoever he was, I had a day or two before the situation with Eden and Chad exploded for real. I decided not to stick around for the fireworks. Or open my big mouth to Eden. Better to let it all play out on its own. I'd paid enough of a price.

That evening I called Chad right after I talked to the PI. "I'm taking off tonight," I said to him.

"Dude, you don't have to go," he said. "I didn't mean for this to blow your whole schedule to hell."

"Yeah, I know," I said. "But I think it's better if I'm not around here until this all settles down." I didn't know if Chad suspected me. I didn't want to know.

"Fair enough," he said. "I like your work. If you want to finish the job you started, let's talk in a month."

Then I went looking for Jimmy. He was, as usual, lying on

the patio with his nap-centric family. "Come walk with me," I said to him. "I need to talk to you."

"Can I go instead?" said Jimmy's brother Gorgeous. He looked happier to see me than Jimmy did. It was tempting.

"Why don't we all come?" Jimmy said predictably.

"No," I said. "It's personal. I'm leaving town."

Jimmy got up and followed me, without complaint for a change.

"Why are you leaving?" he said. "It's paradise here."

"If you mean there are apples and snakes, you've got that right," I said.

"What happened?" he asked.

"Some other time," I said. "I'm taking off tonight and I'd like you to come with me."

"No way," he said, not willing to give it even a moment's thought.

"Would it make any difference if I said we might be going to stay with my family?" I said. "You're the big family guy. They'd be your family too."

"Not interested," he said.

"Well, it pains me," I said. "But, okay. You can stay here. That's how much I love you." It choked me up saying "I love you." Even to Jimmy.

"Excellent" was all he said. "Have a good trip." Then he turned and ran back to his family. And that was that.

I felt pretty blue as I walked back toward the house. My sense of abandonment was profound. I didn't belong anywhere. Everything I'd set up for myself had crashed yet again.

Midwalk, I heard footsteps and turned to see Eden running toward me. "You wanted to talk?" she said, catching her breath. "Can you believe how good I have gotten at event planning? Weren't you impressed? I should probably go into it for a living! I'll talk to Halley about it. Did you meet Sherry? Nicole Richie's producing partner? She has a Chinese baby girl same age as Mai Linn exactly. Well, two weeks younger. Come here. Give me a kiss. I deserve a reward."

"No," I said, jumping back, not sure where cameras were lurking.

"Why are you acting so weird?" she said.

"I'm leaving town tonight. I can't do this anymore," I lied, though not about everything. "Chad writes my checks. I don't like how all this duplicity feels."

"Is this a joke? You're making me feel really bad about myself," she said, sticking out her lower lip. "I thought we agreed we were both having a really nice time. Where are you going?"

"Chicago. Dubai. I don't know," I said. "Maybe I'll go camping. Maybe Yosemite."

"So you're going to just disappear in the middle of a job?" she said. "That's so unprofessional. I thought this was a good arrangement. Win-win, as they say. Boring Chad gets a glamorous, exciting wife. I get to have fun again. We achieve closure. Where's the downside?"

"I'm too old to be sneaking around," I said.

Before she could reach out and touch me, I jumped back. "No," I said. "Aren't you supposed to be dealing with a molestation or something?"

"Oh. Right. Halley's thing. She thinks everyone who uses sex as a negotiating tool was molested."

"Okay," I said. "I gotta go pack."

"That's it? Just like that? You're gone and that's the end?"

she said, a look of spoiled inconvenience on her face. "No 'Thanks for everything, Eden'?"

"Thanks for everything, Eden," I said as I headed back toward the guesthouse.

Now I had one more call to make. This was the one I was dreading most. I picked up the phone and called Sara.

"Hi," she said, sounding very chipper. "Good news! I finally got off my butt and made an appointment with a couples counselor."

"Great," I said.

"I know, right?" she said. "It took me long enough. I was holding out for a male counselor so there was kind of a wait. I didn't want you thinking there were a bunch of women ganging up on you. I know how you get. This is a program called Marriage Fitness. The guy who runs it is supposed to be one of the best in the business."

"That sounds fantastic," I said. "Unfortunately, we have to put him on hold. I'm leaving town."

"Oh?" she said after a long silence.

"I'm going to my mom's," I said. "She's not feeling well. She asked me to come."

"What's wrong with her?" she said, her tone shifting toward suspicion.

"They aren't sure yet. They're running tests," I said.

"This isn't just a way to get out of going to Marriage Fitness, is it?" she asked cautiously.

"Sara! How dare you accuse me of that! No, it is not," I said honestly because I had actually forgotten all about couples counseling. Although looking back at the whole mess, this was among the better of its unintended consequences.

"How long are you gone for?" she asked.

"Not sure. I'm playing it by ear. I'll call you from my mom's house," I said, right before we hung up.

"You know we're leaving tonight," I said to Fruity, Cheney, and Dink, expecting a negative response. But they could not have been more excited.

"Yay," they all said as they began leaping around in a frenzy. At least someone was unreservedly happy about this.

30

A Family Full of Geniuses

I like sunrise over the freeway, especially when I'm going camping. I always used to go camping. I don't know why I stopped. Sometimes you just stop doing things by accident, and then one day you wake up and it's been years and years.

Generally I drive in silence so I can take inventory. But today every thought in my brain pan was crashing into its hyperactive neighbor, like too many agates in a rock polisher. Only one thing was emerging as clear: Eden was officially too expensive for me to mess with. This was the second time our chemistry had emptied my bank account. It hadn't occurred to me that it was possible again. I'd been pretending that this time around she was refilling the coffers as an act of karmic debt. Precisely the kind of crazy idea I probably picked up from Sara, who believes that the universe works in symbolic ways and uses karma to achieve balance. Usually I'd argue with her when she said things like, "Look how often nature uses the circle as a recurring symbol of completion and wholeness." It sounded good, but it didn't take into account that the evidence also shows the circle as beloved by the people, put here just to mess you up. For me, it seems like they have always been women. It was Eden who set the wheels of that detective in motion heading toward me.

I thought about trying to stiff the detective somehow by disappearing the way people do on *Forensic Files*. But that was not what I wanted. I didn't want to live underground or to return to an L.A. full of enemies and paranoia. I wanted to resume my previous life when the Bremners left. So, although it filled every molecule of my being with cyclonic rage, I wrote that fucker a check for five thousand dollars. It was excruciating. I tried to think of it as a down payment on the funeral of my twenty-two-year-old id. The pain might remind me not to resuscitate him when he tried to come back from the dead.

Even worse was leaving Jimmy behind at Eden's house. But I didn't want to take him hostage. Now, as I drove, I worried about the trickle-down effect that Eden and Chad's split might have on their dogs. Was Eden going to get the house? Chad saw himself as the wronged party. I heard him call it "my house." He had the money to fight Eden for it. But he wasn't that much of a dog person. He seemed to run hot and cold. Would the dogs remain with him? Was she going to take them with her if she moved to an apartment?

As we left the L.A. metropolitan area behind us, the road that wound through the desert got increasingly more serene. I loved the balmy, uncomplicated look of all those pale green low-lying plants dotting a pale pink and light tan landscape. One thing I always looked forward to, before we left the I-10, was the big barren area dotted with cactuses that always seemed like they were waving hello. Sometimes when I made this drive, I wanted to run around and put hats on them all.

I'd come this way a half dozen times in the past few years, but this was the first time I was taking Fruity, Cheney, and Dink.

"You know, we've never gone anywhere with you without Jimmy," said Cheney.

"I guess that's true," I said. "I wonder why."

"Jimmy was kind of the star," said Dink. "Now that he's gone, I guess that responsibility falls to me."

"Bullshit," said Cheney. "I'm the acting alpha."

"Why? Because you're a guy?" said Dink.

"You guys, knock it off," I said. "I'm the goddamn alpha. Period."

"Well, then I'm the beta," said Cheney.

"I'm beta," said Dink. "I'm small, but I have more important ideas."

"The hell you do," said Cheney. "You don't even know the difference between inside and outside."

"I totally know the difference, I just don't let it define me," said Dink. "How do you think I so consistently know to pee inside if I don't know the difference?"

"You're supposed to pee *outside*," I said hopelessly. Talking to Dink was like talking to a drunk.

"Exactly," said Dink. "What great ideas does he have?"

"Well, whether you know it or not, I'm the one who came up with licking people's faces to make them think I like them when I'm actually grabbing a quick and easy snack. It doesn't occur to them that their faces are loaded with crumbs and oils and creams and, best of all, salt," said Cheney.

"*You* came up with that?" said Fruity. "I had no idea. I do that all the time."

"I also invented moving forward when they're scratching your ears until they're scratching your butt," he said.

"Bullshit," said Dink. "That's a classic. It's public domain."

"Are you saying that licking is *not* a sign of affection?" I said, shocked at what I was hearing.

"Well, I suppose it can be," said Cheney. "I mean, I wouldn't want to cop a snack off of the face of someone I hated. Unless we are talking about gravy residue." He took a deep breath and lay down in the back of the van, content that he had won the argument and could go back to sleep.

"Where did you say we're going?" said Fruity.

"To visit my biological family," I said.

"So even more snotty black dogs?" said Dink.

"No, that was Jimmy's family," I said. "This is my birth mother and my brother, Steve, and my mother's new husband, Milt, who I only met twice before. Shit, I don't think I told her we were coming."

Sunrise was at six-thirty. And it was a beauty. Watching the sunrise over a highway that stretches out ahead always seems to offer a boundless sense of possibility and optimism. It makes me feel like I am headed somewhere exciting where fantastic things might happen. Even though all those other sunrises on all those other roads full of boundless optimism and promise only led me here: to a van full of dogs on its way to visit my mother. One more good reason not to think about things too much.

Yet as I drove on, that sense of excitement felt so big and portentous that I put off calling my mother to tell her I was coming until the sun was up. Nothing can ruin a sense of imminent possibility quite as effectively as earnest questions about your future plans from the people who raised you.

"Milt Hruczak," said a man's voice when someone finally picked up.

"May I speak to Vera?" I said.

"Who may I say is calling?" he replied in a very deep, almost Johnny Cash–like voice, the pitch and speed of a cartoon villain.

"Her son Gil," I said. Instantly his tone got friendlier.

"Oh, Gil. Hi. Sorry, I didn't recognize your voice. Let me get her," he said. "Vera, it's your son."

"Oh my God. So early? Is something wrong?" I heard her squeal. "Gil? Is everything okay?"

"No, Mom. I mean yes," I said. "I'm about to get on the I-17. I was thinking I'd come visit for a few days."

"You're coming here? Today?" she said. Now she sounded agitated. "I wish you'd have given me a little advance notice. It's going to be tight. You know Steve's staying here for now, right?"

"I can sleep in my van," I said.

"Oh, don't be ridiculous," she said. "Of course you don't have to sleep in your van. It will be so wonderful to have both my boys here with me. Even if they only come to see me when they're broke."

"That's not why I'm coming," I said. "Well, it's not the *only* reason."

"Oh, you know I'm just giving you a hard time," she said. "Milt and I can't wait to see you. What time will you be here?"

"Maybe ten, ten-thirty," I said.

"Good. If I can wake up your brother by then, we can have brunch together. You remember how much Steve sleeps. Geniuses burn at a faster rate than the rest of us, I guess," she said. "I'm going to make your favorite: Belgian waffles."

"That's Steve's favorite," I said.

"But you'll eat them too, right?" she said, a note of panic edging into her voice as she ran down the list of other potential entrées also on tap. "I have a nice steak in the freezer. You can have an omelette. I could make hash."

"Mom, it's fine. I like your waffles," I said. What was it about spending time with my family that made hour thirty-seven of any visit the opening slip in an unstoppable slide down a slippery slope? Maybe we needed some bonding activity equivalent to the way lying on your side in the sun worked for Jimmy's family.

"How long is Steve in town for?" I asked.

"Now you sound like Milt," she said. "I haven't asked him yet. I don't want him to think that I'm giving him the bum's rush. He only got here two weeks ago, but he brought a lot of suitcases. You two have a nice rapport. You can ask him for me."

If Steve and I ever had a nice rapport, it was because he was never around. He dropped out of high school when I was in eighth grade. Then he didn't come back from Europe until I was in college. No one in our family heard much from him during those years. In my mother's mythology, he was off spreading his wings or sowing his oats or any other of a number of overused nature metaphors that supposedly describe the rites of passage for young men. I'm still not sure where he went. In some of his stories, he was on tour with a band. Maybe he just needed to get as far away as possible from my mother so he didn't have to fight with her over every decision he wanted to make for himself. She had her plans for him. He had his own.

I'd be lying if I said I'd missed him when he was gone. During that time, my status in the family changed for the better. I became the designated musical prodigy, wowing my mother with Mozart and Chopin and even the occasional original composition.

I probably pursued classical music because the Steve and his local legend had rock and roll all sewn up at our high school. I didn't want to be compared to him. I wanted my own identity. And I was fine until Steve wrote that bona fide hit. After that, the title of musical genius in our family was his alone. He ascended to the pantheon of the gods, and took my mother along with him for the ride. So eager was my mother to share this upgrade in her status with everyone that she had a shirt printed up that said UNDERCOVER ANGEL'S MOM.

Years later, when Steve was struggling unsuccessfully to write another hit, "coping with the burden of genius" became my mother's favorite topic.

I wasn't totally off the hook. All through high school I had to keep up the lessons and the recitals. I still had to enter the competitions so my mother could brag about them to her friends. I kept this whole part of my life a secret from the kids who knew me at school, since it offered no social advantage involving girls or cars. Those I was able to get from hanging out with wisecracking troublemakers and juvenile delinquents. Beautiful losers were unreliable, but they had sex appeal. Being part of that group provided me with just what I wanted: an identity that I could embrace without fear, because no one else in my family wanted anything to do with it.

Least of all my identity-starved mother. Back then, that meant everything to me.

Still, no matter how busy I was ascending the ladder of cool by flunking my classes, Mom continued to trot me out like a trained seal when her friends came to visit. "He's very talented," she would say to the ladies. Steve is our creative genius. But Gil is talented the way I'm talented. We're helpers, we're appreciators and organizers. We're facilitators."

Sometimes when I listened to my mother talk about my glorious abilities, it was almost like I was the one completely interchangeable element in my own autobiography.

{ 31 }

A Lot of Red

I pulled in to Sedona at about eleven-thirty, a little later than I'd expected because I stopped a few times for caffeine and to give my passengers bathroom breaks.

Sedona was such a stunningly beautiful place there was no reason to ever take photos, since hundreds of breathtaking photos of every scenic vista that looked just like the one you might take, but a little better, had already been posted online. Those eroded, ageless red cliffs rising out of forests in some places, deserts in others, looked like snapsnots from the dawn of time.

I was glad Mom and Milt had a condo there, even though it seemed like neither of them paid too much attention to their surroundings. Everything in Sedona, even their condo complex, was framed by a breathtaking, awe-inspiring view of some red rock horizon. At least this way even when they were in a mall arguing about where they'd parked the car, they might accidentally see something spectacular.

"A lot of red," Milt said to me the first time I gushed about it all. "After a while you get used to it. You don't see it no more."

"But you know what I like best about it?" my mother chimed in. "No matter how far you go, you're only five minutes from stores."

Before I pulled into their driveway I was hit by such a wave of anxiety that first I circled the block to stop at a market and buy a six-pack. Then I drank two bottles of Corona before I had the courage to drive up and park. The closer I got to their condo, the more I was haunted by an imaginary interrogation.

"So your mother tells me you lost your job," I imagined Milt saying.

"No! He did not! It just ended!" my mother would rush to my defense, shortening the length of my penis with every excuse she made for me.

I barely made contact with the doorbell before my mother appeared. She still looked, for her demographic sample, very attractive in a wholesome all-American way. When I was in grade school, all the kids used to say she looked like the lady in the Dentyne commercial. Now that she was in her seventies, with her dyed bright red hair and her tan, she was closer to the woman with the tennis racket who took Metamucil. Thrilled by my arrival, she enfolded me in a big perfumey bosomy embrace before I could say hello. Usually I broke away from her hugs before they were finished, because I was afraid they might never end on their own. This one ended abruptly.

"Are those dogs all yours?" she said, stepping back and lowering her voice as she looked down at the three dogs on the stoop with me.

"What dogs do you . . . ? Oh my God! Where'd all these dogs come from?" I joked. And then seeing no comprehension at all on my mother's face, I added, "Yes, they're mine. But they're all really mellow. They're a nice bunch. You'll like them."

"It's not about me," said my mother, lowering her voice to a stage whisper. "I told you, Milt doesn't like dogs. He doesn't want them in the house. Why don't you leave them in the van for now. Come in first and say hello. Have a cup of coffee. We'll break the news to him casually after he's eaten."

"Oh," I said, deflated, sorry I had no place else to go.

"Right back, you guys," I promised as I led the three dogs to my van.

"Bring us some of whatever that is she's cooking in there," yelled Cheney as I followed my mother back in through the front door. The little wooden table in her kitchen was all set with a white lace tablecloth and linen napkins. My mother was a flamboyant hostess who relished the spotlight that offering people a meal provided her.

"Coffee?" she asked. "I'm making waffles. In honor of having both of my boys here. Remember how when your father left the first time, we all used to sit and eat waffles?"

An image came to me of a very dark room years ago that smelled like syrup and corn bread. Somewhere in that room I could hear what sounded like crying. After Dad left, it felt cold and dark in that house. In my mind it looked like a burned-out bulb.

"We were the Three Musketeers on our first big adventure," my mother said, apparently remembering it differently. "The dragon was finally slain. At last we were free!"

"Well, I was only five. I remember being sad," I said.

"Oh, come on. You weren't sad. You were a happy child," she said. "You were already a whiz on the piano."

I could hear the dogs barking out in the van.

"Hey, dude," said Steve, appearing at the kitchen door wearing plaid drawstring pants and a gray T-shirt that said MOTÖRHEAD. *"Hola. ¿Cómo estás?"*

"Hey, bro," I said, getting up to shake his hand. Steve had put on some weight. He was four years older than me and my height, but at least forty pounds heavier.

"Gil?" I heard another voice, and Milt appeared at the door. Dressed in a perfectly ironed plaid shirt and tan slacks, Milt was slim, straight, and tall. He always reminded me of the postpresidential LBJ. "How are you, son? Nice to see you," he said, shaking my hand. "You look good. You been working out? Waffles again, Vera? You trying to kill us? This is the third time this week."

"Milt, when my boys are home, I always make waffles. You can have a poached egg if you want to be a pickle."

"Good! Don't overcook it like last time. So how was your trip, Gil?" asked Milt, hoisting up his slacks at the knees to prevent bagging as he sat down. My mother handed him a cup of coffee and he blew on it. "What're you driving?"

"I've got a Ford van," I said.

"What kind of mileage you get on that thing?" Milt asked. Slowly and methodically, he opened a packet of Sweet 'n Low. After first tapping it against the table a few times, he poured it into his coffee and began to stir it endlessly, as though it were difficult to dissolve.

"I don't know," I said, realizing I was out of things to say to him. "Fifteen, twenty."

"Not bad at all! What the hell is all that barking?" Milt looked puzzled and concerned.

"I have my three dogs waiting out in the van," I said. If Milt wanted to kick me out now, fine. I was foolish not to stay at a campground or a motel. Why hadn't I just gone to Sara's?

"Don't you want to bring 'em in?" he said. "It's not good to lock dogs in a car in the summer."

"That's what I told him," my mother chimed in as she removed two waffles from the iron. "I said, 'Bring 'em in, Gil,' but he was afraid they might upset you. I told him he had nothing to worry about." She winked at me.

"Don't be silly," said Milt. "I grew up with dogs, Gil. I love dogs. Go get 'em. They need water. It's hot in that car!"

{ 32 }

Before vs. After

*M*ilt fell in love with Dink as soon as I carried her into the kitchen. Cheney and Fruity followed behind.

"Look at that little wiener dog. Give her here. Let me hold her," Milt begged, reaching his arms out to me until I set Dink in his lap. Immediately she began to circle to get comfortable. By the time she had burrowed her pointy snout into the crook of his arm, she had won Milt's undying affection. "See what I mean, Vera? Dogs are crazy about me. I've been nagging your mother to let me get a dog, but she don't want to hear it."

"I had a dog once and she didn't like me!" said my mother petulantly. "Anyway, who do you think will get stuck having to walk the damn thing?" She handed me and Steve each a big plate of waffles adrift in a vast ocean of syrup. "How ironical that both of my boys are home at the same time. Something bigger than we are must be at work!" she said as she poured more batter onto the hot waffle iron. "Start! Eat your breakfast! Don't let everything get cold!"

"So why you in town, bro?" Steve asked, his mouth so full of syrupy dough that tiny little specks shot out when he talked, like sprays of sawdust from a rotary sander.

"The people I work for came back for a few weeks," I said. "Thought I'd do some traveling."

"What did I hear about you working for Eden or some crazy shit like that?" said Steve, shoveling in more waffles.

"Yeah, for a minute I did," I said, pretending to be preoccupied with stirring my coffee.

"Well, that's asking for it!" Milt laughed.

"And then asking for seconds," said Steve, giving a thumbs-up.

"Gil has been through so much!" clucked my mother, her voice filled with way too much empathy as she forked three big unasked-for pork sausages onto my plate. "When I think about everything we have all been through over the years . . . We should feel very good about ourselves. We are survivors."

"No wonder I'm bursting with pride," I said, rolling my eyes at my brother.

"I think my little grand-dogger here would like a snacky," said Milt, now using both hands to restrain the squirming Dink from charging the tabletop. He broke off a little corner of a sausage and held it in front of her as an offering. When she snapped at his fingers like a starved piranha, he dropped her suddenly. She landed on the floor with a thud. "Whoa. She tried to take my damn finger off," he gasped.

"Ah!" said Dink as she righted herself under the table. "It's good to be outside at last."

"Nooooo!" I said, diving for her a second too late. She

had already begun to squat and let out a big stream of urine. Leaping to my feet, I dropped a stack of napkins on top of it as camouflage, then hastily mopped up the mess before my mother noticed.

"See?" Dink said to me. "You thought I'd never learn."

"This is *inside*," I whispered urgently to her under the table. "Listen to me, Dink. This is important. While we're here at Mom's, give me a sign *before* you have to pee. I'll carry you outside."

"When you say 'before,' you mean like now?" she asked.

"This is *after*. We'll talk later," I said to her as I casually tried to rejoin the group.

"When you're done eating, Gilbo, move your suitcases into the guest bedroom," said my mother, tucking into the plate of waffles she'd made for herself. "Did you already tell him, Steve? I moved your old bedroom furniture in there. How much fun is that?"

"I don't think I can quantify it," I said, my head spinning at the thought of a forty-seven-year-old man and a fifty-one-year-old man side by side atop the same beds they had occupied when they were eight and twelve.

33

Starting Another Empire

*A*fter I moved my suitcases, I took out my phone to call Sara. She picked up on the first ring.

"Hi," I said. "It's me. I'm at my mom's."

"You sound tense. You must be eating red meat," she said.

"Just breakfast sausage so far," I said, "but it's still early in the day. My mother's a pretty meat-intensive menu planner. I think she even puts beef in her chocolate pudding."

"How anyone who has given birth to an innocent creature herself can endorse the wholesale slaughter of other sentient beings, I don't know," she said. "If you want to endorse cruelty, I suppose you have that right. Although it certainly seems to me that a forty-seven-year-old man should be able to make his own dietary decisions with a clear conscience."

"My mom's cooking is the best thing about being here," I said.

I could hear Sara exhale through her nose. Why did every

damn one of these broads care so much about what I ate? "Everything else okay?" she said. "How's your mother? What was wrong with her again?"

"Well, all different things. Ladies' problems," I said, not eager to try my luck by picking one. "They're running tests. How are you?"

"Fine," she said. There was a silence.

"Something wrong? Are you mad at me?" I said.

"What do you think?" she said.

"I think yes," I said. "But I am not sure why exactly."

"Well, then, I suggest you sit quietly sometime during the next twenty-four hours and replay the last few weeks of our relationship in your head. See if anything comes to mind," she said.

"So I should call you back some other time?" I said, trying to sidestep the whole thing. I turned to see that my mother was standing in the doorway, watching, listening.

"She's not the one for you," my mother said, shaking her head slowly, as I clicked the phone shut. "A mother knows that sort of thing." She came into the guestroom and shut the door behind her. Then she sat down on the edge of Steve's empty bed and stared at me, her eyes filled with far too much sympathy. "Don't let a woman like that wear you down! Because they will! I have seen it! They will wear you down!" she cautioned. "She knows your value. She knows that you're a catch. I brought both you boys up to be the kind of husband I would want."

"Too bad you and Milt got married before I could make my move," I said.

"Oh, you!" said my mother, rolling her eyes and laughing. "Speaking of which . . . Gil, can we talk about something?"

"Would it make any difference if I said no?" I said.

"I'm worried about your big bwudda," she said, her face assuming a wide-eyed look of concern.

"Why?" I said, hoping if I didn't react it might all go away. "He seems okay."

"I think he's depressed about his career," she sighed. "He hasn't made much progress with his music in a while now. His income's down. There are those back taxes he owes. He won't talk to me about it the way he talks to you."

"What about all the royalties from 'Undercover Angel'?" I said. "They still play that damn thing on oldies stations. I hear it at the supermarket. I hear it at the gym."

"He says the government is trying to screw him." She sighed again. "You know how Steve is about business details. He's not levelheaded like you are. It's the blessing and the curse of his creative genius. I'm so proud of you both. You two are my gifts to the world, but I believe we were all put here to help each other. Steve still has his God-given star power. No one can take that away. But we need to help him focus and pull out of his slump. Would you mind talking to him?"

"About focusing his star power?" I said.

"Well, I think the burden of it all has pushed him off the right track," she said. "All the kids out in Hollywood these days are having this problem." She looked very dispirited for a moment. "Oh! I almost forgot! I saved this to show you!" She reached into her front pocket and handed me a scrap of plastic-coated paper that she had cut from a package. It was a picture of two blond men in their thirties labeled "Mitch and Kyle McMullen: Our Story." "Read it. It's short," she said, staring at me, waiting for me to begin. "It's all about how these two handsome brothers shared a love for coffee. So they pooled their talent, and the next thing you know, they had their own empire. See? It can be done!"

"What can be done? You're thinking I should open a coffee business with Steve?" I said.

"No, no. The point is that when brothers work together on something they love, two heads are bigger than one," she said.

Like clockwork, Steve stuck his head in the doorway.

"What's going on?" he said.

"I'll leave you two alone," said my mother, winking at me as she exited. "A word to the wise: Instead of coffee, think music!"

Steve sat down on his bed. "What was that all about?" he asked me. Between his height and weight, the bed vanished beneath him and he almost appeared to be levitating.

"You don't want to know," I said.

"These are some skinny-ass little beds," said Steve, leaning his back up against the faded plaid headboard, cowboy boots straight out in front of him. I'd looked at that headboard and found it depressing even in junior high. Now it was repeating on me like spoiled shrimp salad. There were oil spots that wouldn't come out from where Steve had been leaning his product-filled hair.

"Kinda weird that Mom saved 'em," I said, nodding, aware now of a creeping dark shadow growing larger inside me.

"Yep," said Steve. "Bizarre. You got any dope on you?"

"No," I said, starting to worry that the shadow might smother me, suffocate me.

"Damn," he said. "Well, Sedona. Shit, it should be pretty

easy to score some weed around here, wouldn't you think? It's so spiritual-retreaty."

"I would think. So how's everything, Steve?" I said, suddenly an obedient little boy on a fact-finding mission for Mommy.

"Fine," he said. "You?"

"Fine," I said. "Anything bothering you?"

"Nothing a nice juicy blunt wouldn't help," he said. "If you could help me figure out who the go-to guy is in this town. You got friends here?"

"Nope. 'Fraid not," I said. "Anything new? You seeing anyone?"

"You heard about Kaitlin?" he said.

"No, I don't think so," I said.

"Belly dancer at the Persian restaurant where we used to play in Portland? Gorgeous set of knockers. I still think of those girls and weep."

"And?" I said. Steve seemed stoned already.

"She flipped out on me," he said. "Went completely bonkers. Caught me with her friend Alyssa. She's in prison now for forgery. I'm 0 for 2 in the great city of Portland."

"Sorry to hear that," I said.

"Yep," he said, taking out a pack of Camels and offering me one. I grabbed for it eagerly.

"You playing out much these days?" I asked, lighting up. Nothing like spending time in the bosom of my family to make me happy I had started smoking.

"Yeah, sometimes. Mostly sixties and seventies covers. We do 'Angel,' " he said, lighting his cig and inhaling deeply. "Shit like that."

"Been writing at all?" I asked him.

"Yeah. You know," he said, puffing, exhaling, looking up at the ceiling, "this and that. I've got some demos. Someone is thinking of a musical based on 'Angel.' I said, 'Right on, man. Send me a check.' I'm waiting on that."

"So you've got a couple irons in the fire," I said.

"Exactly," he said. "Irons in the damn fire."

"How long you here for?" I asked him.

"Till Mom freaks out," he half giggled, "or Milt kills me with a claw hammer." He took a big drag on his cigarette.

"So you're cool with that?" I asked him.

"I told you I lost my apartment, right? So here's what I'm thinking: She cooks, she cleans, she does my laundry. That's three things Kaitlin never did. I've got my laptop so I can download. Know what I'm saying? Want to go shoot some pool later? I'm thinking a pool hall might be the place to buy dope."

On my way out of the house to walk the dogs, my mother stopped me. "So?" she said, her eyes searching for answers.

"Well, I talked to him," I said.

"Is he okay?" she asked.

"Seems fine to me," I said.

34

A Parade of
Meaningful Moments

$\mathcal{H}$ere's what my mother had in common with Sara: an obsession with meaningful moments. Every time I saw her she'd try to engage me in a round of mommy worship. When we passed in the hall, we had to have an intensely familiar personal exchange—a bigger than necessary mutual experience that only we two could share. My mother's glances were never neutral. Every time she looked at me, I could see her assuming, expecting, or inferring something about me. Every facial expression I made was a thing she used to define me.

"Oh, here comes Mr. Grumpy Face," she'd say if I looked taciturn. Or "Here he comes, the Maestro! Arturo Toscanini!" if I looked confident. Everything I did was something typical I always did. If she approved, then it was the family genetics shining through me. And if she didn't, then it was an example of how I was Just Like All Men.

Even that very first day, I had to get out of there right after breakfast to clear my head. Somehow Mom, Milt, and Steve seated at the same table seemed to lower the oxygen level in a room.

"I'm taking the dogs out for a hike," I said, heading out the front door, the dogs in tow. "Need anything at the store?"

"Yes! Will you pick up a container of orange juice for me, sweetie? And a thing of low fat cottage cheese!" she cooed. "What a lovely guy. You were always the considerate one."

"You know I never drink Tropicana," she said, scowling when I returned a few hours later with her order. "How can you possibly not know that by now! You don't pay attention. Your father did that too. Why are men so selfish and self-absorbed?"

"I don't think all men are selfish and self-absorbed," I said reflexively.

"Oh, come on. Not you," she said. "You boys take everything I say so literally."

Of the dozens of repetitive daily rituals in my mother's household, the most difficult one for me was right after dinner.

The meal itself I could handle because my mother was a great cook. Dinnertime was her chance to take center stage. All we had to do was show up with clean hands and enjoy the show. Everything my mother cooked came with a lesson plan. "This is Kobe beef from Japan, where they massage the cattle before they kill them. It acts like a tenderizer," she said, casually broaching a topic that would have made Sara's blood vessels burst.

The difficult part came during dessert, when my mother liked to encourage (read: force) her sons to provide her with postmeal entertainment. In grade school, when this grating tradition first got a foothold, we volunteered willingly, eager to compete for some extra attention from our bickering parents. Dad was still in residence then, but drinking too much. He was in and out of our lives for six more years before he sat us both down, pretty much out of the blue, to explain he was moving to Norway. "Take care of your mother," he said. Then he showed me how to write a check. The next day he was gone, never to return.

Once she was alone, Mom became more emotional and demanding. She also became needier and more melodramatic. The more I tried to be helpful, the more Steve tuned her out. We were both relieved when she finally married Milt on her fifty-seventh birthday. Milt became her focus. The pressure was off of us. It was unsettling to see that she was hell-bent on reviving this embarrassing ritual.

The second night I was there, my mother invited the people who owned the condo next door to come over for pie and coffee. I don't remember their names. They had vague older people's names like Irv and Betty or Morris and Helen. I never learned them because my mother dominated the conversation so hard that their names became completely irrelevant.

"Vera was telling everyone at the last tenants' meeting about how talented the two of you are," the female neighbor said. My mother smiled proudly as she divvied up her homemade chocolate pudding pie into six equal portions.

"You're going to get a chance to see if I was exaggerating!" said my mother, smiling and confident.

"No, Mom," I said.

"Seriously, Mom. No," said Steve.

"Come on, Mom. No," we both said repeatedly for a full

five minutes. Soon she was giving us each the "How much do I ever ask of you? Don't let me down" stare. And even after that, I still fought for a while longer, trying to set a precedent for the rest of my stay.

But she won eventually. Depriving a woman in her mid-seventies of a chance to be proud of her family seemed somehow sadistic. So I sat down at the piano and played Beethoven's Piano Concerto Number 5 in E-flat major. I knew she loved Beethoven. I figured if I acquitted myself of this obligation at least once, it would be over and done with. She gazed at me worshipfully when I was finished, with a glazed-over expression that reminded me more of a fan than a mom.

Then she cut short the business of accepting kudos on my behalf in order to introduce the headliner. Her pièce de résistance.

"My older boy, Steve, is an accomplished musician of a very different sort," my mother began. "Both my sons are multitalented. But Steve is particularly beloved for a certain song that became an American standard in the seventies when it rocketed up and up the charts to the very top, where it stayed for five weeks. Five full weeks!! In the top five! More than a month! And after that, another eleven weeks in the top forty. A total of sixteen weeks! That's four months for one song! That must be some kind of a record! Do you want to tell them how you came to write it, Steve?"

Steve stood there, looking at his feet, biting his lower lip, and strumming his guitar nonchalantly. When he didn't jump into the story quick enough, my mother jumped in for him. "He was playing at a club in Prague. Correct me if I'm wrong." Steve nodded. "It was dark and cold and Steve was homesick from touring. And while he was waiting to go onstage, he started to remember a time when he and his mommy were watching *Charlie's Angels* together on the TV. We were eating popcorn and drinking cocoa like we always did, and Steve looked over at his sweet little mother all bundled up in her quilt and thought that she looked like an angel. So he started to make up a song, right, Steve? A little song, to make him less homesick. All about an angel under the covers. And now you know the rest of the story." She ended with a very bad Paul Harvey impression that made her neighbors laugh. "Did I do that justice, Steve?"

"Yes ma'am," said Steve, still looking at the floor, plucking at his guitar.

"Do you know how thrilling it is to have been present at the birth of a moment now etched in the fabric of American culture?" said my mother, making a waving hand gesture she must have learned by watching *The Price Is Right*. Steve obediently took her cue and launched into his song.

The faces of my mother's friends lit up with delight as Steve began to sing "Undercover Angel." They even clapped along with the beat and then sang the "I said, Whaaat? Oooo weee" part in the chorus. People always liked that part for some reason. That was the part that gave me the butt clench.

"Vera! Who knew you were such a muse!" said Mr. Condo Next Door.

"I am blessed!" said my mother, biting her lower lip and nodding. "It's hard to comprehend that my little body created all this musical talent!"

I looked over at Steve, then looked down at my watch. "Beer-thirty," I said.

"I'll take one," Steve said.

"Get you a beer, Milt?" I offered politely on my way to the

refrigerator, before I realized that my mother's husband had fallen fast asleep. His mouth was slightly ajar and he was snoring gently.

"Well, we'll say good night to everyone now," said Steve after drinking his beer in one enormous swallow. "Gil and I are going to go look for a place to shoot pool."

"You boys be good!" said my mother. She winked happily as I followed Steve out the door to his pickup truck. "The way those two fought as kids, it's so nice to see them be friends!"

"Bro, do you mind driving?" Steve said when we got out of earshot. "I'm a little wasted. I couldn't face that shit tonight without getting loaded."

"I'm glad to hear that bothered you as much as it did me," I said.

"Doing the trained-monkey thing for guests? Someone please kill me," he said. "I mean, Mom doesn't ask all that much of us. But Jesus fucking Christ."

As we drove, I realized how comforted I was by his brotherly camaraderie. It made me feel bad about all those years we'd blown being hostile and competitive with each other for no good reason. Maybe it was a buildup from feeling so alone and backed into a corner by everything that had happened with Eden and Chad and Sara, but I wanted to make amends. Steve and I were blood. We had a lot in common. It seemed a shame we weren't closer.

"Steve," I said, "I just want to apologize for being a shit to you all these years. We've had a lot of stupid pointless fights. Seems dumb to me now. I'm ashamed of myself."

"Hey, no big deal, bro," he said. "Don't even think about it."

"Well, thanks," I said, noticing that he didn't apologize back. "I think I've always been on your case because I was jealous of the way Mom admires you so much," I went on. "Seems ridiculous now. Who wants all that attention from her? Besides, you deserve the praise. You did real well for yourself. I'm impressed with you, bro. And I'm proud of your success."

"Wow. Thanks," said Steve. "Right back at ya."

"Nah . . . I'm still struggling," I said. "I waste too much time. I'm a fuck-up. I'm always a paycheck away from being a homeless bum. It took me to forty-seven to start straightening this crap out. I'm a late bloomer. But I guess there's still hope."

"Ain't no bum that can play no Beethoven's sonatas," said Steve as we slowly cruised the town of Sedona, looking for the dive with the rowdiest clientele so he could score. We made a couple of stops at different bars. They all looked too clean, too full of amethyst crystals, fake Tiffany glass, and kachina dolls.

Finally, way at the end of a strip mall that was mostly turquoise jewelry stores and souvenir shops, we saw the reflective front window of a pool hall. Steve was ecstatic.

I sat down at the bar out front and ordered a Guinness. "I'll meet you back here in a few," Steve said, heading off to the back room.

By the time I was nursing my third beer, I was tired and growing resentful that my brother was still missing in action. Only an hour after our big reconciliation, Steve was pissing me off. I paid my tab and set out to find him.

He wasn't in either of the two big pool rooms off the bar, so I followed the exit signs out to a crowded back parking lot.

There, at one end, was my brother, all stretched out in the back of a Lexus, smoking a doobie with a couple of women. He wasn't hard to find. I just had to follow the strains of "Undercover Angel," which he was singing a cappella at full volume. I couldn't believe my ears.

"Dude, come join us. This is Lynn and I forget your name?" he said to the fiftyish platinum-haired one in the front seat when I came up to the car window.

"Sandra," she said.

"Sandy!" he said. "This is Gil, my bro. Here, dude. Sit down. There's room right here by Sandy."

"Nah," I said. "No offense, but I'm beat. I'd like to get out of here."

"Come on! It's early! Join us!" said whichever one was younger.

"You can take my truck," Steve said. "The ladies will give me a ride home tonight, right?"

"Of course!" said the one sitting next to him. "Let us buy you some dinner. How often do we get a famous rock star to give a free concert in our very own car?"

{ 35 }

The Price of Stardom

From the moment I woke up the next morning, I felt embarrassed about everything. Especially about agreeing to play music for my mother and her friends. I knew my mother. Now she'd be drunk with power from the praise and compliments she'd collected last night. She would be jonesing to do it again. She would invite more people to dinner. She might even try to make it happen every night that Steve and I were both here.

"How many more days?" said Cheney.

"I'm not sure," I said. "Why? Do you like it here?"

"I like that we get to sleep outside," said Dink sweetly as she lay beside me on my pillow. "It's easier to remember where to pee because all I have to do is—" I jumped out of bed, scooped her up in my arms, and raced outside with her. That was the first time I noticed that Steve's bed was unslept-in.

"Remember our new plan, Dink," I said while I waited for her and the other dogs to finish their business in the back-yard. "Let me know *before* you have to pee. Like you just did. That's what you need to do next time."

"Okay," she said, beaming with pride when she was done. "I had to pee."

"Yes. Very good. But you just told me *after*," I said. "When you first woke up was *before*. We had time to take you *outside*. So do that again, just that way. You are a good girl!"

As I was cleaning up the yard after everyone did their business, I began hatching a plan. I really resented being an opening act for Steve. If my mother was going to drag us through this same mud again tonight, I needed to figure out a way to make it all tolerable.

I took out my laptop and Googled the Billboard top ten for 1977. My idea was to assemble a classically styled piano medley made up of all of the lamest seventies hits from Steve's big moment of glory. I would place "Undercover Angel" into the context in which it originally ascended, alongside the other contenders for the throne, like "Car Wash" and "Rich Girl." My mother and Milt would miss the sarcasm and think I'd been very creative. Steve would laugh, though it would also piss him off a little. First thing I needed to do was download the sheet music to all the songs.

That was when I saw for the first time that "Undercover Angel" was registered to BMI and was written by Alan O'Day. After the initial shock, I seemed to recall Steve explaining something about using a pseudonym in order not to blemish his metal-shredding credentials. I remembered him fretting that a mainstream pop song might ruin his street cred. It all seemed silly. I never gave it any more thought.

I had never done a Google search on Steve before because in the late seventies, when the song came out, the Internet wasn't around. I got my first computer in the mid-nineties. When I finally did, the last thing I wanted to do was hear any more about Steve. But now, sitting there on our old beds, I was suddenly curious. I typed his name into the search engine, and then I braced myself for an onslaught of praise and publicity. It would make me jealous. It would piss me off. But so what? It was high time I got over this crap. Having lectured myself at length in this vein, I inhaled and clicked.

And there it was: Nothing at all. No mentions of my brother whatsoever. But oddly enough, there were ten million mentions of Alan O'Day. And videos too. Full of someone who was not my brother but who sounded like my brother. There with all kinds of interviews, links to his other music, fan sites, downloads.

It was so weird that I just kept trying different tag words, looking for different results. Nothing produced a reference or a link to my brother. There were even a couple other guys named Steve Winowiscz. One was a chubby red-faced sales rep for a packing materials manufacturer. The other one was a firefighter. Just for the heck of it, I tried Googling Chad and Sara. Both had pages of listings. Even Jimmy's name came up four times. But there was not a single entry about my brother. Not one reference to his musical career. How was it possible that this had never occurred to me before? Why had I never gone into the store to buy the sheet music? Well, for one, I didn't want to waste my money. And I didn't own a copy of the song or the album because Steve had given me a special cassette of the recording session. When I'd listened to it that first time years and years ago, I remembered, I'd thought that the song sounded like the kind of fluff I expected from Steve. He always wrote dumb songs full of silly, catchy riffs and pop references. Nothing had really seemed out of place.

But today this revelation was so unsettling and disorienting that I left the house without even having a cup of coffee.

"Where are you going?" my mother called to me as I was leaving. "Where's your brother? Tell him to wake up and come get breakfast."

"I guess he's still on a date," I called to her as I led the dogs out to my van. "I'll be back in about an hour."

We drove to one of the many breathtakingly beautiful state parks that were only a few minutes from my mother's condo. I parked in the lot, and the dogs and I headed down a steep trail toward some big smooth boulders that followed the path of a creek. They were so slick and eroded from centuries of rivers and oceans rising and falling that they now provided an almost level path. Fueled by anger, but also in a strangely dissociative state, I hiked toward a wooded area where signs warned us that dogs were not permitted. I didn't care. If the park rangers arrested me, I would take advantage of the opportunity to vent some of this crazy rage.

"How can you be mad in a place like this, where balls are produced naturally?" Cheney said, carrying a big, round, smooth stone in his mouth to drop at my feet.

"I can't throw this for you. If you catch it, it'll knock the teeth out of your head," I said to him as he stared at me relentlessly. "Hey, I've got a question for you guys. What if you found out someone wasn't who they said they were?"

"Like what happened to Jimmy?" said Fruity.

"No, it's not like that," I said. "I never told Jimmy that . . . See, he didn't understand that . . . He, well, the thing is . . . Jimmy jumped to his own crazy conclusions based on . . . Shit. I guess to him it was kind of the same thing."

We walked in silence for a while. The pastel earthtones of the eroded sandstone walls around us provided a sort of a gorgeous but eery diorama of the last few million years of the earth's surface. Dinosaurs were around for 165 million years. Now it was almost as if they had never really existed but were just another set of fantasy creatures from some dumb summer blockbuster. Everything about the way we all lived now was so surreal. Fact and fiction were scrambled every day. So why did it matter who wrote "Undercover Angel"? Who the hell cared, except for my mother, and maybe Alan O'Day's mother? What could be gained by dwelling on such a meaningless family scandal? Although I guess one of the things that galled me was that if Steve just made it all up, he could have had his choice of many much better songs. Now I could say it. I hated that song. And I hated the zesty, impish glee with which it was sung by whoever sang it. I'd been trying to like it all these years, simply to honor my family. I'd assumed my harsh feelings were rooted in jealousy. But no. It was just a song that I hated. Steve owed me big for all the time I'd wasted trying to like it.

But, I reprimanded myself, I had to take responsibility for being so naïve and gullible. Shit. I'd always known that Steve was a liar. I'd known it since we were kids. There had been dozens of examples. He had lied about girls, about grades, about jobs, about money. He'd probably lied about that brand-new Porsche he'd told me he'd owned but totaled. I'd never seen it. Strange that there were no photos.

Steve was a weasel. The last time I'd stayed at his house, he'd shown me a plastic baggy full of pieces of fat that he kept stored in his freezer so he could use them to get refunds taking half-eaten steaks back to Von's market. All that work and risk just to collect *most* of a free steak.

Steve and I had been out of touch when "Undercover Angel" originally came out. Now I wondered about those years. Had Steve ever been in Prague? We accepted it unquestioningly. It wasn't hard to believe that Steve was hitching around Europe. My mother was so into the idea of Steve as a creative genius, it never occurred to either of us that Steve's most creative act had been constructing a really effective web of lies.

To give him credit, he had picked a song that was big enough to be impressive and yet small enough to not really be worth the research. I hoped the real guy who wrote and performed that song had gotten even half as much pussy, praise, and glory from it as Steve had.

I spent the rest of that afternoon and most of dinner debating how to handle the whole thing. Should I let my brother know I'd found out? How would I tell him? What would bringing up the whole subject provide, except a chance to deflate the overblown pride and destroy the bragging rights of a desperate old woman and ruin the high of a stoned guy?

36

The Drummer's
Father-in-Law

*T*hat night for dinner my mother invited Eleanor Pope, the president of her condo's tenants' union. Mrs. Pope was a woman in her seventies. Her big, stiff white hair and white sparkly accessories gave her the appearance of someone who might have been in the original cast of *Dallas* three decades earlier. "Eleanor's daughter teaches ninth-grade math," my mother said by way of an introduction to my brother, who had arrived home from his date the previous night only two hours before. He and I both nodded so matter-of-factly with such identical mute expressions it was almost as if we had been brought there from the same special ed class.

Dinner was my mother's special chicken marengo, complete with oratory about its creation by Napoléon's chef during a battle. Accompanying it was a nice Beaujolais and a big dose of Milt feeling the need to prove that 9/11 was an inside job arranged by government agents. As he wrapped up his conspiracy explanation, my mother brought out her special glasses for serving port. It was a sign that her badgering about after-dinner entertainment would begin in earnest. I had consumed three beers already, along with the wine and now liqueur. The drunker I got, the less enthusiasm I had for my snarky seventies medley. Overcome by compassion, instead I just played Beethoven's Piano Concerto Number 5 in E-flat major for the second time in two days. This time I made a few more mistakes because I was angry. My mother didn't seem to notice. She was preoccupied by gazing at me with that seductive yet off-putting glazed expression that had led me by the nose through the most confusing days of my childhood.

"I still can't get over how I was able to create something so beautiful," she chimed in as soon as I had finished playing, effectively rerouting any praise that might have been directed toward me.

"Vera, time to get over it," Milt said, grinning. He winked at us. "Tell yer mom it's time."

"It's time," Steve and I said in unison.

"You don't know what it's like to raise a child and sacrifice your own opportunities," my mother continued beatifically, as though she were channeling the Holy Spirit. "You do it willingly, out of love and a sense of duty. Sometimes you have your secret regrets. But then you wake up one morning to find that you have suddenly fulfilled your artistic destiny in a way you never expected." My mother beamed at my handsome brother to signal that it was his turn. Steve, however, was so stoned that he hadn't gotten up from the dinner table yet, even though the rest of the group had moved into the living room. He stumbled a little when he tried to stand, knock-

ing over an empty wineglass as he reached to retrieve his guitar from behind an upholstered chair.

"Okay," he said, starting to strum the opening bars of
"Take This Job and Shove It." Apparently he was going to
make them all wait for their orgasm.

"He didn't write *that* one," my mother explained to her
friend in a loud whisper, rolling her eyes. "But he could have.
And so could I!"

"I wish I would have," said Steve. "Fuck."

"Or at least have just said you wrote it," I mumbled.
Luckily no one seemed to hear.

"Both of my boys have lived such hard lives. It makes me
even prouder of all they've accomplished," my mother said
theatrically.

"Beer-thirty!" I said, heading for the kitchen to grab a few
cans from the fridge. Milt, stretched out on the Barcalounger
with Dink snuggled tight into the crook of his arm, held up
his hand to catch one. "This little dog loves her grandpa," he
kept saying, as Dink dive-bombed him with kisses. I suspected it was because his face was encrusted with a thin
glossy layer of marengo.

"Okay. Get ready," said my mother to her friend as Steve
hit the opening chords of "Undercover Angel." Her face was
illuminated with delight as she began to mouth the lyrics, like
she and Steve were Lennon and McCartney.

"The joy of motherhood! My boys showed me my purpose in life," my mother said to her friend as Steve ended the
song with a flourish of Pete Townshend windmill moves. My
mother humbly accepted the smattering of applause and then,
for her encore, brought out a homemade cheesecake. "It was

God's plan for me to bring two great talents into the world," she went on. "Now I'm working on His plan B. My dream is that my two boys will collaborate on something fantastic. Steve, did Gil show you that clipping about the brothers who started a coffee empire? You two could do something like that!"

"Whaddya say, Steve? Should we open a coffee empire?" I joked.

"Yes! You should!" said my mother. "But with music! Not coffee! Gil, you're a team captain, like me. You need someone with a spark. Steve, you have that spark but you need an organizer. Gil can be your nuts-and-bolts guy. What a fantastic pairing. Am I right, Eleanor?"

"Sounds wonderful to me," said Eleanor, finishing up the cheesecake on her plate and licking her fork.

"Eleanor knows a little something about teamwork," said my mother. "Her husband was a basketball coach."

"I'm sure your boys could do whatever they set their minds to," said Eleanor. "Can I have another smidgen of cheesecake? I shouldn't, but it's so light. I don't like cheesecake that's too heavy or rich."

"Come on, Gil. You know I'm right," Mom said, staring at both of us with a face that said, "I know what's best for you."

"Mom, Gil and I don't really sync up creatively," said Steve, slurring his words, when he was finally able to speak. "We're two very different people. He's all fancy and shit. I'm more, you know, basic. Commercial."

"Exactly. A perfect team," said my mother. "You're yin. He's yang. Between the two of you, you have it all. Like Sonny and Cher. Like Hillary and Bill. Like Laurel and

Hardy. Like me and Milt. Tell me you'll give it some thought and make your brilliant mother happy!"

"Gil doesn't even get what I do," Steve said in a peevish tone of voice that I hadn't heard him use since junior high. "It'd be kind of like if Lang Lang sat in with the White Stripes."

"So I'm the novelty showboat but somehow you're Jack White now?" I said, feeling pushed. "I have a better idea. Why don't you team up with Alan O'Day?" It was too late. The twenty-two-year-old dude was uncorked. "You two have a lot in common. Build your empire with him."

"Who?" said my mother.

"The guy who, according to Wikipedia, gets the royalty checks for 'Undercover Angel,' " I said. Steve turned notably pale. And he was a very white guy.

"First of all, I told you millions of times that I am Alan O'Day. That is my pen name," said Steve, impressively calm. "And second, Wikipedia is 100 percent bullshit. Anyone can write anything in there. That is proven."

"Then who is the guy in all the videos and the online archives? Some virtual reality corporate figurehead, like Betty Crocker?"

"What are you two talking about?" said my mother. "What's Wikidemia?"

"Nothing important," said Steve. His voice was full of the kind of anger we'd both been sidestepping since I'd arrived. "More Internet BS."

"Okay, okay," I said. "Forget it. I don't even care. It doesn't fucking matter."

"That picture and those videos were a joke," said Steve. "The guy is my drummer's father-in-law, okay? My band and

I got drunk one night and took his picture. *We* thought it was funny. *He* thought it was funny. Now it's got a life of its own."

"What are these two on about now? I don't get it, do you?" said my mother to her friend. "They've been going at each other like this since they were in grade school. Gil has always given his brother a hard time. And they wonder why I treat them like children."

"All men are children," said Eleanor.

"Amen! You said it!" said my mother. "Enough of the sibling rivalry, you two. You're both superstars in my eyes."

"I gotta go make a few calls," I mumbled, taking my beer and my phone with me into the back bedroom. At the same time Steve disappeared into the bathroom. Seconds later, the unmistakable smell of marijuana began wafting out from under the door.

I tried like hell to place a call to the Bremners, hoping they might somehow be leaving ahead of schedule. They didn't have a service or an answering machine. The Bremners were at an age where they didn't want to be bothered.

"I can't stay here much longer," I said to the dogs as they sat staring at me, expressionless while I checked my messages. I only had one. It was from Chad, so I called him back.

"Hey, buddy. Just calling with an update. Mission accomplished. I busted Eden," he said. "The PI got photos of her in a full lip-lock with that fucking architect. In flagrante delicto. How sick is that?"

"Really?" I said.

"Yep," he said. "I was paying this guy a salary to do my wife. Talk about a sign we're in a recession. The PI thinks there was another guy too. He says he's got footprints, cigarette butts, fingerprints, but can't ID him yet. He thinks the guy got hip to the robot cameras and stopped coming around."

"Wow," I said.

"Dude, this sucks. But it's also a big relief," he said. "I feel calmer knowing I wasn't making the whole thing up."

"Definitely," I said. "So what now?"

"Well, E took the kid and moved into a suite at the Four Seasons," he said. "We think the architect is with her. I'm here by myself, downloading double-penetration videos. Probably going to go visit my folks in Toronto for a few weeks. I need a change of scenery. I'm putting the dogs in a kennel. I'll pick up the tab for Jimmy. But I wanted you to know where he's going to be. Technically he's still your dog, right?"

"I don't want Jimmy in a kennel," I said. "I'll come get him. When are you leaving? I'm in Arizona right now."

"Oh, shit. I figured you were around here," he said. "I'm leaving tomorrow. I have a plane ticket for a four-thirty."

"That's fine," I said. "If I get on the road in the morning, I'll be there by sunset. Leave Jimmy in the guesthouse. I have the key."

"Perfect," he said. "I'll leave him food and water in case you're running late. Dude, I'm sorry about all this. It's been nice working with you. Maybe when I get back you can help me get the place ready to sell. I'm putting it on the market. Maybe get a loft downtown."

"I understand," I said, feeling guilty about how nice he was being, as well as relieved to know that their marriage would have imploded without me.

"Do you mind if I camp out in the guesthouse for a few

nights?" I said. "I'm in limbo waiting for the high sign from the Bremners . . ."

"Fine. That's fine," he said.

"Yippee," I said to the dogs after I got off the phone with Chad. "We're going back to California tomorrow." I was thrilled. In just a few days at my mother's I had begun to have that vague uneasy sense that I used to have when I was in high school—that my life was destined to be a series of airport stopovers on my way to catch a flight that no one told me had been canceled. That was the way I felt when I dropped out of college.

The three dogs, all seated on Steve's bed, stared at me intently.

"In a car. We're going for a ride in the car," I repeated. With that, a feeling of great excitement instantly filled the air.

37

Pleasing a Woman

I stuck around for another plate of syrupy dough in the morning before I left. This time it took the form of French toast.

"Think about the coffee, brothers," my mother reminded us as she was piling loose rolls of toilet paper and paper towels that she had purchased in bulk from Costco into the back of my van. "The McMullen brothers and their self-made empire," my mother repeated again. "I hope you saved that clipping. Great stuff happens when brothers put their talents together: the Wright brothers, the Marx Brothers, the Smothers Brothers, Ernest and Julio Gallo . . ."

"Moe, Curly, and Shemp were brothers," I said. "Talk about flames that burned too brightly. And don't forget Uday and Qusay Hussein! And the Jonas Brothers. I'm still not sure what they do, but I do know that they're brothers."

"Do you need any kidney beans?" she asked me. "I have a whole case."

"Mom, they sell stuff in Los Angeles," I said as I made a last-minute check for things I'd forgotten. "There's no bean shortage that I'm aware of."

"I can hardly stand to say goodbye to my little grand-dog here," said Milt, coming out of the house carrying Dink. "You're sure you don't want to leave her here with me?"

"I don't think you can afford to replace all that carpet," I said as he handed her to me. "Dink, before we leave, do you have to pee?"

"I can hold it until we get inside," she said.

"Then why don't you go right here," I said to her, putting her down on the street.

"I miss you already," said my mom. "Please come back soon." She leaned in the window to give me a kiss. "And remember: Think Jackson Five."

"Then you and Milt get busy and adopt some more kids," I called to her as I drove down the street. "We're three short."

Steve never even came out of the house.

Once I was cruising on the I-17 headed for L.A., I put in another call to the Bremners. And praise the Lord, the tide had turned in my favor. They picked up their phone.

"I have some news that I hope won't upset your plans," said Mrs. Bremner hesitantly. "We're going to cut our stay short by a few days. I hope that's okay. Our place in Geneva is actually finished, in the knick of time. Martin is getting restless. You know how you men are! Why are you men all so restless, Gil?" she asked. "So when do you think you'll be available to come back and watch the place?"

"As soon as you like," I said. Talk about the understatement of the year.

"Well, Martin wants to get going by Saturday morning at the latest," she said. "You still have the key and everything, I assume."

"Yep, I sure do," I said, grinning wildly, so happy was I to be headed back to my home base. I really missed the place. It was Thursday morning. I was almost home free. And this filled me with such a feeling of glee that I decided to celebrate my own homecoming. I pulled off the road at Palm Desert and ducked into a sports bar to treat myself to a nice meal.

I'd had Uncle Ranchero's Savory Chicken Fried Steak at the Ranchero House once before. I liked everything about the experience except the paper tablecloths. Otherwise it was a flat-screen-TV-filled faux-home-cooking beer-on-tap kind of a paradise full of Christmas lights, taxidermied heads, trophies, and sports memorabilia. Just the kind of place where I could suck down beer in dim light and vanish into my own or other people's fantasies, especially if they were talking too loudly. This time I went with the meat loaf, the home fries, and a pitcher of draft beer—the perfect combination of foods for watching NASCAR and college football at the same time.

Then out of the corner of my eye I recognized Patty Pacquette. I had dated Patty a few times back in high school. When I say "dated," what I mean is we had sex twice before I dumped her for a girl with much bigger tits. I know. I'm sorry. In the low-functioning group of chimps that I hung out with back then, that was the kind of precipitous upward leap in status that won me a lot of points.

I was pretty sure it was her because of the way she kept

staring at me. I think she was trying to figure out why I seemed familiar. Her slightly asymmetrical face was sort of the same even after thirty years because she had been one of those sixteen-year-old girls who had always looked forty-seven. Now she had dyed blue-black hair and was wearing it short and spiky like Laurie Anderson. She'd put on a few extra pounds, but it was pretty well hidden under a big distressed-leather bomber jacket. I don't know what you'd call her "look," but it involved a pierced eyebrow, strands of leather necklaces, and a tattoo of barbed wire on her wrist. If she had been eighteen, I might have called it punk. At forty-seven, it was closer to prison matron.

Still, I smiled at her and gave her the revolver finger click-click—the human equivalent of the double tail thump. It was meant as a gesture that hopefully said, "Hey. How ya doing? Sort of (but not all that) glad to see ya." She narrowed her eyes as she nodded back at me, still puzzled. Then she picked up her martini and stumbled over.

"Do I know you?" she said.

"Well, the version of me you knew had more hair in better places," I said. "Gil Winowiscz. We graduated Thousand Oaks High same year."

"Gilbo!" she said, sitting down at my table, a big grin lighting up her face.

"Can I pour you a beer?" I said. She chugged the rest of her martini and held out her empty glass.

"Absolutely," she said. "A beer-tini. Wow. So, Gilbo! You look great. I had such a thing for you back in that other lifetime."

"Really?" I said, wiggling my eyebrows. "That's nice to hear."

"I think we went out a few times," she said. "Didn't we? Am I wrong?"

"I don't know. Did we?" I said, playing dumb. Truly the best thing about getting older was the option to employ selective memory.

"So, what're you up to these days?" she said, asking the number one question that no one wants to answer at high school reunions.

"Not much," I said. "I had more potential when you went out with me last time."

"You and me both," she said. "It's coming back to me now. Didn't you play piano or something? Or am I getting you confused with someone else?"

"That was me," I said. "Though you might also be thinking of my brother. Steve was in bands. Still is. I let it all slide."

"Just like me with ballet and tap," she said, conjuring unfathomable images of the strangest, most frightening dance troupe ever assembled. "Too bad, but I guess that's life." She held up her empty martini glass. I poured us both some more beer, pounded mine back in a gulp, and then poured myself even more. After that I ordered another whole pitcher.

"Now I work at the Do It Center," she said when we got to her details. "I manage hardware and garden tools. Pretty exciting, huh? I don't even know what most of the shit I sell is."

"Well, I can help you there," I said. "I mainly work in construction. Tools may be the only thing I know a lot about."

"Really?" she said. "Ooh. That's sexy." Now she was looking at me with more interest.

"Whaddya want to know? Name something you sell that you don't understand," I said.

"A chain wrench," she said. "I sold one of those last night."

"You don't know what a chain wrench is?" I said, pouring us each some more beer. "Oh, come on. Think logically. You got something this big around"—I held out my hands to make a shape about the size of a grapefruit—"and you need a wrench but none of the standard sizes fit. Are you pulling my leg?"

"No, but if you move a little closer, I could give it a shot." She grinned. "You wanna go over to my place? It's just a few blocks from here. I could use your advice. Maybe you can tell me if I should buy a new dishwasher."

"I don't know appliances," I said, "but I can take a look."

Next thing I knew, I was parking my van in front of a big apartment complex.

"You guys have to wait out here," I said to the dogs after I took them out for a bathroom break. "Daddy's got an errand to run."

"Why do you smell like that?" said Cheney, sniffing my legs. "Is this your mating season?"

"Guess it could be," I said. "I don't know how long I'll be. If you have problems, bark. I'll hear you."

Patty's apartment was small and needed paint. It was on the third floor of a three-story building from the sixties. The front room was full of IKEA cabinets topped by Indian fabric topped by lamps that had shades edged with fringe. It only took part of another beer before Patty was sitting in my lap. I hadn't expected this, but it was a nice surprise. We seemed to get along great, especially when we were laughing about the idiots from high school. "Maynard Keeper. Remember him?" she was saying as she rubbed my shoulders. "He got the lead in *Bye Bye Birdie* because he was the only marginally hot guy who auditioned. But he couldn't carry a tune. I heard he got picked up in Thailand selling coke."

"Well, you don't need to be able to carry a tune to do that," I said.

Patty leaned over and kissed me. Then she began to un-button her sweater. Next thing I knew she was showing me her brand-new enormous breast implants. "How do you like these?" she said. "They were my Christmas present to my-self."

"Wow, very nice. My compliments to Santa," I said as she pushed my face into them.

To my surprise, she then pulled back abruptly. "Let's slow down for a second," she said. "I want you to hit me first."

"Excuse me?" I said.

"Hit me. Slap me across the face. Go on," she said.

"Shit," I said, "I don't want to hit you."

"Why? Because you're pussy-whipped?" she taunted me. "Are you afraid? Are you the kind of wimp who lets women walk on you?"

"Well, there are those who would say that's true," I chuck-led.

"Are you gay? Do you have a tiny dick? Hit me. Asshole. Coward. Moron," she baited me. "Hit me. I dare you. Hit me."

"Are you serious?" I said. "Why do you want me to hit you?"

"Don't be my therapist. You'll ruin everything," she said, growing irritated. "Don't you know not to ever ask why dur-ing sex? If you need answers, look it up on Google when you get home. Come on, play along. . . . Because it turns me on is why. Hit me and then I'll do whatever you like, no questions asked."

"Okay, fine," I said, kind of playfully hitting her in the face.

"Do you need a dictionary? I said *hit* me. That's not hitting," she said, and she spit at me. "You'd get killed in a fight. Don't you know how to hit better than that?"

"I'm not comfortable hitting a woman," I said.

"Since when is sex about comfort? Okay, then choke me," she said. "Can you at least do that?"

She began kissing me and working me into a fever. "Now," she said, "put your hands around my neck and choke me. Like you hate me. Really let me have it. Strangle me."

"Patty," I said, "if I hated you, I wouldn't be sitting here. I'd split. I'm not getting this at all. You bought yourself a smokin' set of knockers. You look great. Why do I have to choke you? Why can't we just fuck?"

"Never mind," she said, exhaling loudly, shaking her head in rage. "Now I know why we never connected in high school. You're obviously one of those guys who only cares about himself and his own orgasm. I don't get it. Men will never do what a woman wants. But let a woman not do what they want . . . Oh my God! The sky is falling! The feminazis! The castrating feminists!"

"I guess I should go," I said. The mood had turned ugly. But when I stood up to put on my pants, the floor made a swan dive toward my face. All that beer was having its way with me. "Do you mind if I lie down for a minute?" I remember saying before I passed out.

It was five A.M. when I woke up alone on her couch, curled in the fetal position, dressed only in boxer shorts. The whole right side of my body was fast asleep. It felt like someone had grafted a cushion of blubber onto my neck. My arm was flailing around. I couldn't feel my leg. *Oh, shit,* I thought. Then I remembered: *The dogs!*

I got dressed and ran out to the van. To my great relief, the three of them were fast asleep in the back.

"I was wondering when you were coming," said Fruity. "I was afraid you drove off without us."

"How could I do that? You are *in* my car," I said.

"You're so smart, it seems like you could find a way if you wanted," said Fruity.

"You didn't have to worry about me," said Dink. "I already peed outside. In the van. On the road. Just like you said you wanted me to. So I am fine for the next few hours."

I looked down and saw that my big new box of nails was sitting in a pool of piss.

After I cleaned it all up, we drove off in search of a coffee place. One large black coffee later, we hit the road again.

"What time do we go get Jimmy?" asked Cheney as we merged with I-10.

"Whenever we get there," I said, glad that our schedule had some leeway. I was so hungover and sleepy. I had to pull into a rest stop to sleep for a couple of hours before we started our drive.

38

Events

*J*ust my luck that my nap had placed us squarely in the middle of the worst of morning rush. It was the full happy meal of L.A. motoring: not just many lanes of traffic stretching into infinity at fifteen mph, but also sixty-mph Santa Ana winds accompanied by reports about the outbreak of multiple wildfires. With conditions this bad, of course there was almost no radio reception. The van was rocking from side to side, knocking Cheney off the front seat and into the dashboard. With Dink tightly curled in my lap, I struggled to hold the road.

Ah, for the good old days when an unpredictable looming catastrophe, like an earthquake, seemed almost quaint.

"The one good thing that has come of all this recent chaos is the opportunity to know the three of you better," I said to them as we inched along. "Anything you want to talk about while we're stranded here in traffic?"

"I have a question that's been bothering me for a long time," said Cheney. "Explain that small piece of plastic that looks like undercooked meat? Do you know the one I mean? There is one in the corner, under that coffee can full of screws. Is it a test to see if I'm stupid? What am I supposed to do with it?"

"Hmm," I said. "It's sold as a toy for dogs. I assumed you found it amusing. You ran right off with it when I gave it to you. I thought you'd know these answers."

"Amusing like how?" he said, perplexed. "It doesn't smell or taste like meat and it squeaks when you try to chew on it. Plus it has that disturbing clown face. What part of that is supposed to be fun?"

"Well, I'm not sure. It didn't come with instructions," I said. "If you want we can write a letter to the manufacturer. Sometimes the world of professional fun rotates on a very unstable axis."

Traveling east on the 101, we were closer to the Bremners' estate than to Eden's. My plan was to drop the dogs off and then head across the canyon to get Jimmy.

It was about nine A.M. When I pulled into the Bremners' driveway, the limo that the Bremners were taking to the airport was backing out.

The driver stopped the car so Mr. and Mrs. Bremner, a handsome-looking white-haired couple in their seventies who always reminded me of the Duke and Duchess of Windsor, could step out and say hello. We shook hands and exchanged the kind of pleasantries appropriate to people who shared a place to live and nothing else. However, today the genial banter quickly escalated to more pressing things. "Looks like we're getting out in the nick of time," said Mr.

Bremner. He pointed up at the sky. "You've heard what's going on?"

That was the first time I really noticed that the color of the sky was almost porno pink. A washed-out yellow layer bleeding into the distant horizon gave everything the glow of a badly timed sunrise. I was thinking how beautiful it was until I heard Mrs. Bremner say, "The fire is only a few miles from here."

"Oh, Jesus," I said. Now I noticed that there was a disgustingly familiar sprinkling of ash swirling overhead. I had lived through a couple of these fires before. They used to come about every ten years. Now they seemed to have become an annual rite, a grotesque parody of a regional holiday. When the hot Santa Ana winds began to blow in late summer, I used to find them romantic, like trade winds, or that line from a Steely Dan song. Now they were the opening shot in a race toward mayhem: a signal to all arsonists that the party had started and there was an open bar.

"We woke up to it," said Mr. Bremner as he climbed back into his limo. "It started about an hour ago. Guess we better get going before they close the roads." He looked pale and stressed. "The good news is that the wind is blowing the fire in the other direction."

"We'll be okay," I said. "I know the drill. I've done this more times than I want to count. I won't let anything happen. You folks relax and have a nice trip."

"And you be careful, Gil. Stay in touch; keep us posted. We'll call you from the airport," Mrs. Bremner called out the window. The limo backed down the driveway toward the main road and then disappeared heading east.

Walking back into the house was a bittersweet moment for me, a satisfying sigh of relief. I was home, surrounded by the space and quiet I had been yearning for. There was room for us all to relax, unobserved, uncommented upon. No mandatory special shared moments. No one to disappoint.

The Bremners had left the TV on local programming because it was all breaking news about the fire. On every channel was footage of hillsides and structures in flames. Here was a house on fire. There was a field full of smoldering embers. Local news teams dressed in rain slickers and wearing surgical masks reported from the tops of mountains buffeted by hurricane-force winds. They detailed the progress of the fire as if it were an invading army. "The house down the street from you has just been occupied by enemy troops. Now their unstoppable death march has moved one street closer."

Footage of airborne sparks igniting hillsides full of un-cleared brush made the Bremners' beautiful old wood house look like a carefully assembled bonfire waiting for a match. One minute there were three hundred acres on fire and two Superscoopers dropping water. In no time at all it was four hundred acres on fire, ten helicopters, two fixed-wing air-craft, and a dozen homes destroyed. Linguistically speaking, this was the first fire I had lived through where the newscast-ers seemed to have held a secret meeting and agreed to inex-plicably use the word "event" wherever possible. Suddenly, the fire was "a fire event," the Santa Ana winds were "a wind event" and "a Santa Ana event." And they repeated that weirdly chosen noun as if it were traditional terminology, passed down through the state's rich history. Every time I heard it, I thought, *How much did I pay for the tickets to this event, and is it too late to get a refund?*

I got sucked inescapably into the tension vortex when I heard that houses on Eden's street were in flames. Watching footage of familiar-looking people standing out in front of that Save-Less speaking too quickly as they relayed their fears for the future, reminded me that I was running out of time. Eden's house was on the other side of the same canyon as the Bremners'. Jimmy was in that guesthouse all alone, waiting for me. There was no one home on the property. No one but me knew he was there.

I rushed to put the dogs back into the van and headed over to Eden's using only back roads. According to the newscasters, the big main roads were closed.

About half a mile from the turnoff to Eden's street, I was stopped at a police barricade.

"I need to see some ID," an exhausted cop said to me. "We're only open to residents."

"My dog is locked up in a guesthouse down the street. I have a key. I have to go get him. I was a resident but I left town," I said.

"Driver's license and registration?" said the cop. As I handed him my driver's license, I realized how I must look to him—unshaven and unshowered, smelling like beer and Patty Pacquette. I hadn't slept or brushed my teeth. I was bleary-eyed and hungover. Now I was asking to be let into Eden's tony neighborhood with no ID while all the real residents were being evacuated.

"I know my ID has a different address," I said, "but I was living there and working, and my dog—"

"I can't let you through," he said. "We're only open to residents at this time."

"You have to let me through," I said. "I have to go get my dog."

"Do you have anything to prove residence? A utilities bill?" he said. "A piece of mail?"

"I don't think so. I had free room and board," I said to the cop, realizing that I was starting to sound like a belligerent deadbeat. "Hey, pal, it's an emergency. I need to get in there right now. It's just a short ways away. What if you drive me? You can sit and watch while I run in and get my dog. That's all I want to do." I showed him my key chain. "These are the keys to the place."

"Wait here," he said as he went back to his squad car to check on me.

He had been talking into his police radio for four or five minutes when something inside me snapped. I got out of my van and started to run down the road on foot. The cop in the squad car saw me right away and called for backup. I was almost to the corner when a second cop car came roaring toward me from the opposite direction. Cop number two blocked my path with his car, then got out and charged me. He dove into me like I was a heated swimming pool. When he tackled me, it hurt. He was a big guy. He knocked me onto my stomach, in time for the first guy to race up and pin my arms behind my back. Someone put handcuffs on me and snapped them shut.

"Whoa, dudes," I said. "Come on. I'm not a Blood or a Crip. I'm just a local guy trying to save my damn dog."

"Gil?" said cop number two.

"Wayne," I said, recognizing his voice even though I was lying facedown in the dirt with my hands cuffed behind me. Wayne was the cop I hung out with at the sports bar on Agoura Road.

"Wayne, dude . . . I'm sorry about this," I said, "but your partner here wouldn't let me go get my dog. He's locked in a guesthouse down the street. I'm just back from a trip. I was supposed to go pick him up yesterday." I realized I was starting to cry. It surprised me that I was so out of control. I was frazzled, a torn, shredded mess. "I had a gig down the street at my ex-wife's place. They were taking care of my dog Jimmy," I tried to explain, thinking it was too much information. "I almost called you and asked to stay on your couch. I had to go see my mom."

"Gonna cost you five hundred dollars for that little stunt," said cop number one, apparently unimpressed by my tale of woe. He was already writing the ticket.

"Perfect," I said. "Between the state of California and that goddamn private eye, I have a bank balance of zero. Fine. You can all have my fucking money. I don't give a shit. Just let me go get my dog, okay? That's all I want."

"I'll take custody of him, Mike," said Wayne, unlocking my handcuffs. "It's pretty bad down there, Gil. Another house just burned."

"Can we please hurry?" I said, increasingly panicky. "You met Jimmy. He's like my family," I said, wondering if I would have worked this hard to save Steve.

"Take it easy," said Wayne. "Why don't you pull your van to the side of the road so you're not blocking traffic. Mike, can you keep an eye on this guy's van?"

By now the other three dogs were all staring out the

driver's side window. Was it a hot day or was all that heat the fire?

"Looks like you've got a full house in there already," said Mike.

"Jimmy is special," I said. "Well, I guess they're all special. If you don't have dogs, maybe you don't know how that is."

After I moved the van, Wayne and I drove about half a mile in his squad car until we were stopped by another blockade. This time it was fire trucks.

"No admittance beyond this point," said a fireman.

"He's got a dog locked in a house down there," said Wayne. "Got the keys right here."

"Will someone please just go get my dog?" I screamed at the firemen. "If you let me run in there for a minute, I'll be fast. Just drop me off as close as you can."

"Can't let you go down there, bro," said the fireman. "We've got the trucks down there. We have a crew working the area. No one else is permitted. But I'll let 'em all know about the dog. I'll give 'em your key. They're good about that kind of thing. We've been pulling quite a few animals out of these places." I could see billowing black smoke coming from down our road.

At this point I was so agitated and full of foreboding that I made one last attempt at an end run. I jumped out of Wayne's car and went barreling past the firemen and cops. I busted through a barricade. But I was exhausted and such a wreck from too little sleep and all that had happened that it didn't take much for a bunch of guys half my age to restrain me. I was like some poor wounded rhino charging a line of tanks.

By the time Wayne drove me back to my van, the whole

Bremner neighborhood had been evacuated. I was turned away when I tried to drive back down our road.

Now I had no idea where to go. I was on the lam with three dogs and a van full of tools. My nervous system was shot. I felt like a prisoner of war. The radio said that there was a community evacuation center at the high school where I could stay the night, but dogs weren't permitted.

"Fifty-five houses have burned so far," said the newscaster on the radio. Now there were five hundred acres in danger and no estimate on the damages. "Zero percent containment of today's fire event," said the news zombie.

"I've got to do something," I said to Fruity, Cheney, and Dink. My skin felt like it was burning. "I can't live without Jimmy," I said.

"Does that mean you're mad at me?" said Fruity. "I still love you and everything. So don't kill me, okay?"

"For Chrissakes, stop it," I said. "I love you too. If I was going to kill you, why am I working so hard to keep you alive? But we're talking about Jimmy, for Chrissakes. I raised him from a puppy. He's like my flesh and blood. Only he's more honest than they are. And he's much hairier."

I was so upset I felt like parking somewhere and refusing to leave the neighborhood. But when patrolling police gave the order to get out, I had no choice but to start driving north on the 101 toward Oxnard.

Next thing I knew, I was pulling up in front of Sara's house. I was on autopilot. I had no other place to go. Sara and I hadn't spoken in . . . was it a week? Was it a month? I'd lost track. But I knew she hadn't.

Sitting in her driveway in my car, I called her on my cell.

"Gil?" she said when she heard it was me. "Where are you?"

"In your driveway," I said.

"You're kidding, I hope," she said, shocked.

I saw her peek through the curtains in the windows in the front of her house.

"Oh God. You're serious," she said. "I wish you'd given me a heads-up."

"Sorry," I said. "My neighborhood is on fire. I didn't know where to go."

"Oh Jesus, oh Jesus," she said. "I haven't put on the radio this morning. Where's the fire? Is everything okay?"

"Jimmy's stuck in Eden's guesthouse. Her goddamn street is on fire. They won't let me through," I shouted.

"Oh Jesus, oh Jesus," said Sara. "What can I do? What are we going to do?"

"I spoke to some firemen. They know he's there. I gave them my keys," I said, hoping it would sound like I'd done the right thing. As I spoke, I was surprised to hear my voice crack.

"Oh, shit," she said. "Let me put on my pants. . . . Come in. Bring the dogs."

"Thanks," I said, relieved to stop talking until I pulled it together.

"Um, Josh is here," she said. She put her hand over the mouthpiece. I could hear a muffled "A friend. His house is on fire."

"Your ex?" I heard a man's voice say. That was the first time it hit me. I was somebody's ex again.

I let the dogs out of the van and they all ran to her front

door. When she opened it, they were so happy to see her, it was like I was releasing kidnap victims.

"Hi," said Sara. She was wearing a robe over a nightgown. Beside her was a nice-looking guy, shirtless in drawstring pants and Crocs. Was she fucking this guy? He put his arm through her arm and I knew the answer was yes.

39

Crocs

*D*amn. How could Sara be fucking a guy who wore Crocs?

"This is Josh," she said, sounding tense. "Josh, this is Gil."

"Can I get you some coffee or an English muffin?" he offered. "We were just having breakfast." He was being polite, but he totally pissed me off. His voice was soft and lilting, the gently modulated, whispery voice of a sensitive man. Who was he to be offering me food in Sara's house? It hadn't been that long since I'd been living there. Didn't I still have some seniority?

"Nah," I said, even though I really wanted both. This was my payback for tuning out on Sara. What was I thinking, stepping back into her life without any warning? I would have killed her if she'd done that to me.

"I'm sorry about this," I said, "showing up unannounced.

I wanted to drop off the dogs somewhere safe, so I can go back and find Jimmy."

"No, man. It's cool," said Josh, embarrassingly nice.

"Of course you can leave the dogs here!" said Sara, supportive and concerned. She picked up the remote and turned on her 1991 model TV, where a different set of virtual-looking newscasters were droning on about "the fire event" and "the wind event." "I don't think you're getting back into your neighborhood today," she said. "Sounds like they've got the roads closed. Zero percent containment."

"I'll crash the goddamn roadblock," I said, trying to sound like a monolithic male force for good in front of Josh, but knowing I was all out of energy to try it again. "I gotta go get Jimmy."

"I think you better sit tight," Sara said, "and wait till the wind dies down."

"If he's in danger," I said, "it's because of me. I am such an asshole."

"You said you told them about him," she said. "You did the right thing. They'll get him. It will all be okay. Those guys are good with animals. . . ." And then she got pale and looked nauseous. "I think what we need is to sit still and do a positive visualization. Sometimes that will help direct the energy."

She closed her eyes and we all sat quietly. When I peeked, six dogs were staring at me. Their eyes were alert like they thought I was planning something fun!

After the meditation, I tried not to notice the little eye darts that Sara and Josh were now sending to each other—supportive little head movements and affirmations to show they were successfully coping with me.

"I am so sorry about this whole thing, you guys," I said.

"Hey, no biggie," said the benevolent Josh, nonchalantly picking up an acoustic guitar that was leaning against a bookcase. Absentmindedly he began knocking out some little chord changes. Now he was pissing me off again by being allowed to play the talented musician while at the same time showing he was able to handle me in stride. Crocs. How did he expect to pull that off, wearing Crocs? And yet he did. What an asshole.

Why the hell was this bothering me so much? I wondered. I had been jerking Sara around for years. I should have been happy she'd met someone else so quickly. Josh was the kind of "man blessing" I should have been praying she'd find. Now she and I could be "friends" and she'd be off my case. He could serenade her by cool mountain streams. He could sing her romantic poetry about a love that would never die. Maybe he would liken her unto a sunset or the arrival of spring. All that crap that I had no intention of doing.

"Josh is a singer-songwriter," said Sara.

"Ah. A fellow traveler?" I said, surprising myself by suddenly donning the cloak of musician after shrugging it off for decades. "So, unemployed?" I asked.

"No. I have a deal with Universal," Josh whispered, cool, calm, and casual under the weight of so much responsibility. So nonchalant and comfortable with his rising fame.

"Gil plays the piano. His brother is a famous singer-songwriter who had a big hit song in the seventies," said Sara. "'Undercover Angel.' It was number one for how many weeks?"

"I don't know," I said, growing sullen. "A million."

"Oh, right!" said Josh, immediately starting to play the first few chords of the song to show his familiarity, then stopping abruptly, as though it weren't worth the effort.

"Well, guess we should go get dressed," Sara said. "Looks like life is calling."

"Time to start our busy day," sang Josh. "Got to call life back when life is calling. No call-waiting. Call your life back. Your life wants you to call her right away!" As he sang, he improvised a tune on the guitar that sounded like a lesser song by the Eagles. Then he started to sing the whole thing through a second time, as though he were now considering it more seriously as a work in progress.

Wasn't it impolite to be making up light verse when someone in the room had a dog in danger? Wasn't that kind of bad form? It also pissed me off that he'd said "Time to start *our* day." Why were they already co-piloting their days? How long had she known this prick? Weren't her feelings for me supposed to run deeper than this? Where was the fretting and mourning and grieving over what might have been? Could everything about me be so easily filed and forgotten?

What hurt most of all was that even though I'd never really been sure how I felt about Sara, I'd always been very sure how she felt about me. How did I lose my place in line so fast?

When Sara and Josh disappeared into the bedroom to get dressed, I could hear their muffled laughter as I watched the news coverage of the fire event. What could they possibly find funny on a day when everything I cared about was threatened? Didn't they see the ashes falling from the sky right in their own front yard, carrying pieces of other people's destroyed lives? How fucking insensitive was that goddamn Josh? Why were the assholes who were supposed to be sensitive for a living always so damn cold to others?

I heard another short burst of laughter from the bedroom and knew I had to get out of there fast. I was too hot one minute, too cold the next, like I had on the wrong clothes or my thermostat was broken. I needed to get a hotel room. I couldn't afford a hotel room. So I put my three dogs on leashes and headed out to the store to pick up a six-pack. I could at least observe my beer-thirty ritual in the back of my van.

But when I curled up and listened to the fire coverage on the radio, for the first time in a long time, I didn't want to drink. It was the goddamn beer that was behind this whole mess.

Even without it, the day went by in a blur. I listened to the news freaks speculate on a million worst-case scenarios, haunted by images of Jimmy in danger, in terror, in pain, waiting for me, counting on me. He was feeling abandoned, and he had been—by me. I loathed and despised myself and Patty Pacquette. It was all her fault. If I could have had do-overs, now I would have been willing to hit her as hard as she wanted. None of this would have happened without her and all of that beer. I would have been back at the Bremners' house the previous day. I would have gone to pick up Jimmy way before the fire had started. But I was only in Arizona because I'd gotten thrown out of Eden's. And that whole mess would never have happened if I hadn't been such a dick to Sara. All of the bullshit with Eden could have been avoided. That detective wouldn't have been able to strong-arm me. I would have my money. But most important of all, I'd have

Jimmy. This was a wake-up call. My jerry-rigged life was a big fucking mess because I didn't have the maturity and guts to devote myself to the only woman I'd ever known who meant me no harm. Sara was the only good thing to come into my life since my divorce. She was the only one who could save me from my twenty-five-year anniversary celebration with the twenty-two-year-old motormouth douche bag who'd repeatedly ruined my life. Why had it taken me so long to see that she was the missing piece of my soul? I needed to get her back.

Now that it was so clear, I was in a real panic. I felt like a little kid who'd been spinning in a circle just to make myself dizzy. Now there was nothing to do but drink beer and listen to fire bulletins on the radio.

At some point Sara and Josh came out of the house and rapped on the back of my van. They were headed out to dinner and invited me to join them. I could tell from their facial expressions they were hoping I'd say no. I didn't want to go anyway. I'd seen enough of The Sara and Josh Show. My only thoughts were about Jimmy. Otherwise I was numb. Better to remain alert, immersed in anxiety and fire bulletins. If there was a window of opportunity for me to save Jimmy, I wanted to know about it.

Now as I watched Sara get into Josh's Prius, lean over and give him a peck on the cheek, my feelings for her descended on me like a road map of destiny. They were as vivid and simple now as the sensation of hunger or thirst. Maybe it wasn't too late. Sara and Josh were a new couple. But Sara and Gil had a history. My leverage couldn't be over.

Before I left Sara's house, I went inside and took a shower.

After I mopped up and carefully restored all the miniature marine mammals and mermaids to their original upright positions, I left a little note for Sara in her office by her computer. "I miss you," it said. "I hope you miss me too. I love you. Please call me. We need to talk. Love, Gil."

(40)

A Judgment Call

About six o'clock the following morning, I was able to get back into the Bremners' neighborhood. I was not, however, prepared for what came next. The largest section of the Bremners' house was completely gone. There were piles of charred rubble in some places, blackened remnants of wall in others. The piece of living room that was structurally intact was so water damaged it was as though a flood had hit it. It looked like a scene from the nightmare I'd had the night before.

The dogs loved the way it stunk like rot and fungus. There was so much to investigate. I tried to call the Bremners on their cell, but the lines were blocked. More important, of course, was that I still had to find Jimmy. I guessed the fire department must have evacuated him to somewhere.

So I put the dogs back into the van and drove as fast as I could over to Eden's estate. The road remained closed by a police blockade. Only residents could pass, or ne'er-do-well handymen with a written permission slip from a policeman friend, God bless Wayne. A different roadblock bully called headquarters to check on me, but this time he let me through.

Now I was in for an even bigger shock. Eden's house was gone. There was nothing there but a chimney and the slab from the original foundation. It was weird how much smaller her property looked without all the things that had divided it into vertical levels. A lot of what had once been many enormous rooms was now just undifferentiated open air. Part of the kitchen plumbing remained. Part of the downstairs guest bathroom and shower stall were visible but blackened. The guesthouse seemed to have never existed. It was even hard to locate. I kept looking in the right direction, thinking I'd misplaced it somehow. Where did it go? It had to be here somewhere if I looked carefully enough.

The dogs and I got out of the van and began to walk around the lot. Everything now seemed unfamiliar. The trees and landscaping were gone. There was no sign of anything alive or dead, including Jimmy. Only after I found the stone path that led to the front door could I tell where different rooms had been. Finding no obvious bones seemed like a good sign. But looking too hard for them also seemed like bad luck.

Next thing I did was put the dogs back into the van and return to the roadblock to ask where the rescued animals were kept. The cop gave me a number at which to contact the fire department. But since the fire was then only 65 percent contained, that number was a constant broken dial tone, impossible to reach. When I finally did get ahold of a human being, not a recorded message, they quickly transferred me, then transferred me again. The end result was that I needed to call

Animal Control, the first step into another bureaucratic morass that sent me back to square one.

Through it all, the only thing I didn't learn was what had happened to Jimmy. Rescued animals were at the Agoura shelter, they said.

Unable to bear any more menus of computerized options that led to more menus of computerized options, I drove over to the Agoura shelter. There I viewed a heartrending assortment of strays and rescued animals and wildlife: not just dogs and cats but deer, opossums, a coyote, a bobcat, baby squirrels, assorted birds.

But no Jimmy. The people at the shelter directed me to the nearest fire department. I tried to find out the names of the firefighters on the scene during Eden's blaze. This was apparently impossible.

"All the animals we rescued are at the Agoura pound," said the guy manning the desk. "We're under strict instructions to bring them there."

"My dog wasn't there," I insisted. "So where else could he be?"

The guy was quiet while he thought about his answer. Then he shrugged and shook his head slowly. "Well, depending on your personal religious beliefs . . . I happen to believe that our animal friends are family and wait for us on the other side in the very same heaven where we are all headed one day."

"What if we're all going to hell?" I said. "Will they be waiting there too? Is this fire another one of those sketches from the intelligent design pad?"

That was the first time it dawned on me . . . what if no one had rescued Jimmy? That didn't seem possible. The area had been crawling with firemen. Jimmy would have been barking. Someone would have heard him. I'd given them my keys. And I had a five-hundred-dollar ticket to prove it. Obviously they would have gone in to get him. I had worked so hard to get down to the scene and alert everyone. This really couldn't have happened. If it was true, then I wanted to die. I started to run through the whole pointless careless tragic Rube Goldberg diagram again. From Sara to Eden to Mom to Palm Desert with a stop at too many beers. That was the bottom line. I had left Arizona in plenty of time. I could have been in L.A. long before rush hour. I could have stopped at Palm Desert, eaten meat loaf, boned Patty Pacquette, and still been home by two A.M. That twenty-two-year-old alpha who'd had me by the testicles for twenty-five years was trying to kill me. I wished he would hurry.

Now all I knew was that I had to find the firefighters who'd been at Eden's. I had to hear directly from them if they had seen Jimmy. Simple but apparently impossible. Most were still fighting "the fire event" at that very moment.

Thank God I'd finally lived in one place long enough to be connected to someone who could be helpful. The only thing left was to ask my buddy Wayne to make a few calls for me. He was nice enough to arrange for me to speak to a fire captain, though at the same time careful to let me know he had other things to do besides grant me any more favors.

"We got so busy with the main house, we had to let the guesthouse go," the fire captain said as I sat in the back of my van in the parking lot behind the police station talking to him on my cell. "We figured once we were out of the woods, we'd get back to it. . . . We never had time."

"But my dog was in there," I said. "He was the only living

creature on the property. The rest of the buildings were empty."

"I'm sorry we didn't know about that," he said. "We had to make a judgment call."

"But I went all the way down there to tell everyone," I said. "I was right there at the roadblock. I got stuck with a five-hundred-dollar ticket. I gave you guys my keys."

"I am so sorry," said the fire captain. "I love dogs. I wish I had known."

Now it hit me. I felt absolutely sick. I've always heard people say "weak at the knees" but never knew what it meant until that wave of physical frailty and nausea overtook me. Next thing I knew, I was heaving my guts out right there in the parking lot. Then I was lying on my side on the asphalt, sobbing.

"You okay?" a guy in a policeman's uniform asked me. "You want to come into the station and lie down for a minute?"

"No," I said, embarrassed by the big deep howling wail of mourning that escaped like a bat from the center of my soul. It was coming from a place I purposely never went. But when I fell into that hole, odd things came splashing up at me. My father's face; a scene from my childhood where I was all dressed up at eight years old, waiting for someone who never came; a million scenes of Jimmy: the feeling of his wet spongy nose and lips and muzzle against my neck. The proud silly way he strutted when I walked him on a leash. The way he woke me up by jumping onto my chest at seven A.M. and washing my face for me. The way he knew how to manipulate me into doing pretty much anything he wanted, all the while making me think it was my idea. He was irresistible to me. Maybe it was all that eye contact he made. Something about his intensity was so singular, so familiar and deep.

I tried hard not to imagine his last minutes. Then I started to feel a rage so big that it filled the whole world, a rage that wanted to strike back at whoever was making the innocent have to suffer, whoever had done this to Jimmy and to me. Patty Pacquette was lucky she hadn't asked me to hit her right then.

I loved the other dogs, but I didn't know if I could handle tomorrow without Jimmy. My carelessness had destroyed a life that meant more to me than my own. Jimmy was gone. What was the point of my existence if I put loved ones at risk?

Unintended Consequences

I climbed back into the van too upset to drive as I listened to the sounds of policemen hosing away my puke.

Dink jumped from the passenger seat into my lap. Fruity came from behind and plunked her big head onto my shoulder.

"Anything I can do?" said Cheney. "If you want to throw some shit, I'll bring it back. I know I've made that offer before, but this time I will do it so effectively that you'll never know it was gone. I'll put it right in your lap. It'll be right by your hand in case you want to throw it again."

"No," I said. I couldn't talk. "Jimmy . . . No one knows where he is," I finally said.

"That's too bad," said Cheney, "but we haven't seen much of him in . . . How long has it been? A year? Two years?"

"I like spending time with you," said Fruity. "You're not mad at me, are you?"

"You said to tell you when I was thinking about peeing," said Dink, snuggling toward my belly.

"You want me to take you out?" I said. I looked into the back of the van and saw a wet spot by the side door. "Ah, who cares? What difference does it make?"

We sat there in silence for a long time. And then when I thought I could drive without getting into a wreck, I drove us back to the Bremner property.

A short while later the phone calls started. The Bremners had just arrived in Switzerland by way of France. Mrs. Bremner called to get an update. They were shocked to hear that the house was mostly gone. Mr. Bremner tried to put a bright face on it. He had been thinking about remodeling the place, he said. "Can you supervise it for us?" he asked me. "And while I'm trying to get in touch with our insurance broker, can you stay on the property and keep an eye on things? Maybe rent a trailer? A nice one. The neighbors have enough to cope with at the moment."

"Sure," I said.

"Good man," he said. "Everything else okay? All the animals tip-top?"

I didn't say anything. I couldn't bring myself to talk about it.

Next Chad called from the Toronto airport. "Sorry I've been out of touch," he said. "The neighbors told me what happened. I thought I should check in with you. Everything okay? Good thing I thought to put the dogs in a kennel, huh? Did you get Jimmy?"

"No," I said. Then I couldn't speak. The pain rushed forward inside of me like a flash flood. "I didn't get there in time," I said.

"No! How could that happen? That is horrible. What can I do for you?" said Chad. "Are you sure he didn't get out? I bet someone heard him barking and let him out. I left the windows open. I bet he panicked and jumped through the screens. They always do that. Do you need anything? Money? A place to stay? How can I help you?"

I couldn't speak now. I had to get off the phone. I wasn't comfortable having anyone hear me make those weepy nasal sounds. I held them in, but tears were running down my face.

"As far as I'm concerned, you're still on the clock," said Chad. "If there's anything I can do for you, please let me know."

Chad flew in that night. When he called me on his drive back from the airport, I was sitting in the back of my van, parked in the middle of what used to be the Bremners' front lawn. Now it was a big patch of scorched dirt and unidentifiable stuff. I was in a beer stupor, starting on my second six-pack. I'd told myself if Jimmy was okay I'd stop drinking. Now I didn't see the point.

"I had my assistant get me a rental," said Chad. "In a way it's a blessing to be out of there. I was dreading having to sort through Eden's crap."

"I know that feeling," I said.

"What are you doing tomorrow? Could I hire you to go over to the kennel where I boarded the dogs and pick them up for me?" he said. "I'd be happy to pay you whatever you want to charge."

"Sure, I'll go get 'em. Don't worry about the money," I said, trying to return some of Chad's kindness, though I was ambivalent about seeing Jimmy's surviving family. Maybe it would be gut-wrenching.

That night I unpacked a bunch of the larger tools from the back of my van to make room for the three big dogs I was picking up. I took out the saw horses and the biggest power saws and assorted power tools and put them into the Bremners' garage hacienda. Built like a bunker, that thing had survived intact. Or maybe the firemen just hadn't been able to stand the thought of such expensive vintage cars going up in smoke.

Then I curled up in the van with Cheney, Fruity, and Dink. It felt good to have them coiled tightly against me. "You guys have been a real comfort to me," I confided. "I know things have been kind of rough since we first left the Bremners', back in the 1800s or whenever that was," I said. "The only good thing to come of all this is I feel a lot closer to the three of you."

"Seems like you're a lot nicer now," said Fruity.

"Seems like you throw things more often," said Cheney.

"I am thinking about peeing," said Dink. I looked around for the mess. Not seeing one, I picked her up and put her on the ground outside of the van. And lo and behold, she started peeing!

"Dink," I said, "you peed outside! *And* you told me first."

"I'm sorry," said Dink, her tail tucked between her legs.

"No! You are such a good girl," I said as I picked her up and kissed her snout. "You did everything right. I knew if we kept at it, sooner or later . . ."

Now I was so full of appreciation for the scary frailty of the moment that by beer-thirty I found myself giving my own version of that speech in *The Wizard of Oz*.

"I was stupid to not be paying more attention to you three all this time," I said. "You, Fruity, are so enthusiastic in the way you embrace life. So sweet and nonjudgmental and sensitive. I want to help you learn to trust more. You, Dink, are almost ridiculously affectionate. You make everyone feel lovable. And you, Cheney, are consistent and loyal and have so much focus. You're a real partner."

"Thanks," said Cheney. "Can I get you to throw this?"

"I look back at myself and I can see how cut off I was from everyone," I said. In the name of progress I was trying for a wrap-up with a learning curve that made sense of it all. "Maybe I felt like if I loved too many things at the same time, it would dilute me. Or make me disappear. It felt like too much work. It made me tired. But you know what? You three guys make it easy for me. It's less work than I thought."

"We all miss Jimmy," said Dink.

"But I hope you don't blame it on me and put me to death," said Fruity.

I turned off my reading light and just lay in the dark, feeling sadder than I ever had. I wanted to cry. But I was all cried out. So I just let the sadness carry me along like a river, because by drowning in it, I was keeping Jimmy alive.

(42)

A Little Goes a Long Way

𝒯he next morning I got up at eight A.M. to head for the kennel. While I was driving, the phone rang. It was Sara.

"How's Jimmy? Are you okay?" she said. She sounded
worried. "What can I do to help? What's going on?" I loved
the feeling that she cared about me. I missed it. "Do you want
to bring the dogs and come over here?" she asked.

"No, I'm okay," I said.

"I got your note. I'd be happy to talk. When do you want
to do it? How's Jimmy?" she said.

"Gone," I whispered.

"What do you mean, gone? Where? Is he hurt? What happened?" she said. "No," she said. "Don't tell me something
happened to Jimmy." And when I didn't speak, she started to
moan. Then she began to cry. She cried for him. It really
touched me.

"I'm on my way to pick up the rest of Jimmy's family from

a kennel," I said. "I told Chad I'd drive them to his new house."

"You want to call me when you're done?" she said. "You want to come by after?"

"What about Josh?" I said.

"Don't worry about him," she said.

As I pulled my van up to the front of the kennel, I got a sick feeling in the pit of my stomach knowing I was about to see Jimmy's look-alike family. If I hadn't interfered and I'd just kept my big mouth shut, Jimmy would have been there too. But no. I always had a bright idea. I always had to tempt fate. I never could go along with the program. "Did you bring any leashes?" asked the slightly surly-looking kennel supervisor, a twentysomething girl in a red down vest.

"No," I said.

"We have leashes here, but we'll have to charge you for them," she said.

"Fine," I said as I followed her down a long narrow hallway to the back of the place, a seemingly endless series of connected rectangular fenced dog runs attached to a cinderblock building full of enclosed cages. Down at the far end I could see three big black dogs lying in a row. Their heads were on their front paws. They were staring into space like they used to out on Eden's patio. When they recognized me, they all began to leap at the fence.

"Oh my God," said Gypsy. "It's you. I know you. I know you. Let me kiss you. Let me out of here. You remember me, don't you? I know I ignored you a lot, but those days are *over.* You'll be my favorite now!"

"I knew him first. So say hello to me," said Party Girl,

Jimmy's pushy sister. "I'm the one who knows who you are. You definitely know me. Remember?"

"Jesus Christ, man, what took you so fucking long?" said Jimmy. "I told them you'd show up here eventually. Get me out of here *now*."

I couldn't believe my eyes. Was it really Jimmy?

Yes. It was Jimmy.

When I squatted down, he ran at me with such force he knocked me over. "You were so right about this whole joined-at-the-hip family thing," he said, licking my face. "A little goes a long way. I mean, I love them and all, but these two are so fucking weird. And don't even get me started on my goddamn brother and his alpha issues. If he were in this cage with me here one of us would be dead. Take me home with you. Get me away from them. Now. No kidding."

"Is it really you?" I said.

"As opposed to what?" he said.

I threw my arms around him and hugged him, tears streaming out of my eyes. "Oh God, it's so good to see you," I said, stopping only briefly to worry about Jimmy's brother. Had he been in the house? Maybe Chad was right. Maybe he had escaped. I would put signs up, I decided. I would look for him.

But for now I wanted to enjoy one of my life's great moments as I focused on breathing in the deep, fresh, familiar scent of musty Chinese food that was Jimmy. It was kind of partway between chow mein and wonton soup. It was my favorite smell in the world.

"Can we please get out of here?" he said.

$\left(\begin{array}{c} 43 \end{array}\right)$

A Matter of Degree

J dropped Jimmy's mother and sister off at Chad's new rental. His assistant brought them inside. "Tell Chad to call me," I said to her rather than explain the whole mix-up with the dogs to one more pie-eyed twentysomething who was waiting impatiently for me to finish so she could start text messaging.

"This is unbelievable," I said as I headed back to the Bremners' semi-vacant lot with my four dear pals. "It's the best thing I could have imagined. I've been given a chance at a whole new beginning."

"Me too," said Jimmy, who was sitting in his old spot in the passenger seat. "I'm really happy about this too."

"So now I always have to sit back here again?" said Cheney bitterly.

"No, now you two have to take turns," I said.

"What about all that stuff you said about needing your family to be complete?" said Fruity.

"I never said that," said Jimmy.

"Yes, you did," said Cheney.

"No, I didn't," said Jimmy. "I would never say that. It doesn't even sound like me. I mean, I still like them and all. But it bugged me the way even my mom got me mixed up with my brother. I mean, I know we're both black and have long hair and all, but clearly I'm the natural alpha. I put quite a bit of work into having my own take on things. I have a very unique walk. I try to eat my food a little more slowly than the others. I have a very distinct yawn. I mean, my brother was . . . Okay, this will sound petty, but . . . he was a simpleton. He was a total beta who would spend the day chewing on the edge of his food dish hoping that someone would see and fill it with more food. The dude had no teeth left. I tried to tell him he was going at it all wrong."

"I know what you mean," I said. "I have some of the same issues with my brother."

"Yeah, you didn't meet Gil's brother," said Cheney. "What a guy. Never throws a thing."

"And he chews on his dish?" said Jimmy.

"Well, metaphorically speaking, he does," I said.

"I'm a very accomplished guy," said Jimmy. "At least you noticed how hard I work on my facial expressions. No one in my family ever said a word."

"There are great things about family," I said, "but part of how nature works is that we are all supposed to move out at some point and form our own families. We're meant to create our own little genetic strains within our breed who will over time grow to hate us and want to move away from us. That's the natural order of things. For dogs and for people. Each generation wants to escape from the last one. Talk about intelligent design."

"Well, it certainly worked for me," said Jimmy. "I really wanted out of there. My mother and my brother both tried to have sex with me. Turns out, even I have limits."

"Dude!" I said. "That sucks. I never had it that bad."

"Yeah, when you left and I realized I was stuck there without you, I freaked," said Jimmy. "I felt like just another hairy black mouth breather lying on the patio."

"Well, you guys are family to me," I said. "I know it's a weird kind of family, but most families are weird. It's only a matter of degree."

"A good way to show your appreciation would be to throw some stuff," said Cheney. "See who brings it back. Maybe give them a nice reward."

As we pulled onto the Bremners' lot, I was surprised to see a couple of nicely dressed men with sweaters tied around their necks pacing around the grounds, taking measurements. Judging by the surveyor's level, one was an engineer. The other was that Japanese architect who was having sex with my ex-wife.

"Hi," I said to them as I let the dogs out of the van. "Can I help you?"

The architect didn't seem to recognize me. Maybe if I'd had some linen pants and a sweater tied around my neck, I would have merited more attention.

"Martin Bremner sent us over to have a look," said the architect. "We're going to draw up some plans for a remodel. I guess you're his man?"

"I guess I am," I said. "When do you think we're going to get started?"

"We have to apply for permits first," he said. "It'll take a couple weeks."

"How's Eden doing?" I said to him.

"Eden's good," he said, looking at me quizzically. "She and the child and the dog are at the Four Seasons. How do you know Eden?"

"I was working for her," I said. "Also, I was married to her."

"Oh! You're Gil!" he said. "I don't know if we've been properly introduced. I drew up the plans for the guesthouse. You were living there toward the end, right? Did you know they split up? Chad and Eden?"

"Yes, I heard," I said, watching him closely to see what I could read on his face. Frankly, I couldn't see much of anything.

"I guess there were problems. From what I hear, Chad wasn't the nice guy he made himself out to be," said the architect. "You know their house burned down, right? Did you hear about how he took off right before the fire and left a dog locked up inside? I drove Eden over to get her clothes—right before they shut down the roads. We found the poor animal howling hysterically in the damn guesthouse! What kind of unfeeling jackass locks up a dog and leaves town when the city is on fire? Where were the other three dogs? No one seems to know!" he said.

"They went to a kennel," I said. And I kind of explained, leaving out the part about Jimmy and the mix-up.

"I can't wait to tell Eden," he said. "She'll be very relieved."

"Looks like we're going to be doing some camping," I said to the dogs when the engineer and the architect finally left. I went back to my van and began searching through my stuff for my old backpacking tent.

Then the five of us walked all around the Bremners' three-acre lot, until we picked out the most level spot. We set up camp on a nice little flat sandy patch in front of some cypress trees. It was the part of the yard that the fire had missed.

"Whaddya think of our new digs?" I said to the dogs. "Now the whole yard is our living room."

"I like it. But does that mean that *out* here is now inside?" said Dink.

I liked living in the Bremners' backyard almost as much as I'd liked living in their house. It was a different view of their world that I hadn't been seeing: Now there were hawks, crows, mockingbirds, sparrows, and finches. There were also more parrots, deer, raccoons, opossums, snakes, owls, and coyotes than I had ever noticed in all my previous years of living there. The insects became more interesting. The snails started to seem cute. I even saw a roadrunner.

It made me feel kind of peaceful until I checked my messages. I didn't even listen to the two from Jenny, the lolcat woman. But I also had three from Sara, each one increasingly concerned. It had been two days since I'd left her that note that said I wanted to talk. I hadn't called her back. Was I okay?

"Hey," I said to her voice mail, feeling very ashamed. I now realized I had been intentionally avoiding her calls. Why was I avoiding her? I wondered to myself as I left my message. I thought I couldn't live without her. But now that all seemed wrong. "I'm fine. I'm sorry I didn't call," I continued, "I set up camp in the Bremners' yard. You'll have to come by and see the tent. And I got good news about Jimmy."

"What good news about Jimmy?" she said when she called back a few minutes later. By then I was building a charcoal pit to cook us all dinner.

"Turned out he was in the kennel with his family," I said, realizing I didn't want to repeat the whole story again despite all the concern and kindness she had shown me. She wanted to hear it. She begged me to tell it. She was doing whatever she could to extend herself and show that she cared. And here's what was weird: The more she reached out to me, the more I could feel a million switches being pushed to OFF inside me. I could almost hear them clicking shut one after another. A giant motherboard of electrical circuits was closing down.

"Great," she said. "You said something about wanting to talk?"

"Well, yeah," I said, realizing I no longer did. What was it with me? What did I want from this woman anyway? Did I want way too much, or almost nothing at all? Did I like sharing my life with dogs because they asked for so *little*? Or was it because they were willing to bend to my rules, no questions asked? "Maybe sometime next week," I said to Sara, thinking about the way I was now visualizing a mental scorecard for the basic elements of our relationship: sexual compatibility, ease of conversation, a nice place to live, personal attractiveness. I was always adding up columns of numbers, and then checking the totals to see how Sara's results fared against my gold standard. Maybe aiming for the impossible wasn't the best way to conduct a relationship. I was always waiting for everything to turn to gold.

Here's what I liked most about Sara: the way I inspired feelings of love in her. I enjoyed being adored. But did I love Sara, or did I just love that she loved me?

"Oh," she said quietly. "From your note you made it sound kind of important. I'm available tonight if you want to come by."

"I've been through the wringer," I said, resisting her invitation. I didn't really want to come by. I liked lying in my tent alone, listening to the snoring dogs and the sounds of creatures outside in the yard. I liked reading by the light of my flashlight. And I loved not having to make polite conversation. "I'm too exhausted," I said.

The truth was that after all this, I still didn't know what I wanted from Sara. *Be a good guy for once and just leave the poor woman alone,* I thought to myself. *You've had five years to give her what she wants. Stop lying to her. Do what you have to do.*

"I guess I kind of want to hang here by myself," I said. "Hey, I meant to tell you. That guy Josh seemed like a good guy. I'm glad that's working out for you two. I'm really happy for you."

"Oh," she said again, very quietly.

(44)

Nice

In the coming weeks we started construction on the Bremners' house and on Chad's place. I was the foreman for both.

Eden took her child and went to Spain, where she and that architect apparently knew someone with a villa.

Jimmy fit right back into the pack. It was even better than old times.

However, he wanted nothing at all to do with his Their-Space page. So I closed it down. In two minutes it was completely gone. His four hundred and fifty friends were set loose to find some other incredibly thin pretense for knowing each other. Goodbye, blog. Goodbye, lolcat ladies and their whimsical spellings.

But I found that I missed having something on the Internet to check in on. I missed pretending to like people I didn't know because they pretended to like me. So I took the plunge with my own brand of BS and put up a Gil the Handyman site. My logo was a picture of me and all four dogs standing in front of my van. I offered tips on how to clean the grout on your countertops. I did a Power Point presentation on how to add another fifteen feet to the size of your bathroom for cheap. I put up a video showing how to plug a hole and another one about how to unplug a drain. Of course there was a link to my hilarious, underappreciated T-shirts. I had my fingers crossed that FIX IT YOURSELF, ASSHOLE might be the first to go viral.

That didn't happen but I began to get quite a few page views. I even got an invitation to speak at a home remodeling convention.

Meanwhile, things were rolling along on an even keel and after all that had happened, an even keel felt like heaven. Until that one unfortunate evening when Cheney got sprayed by a skunk. I rushed him into a tomato juice bath, which is what I'd heard that you should do. All it did was make him smell like a rotting lasagna. It was as impossible to be near him as it was to be far away from him, since far away is out of the question when you live in a tent. That is how it came to pass that I called up Gina the dog groomer. When I heard her voice, a coiled spring in my head went *boing*.

"Would you have time to come by and de-skunk my dog?" was the message I left her.

"I am only working weekends this month because I'm going through a breakup," she said when she called back.

"Oh, I'm sorry to hear that," I said, hearing that coiled spring *boing* a second time.

"Last time I saw you, you were taking Jimmy to see your ex-wife," she said. "How'd that all turn out?"

"Long story," I said. There was a loaded silence that ended

when we both laughed at the same time. I said, "Okay. Wow. See you on Sunday!"

Afterward, I was feeling kind of energized and euphoric. So I put the dogs into the back of the van and I drove down Agoura Road. I went into that Italian restaurant with a bar where I used to see Wayne the cop, hoping he might be there so I could buy him a couple of drinks to thank him for all his help. But it was only four-fifteen. I was much too early.

The place was completely empty. A bartender I didn't know was polishing glasses and straightening up. I ordered a draft beer and then sat down at a table, looking around at the paintings of sunsets, casually watching the Dodgers game. As I was surveying the empty stage, wondering who was playing there that night, I had an odd impulse.

"Do you mind if I check out your piano?" I called to the guy as he mopped the floor.

"No, go right ahead," he said.

So I sat down on the bench and lifted the cover. It was a nice instrument—not the best, not the worst. So I just started playing everything I knew by heart. I was shocked at how much stuff I remembered. I still knew most of Liszt's Sonata in B minor. Amazing the way certain things stay with you.

"Wow," said the bartender. "Nice."

"Thanks," I said, as I followed up with Mozart's Sonata in C, or the two thirds of it that I could still recall.

When I finished, the bartender and two Mexican guys from the kitchen gave me a round of applause. Felt pretty good.

{ 45 }

Indicators of Longing

*L*ater that night, I was woken up from a very pleasant sleep by a lot of noise just outside and toward the back of my tent. At first I was alarmed. Then I realized that Jimmy was lecturing the others again. I could see the group through the mesh tent window.

"I'm still having problems getting what I want from people," said Samson from down the street. "What is the best technique to use every day?"

"Great question," said Jimmy. "Well, I think you know that a lot can be done with cute faces. Some of those you seem to have in your rotation already. I know we've talked about employing IOLs—indicators of longing. Such as rubbery drools and tiny high-pitched whimpering noises. But how about if we do a brief refresher course just to get you jump-started. Watch closely as my wingmen and I demonstrate a few standards."

Now Jimmy shouted out numbers. With each new command, Fruity, Cheney, Dink, and Jimmy would change their positions.

"Number one," said Jimmy, and the four of them lay down with their heads resting on their front paws, eyes staring up, filled with sadness.

"Number two," said Jimmy, and the four of them immediately sat up on their hind legs and began to paw at the air. "This flailing-hand thing is irresistible. Use it very judiciously," he noted.

"Number three," he yelled, and now they all sat very still on their haunches and did "Nose down, eyes up."

"There are dozens more," said Jimmy. "As I mentioned before, most human beings function through empathy. So seeing your naked yearning motivates them to do your bidding." Jimmy stopped suddenly, frozen in his tracks. "Gil might be awake now. I think I feel his presence. So let's stop here for right now. When you have mastered all of these, then we can move on."

Acknowledgments

The author would like to thank Bruce Tracy, Beth Pearson, Melanie Jackson, Andy Prieboy, Jimmy, Ginger, Hedda, Puppyboy, and Marc Germain. The author would also like to thank David Attenborough for all those great BBC documentaries, but she doesn't know him so: here.

ABOUT THE AUTHOR

Emmy Award–winning writer MERRILL MARKOE has authored three books of humorous essays and the novels *Walking in Circles Before Lying Down* and *It's My F---ing Birthday* and co-authored (with Andy Prieboy) the novel *The Psycho Ex Game*. An overly long biographical résumé can be found at www.merrillmarkoe.com. She lives in Los Angeles with four dogs and a man.